the
love
&
lies
of
rukhsana
ali

sabina khan

Scholastic Children's Books
An imprint of Scholastic Ltd
Euston House, 24 Eversholt Street, London, NW1 1DB, UK
Registered office: Westfield Road, Southam, Warwickshire, CV47 0RA
SCHOLASTIC and associated logos are trademarks and/or
registered trademarks of Scholastic Inc.

First published in the US by Scholastic Inc, 2019
First published in the UK by Scholastic Ltd, 2019

ISBN 978 1407 19457 8

A CIP catalogue record for this book
is available from the British Library.

Printed by CPI Group (UK) Ltd, Croydon, CR0 4YY
Papers used by Scholastic Children's Books are made
from wood grown in sustainable forests.

1 3 5 7 9 10 8 6 4 2

www.scholastic.co.uk

the
love
&
lies
of
rukhsana
ali

To my Jaanu, for being my
partner in crime, to
Sonya and Sanaa for inspiring
me every day, and to my beloved
Nikki for all the cuddles

chapter
one

No parties, no shorts, no boys. These were my parents' three cardinal rules. But what they didn't know couldn't hurt them, right? I quickly changed out of my NASA pajamas and into my favorite black crop top and dark blue vintage jeans, liking the way they accentuated my curves. According to Mom no one needed to know that I had boobs, much less a belly button, except for me, Allah, and my future husband. Of course, the whole "no boys" rule was a moot point in my case, but fortunately my parents didn't know about Ariana.

"Rukhsana, Mom is never going to let you out of the house wearing that."

Startled, I spun around to see my brother, Aamir, leaning lazily against my door frame.

"Knock much?" I said, quickly pausing the music playing on my phone.

"I did. It's not my fault you couldn't hear me over that screeching you call music." Aamir smiled as he sauntered into the room and plopped down on my bed.

Of course, my brother was right. I would never be allowed to go out wearing this. Which was why I was planning to throw on my oversized school hoodie to once again become the shapeless blob my parents preferred to think of me as.

"Aamir, you know this isn't my first rodeo." I ruffled his hair affectionately. "Plus, you always have my back, right?"

"Yeah, yeah, don't worry, I'll cover for you," Aamir said, pushing away my hand. He was very particular about his hair. "But it's going to cost you," he added with a grin.

"What do you want this time?" I pulled the bulky hoodie over my head.

"Something good. I haven't thought about it yet." He surveyed my outfit. "Ariana's going to run away when she sees you, but at least Mom will be happy."

I punched him playfully in the arm before going downstairs. The smell of chai led me into the kitchen, where I found the pot bubbling on the stovetop. I inhaled its spicy aroma deeply, allowing the cinnamon and cardamom to soothe my nerves. It was almost five o'clock, time to head over to Jen's house to finish getting ready for the party. But first I had to convince Mom to let me go.

She walked out of the study having just finished with her Asr prayer, absentmindedly rolling up her prayer rug.

She wore a faded blue shalwar kameez, one of the few old ones she kept for when she cooked. Other than the few grey strands escaping the black bun at the nape of her neck, she looked much younger than she really was.

I took a long sip of my tea before placing the cup on the kitchen counter. "Mom, don't forget, I'm going to Jen's house soon."

She removed her head scarf and draped it over the back of a chair.

"Again?" she asked, deepening the worry lines on her forehead. "Why, Rukhsana? You just went the other day." She picked up the pot and poured herself a cup of chai, taking a careful sip before returning her gaze to me.

"Mom, I told you," I said with a deep sigh. "We have a project due on Monday and tonight is the only night we're both free to work on it." I waited, a familiar knot forming in my stomach. I hated how I felt right now, like a child asking for just one more cookie. I could almost see the wheels turning in her head as she decided my fate for the evening.

"I need your help with dinner first. I'm making murgir jhol and your dad will be home soon. You can make the roti and then go." That was that. She turned away to pick out jars of spices from the rack and lined them up neatly on the counter next to the stove.

Great. Now I was going to show up to the party smelling of fried onions and garlic. Just what I needed.

My phone pinged.

Rukhsana!! Get your butt over here!

It was Jen. I knew she'd freak out if I was late.

I darted a glance at Mom. She was busy chopping onions, her face stoic, as if not even the onions could make her cry. I don't know how she did it.

I need another hour. Couldn't get out of kitchen duty.

You suck!!!!!

I pressed the mute button and shoved the phone back in my pocket with a groan.

"Mom, can't you get Aamir to help out tonight? I really need to go. Jen's waiting for me."

Mom laughed as she ground some coriander in the mortar with a pestle. "Don't be silly. Aamir has homework, and you know very well that you need to learn how to prepare these dishes by yourself. When you're married, who will come and cook for you?"

As if on cue, Aamir strolled into the kitchen and Mom's face lit up. Typical. Mom could be such a cliché sometimes. Of course, she doted on my brother, but me? I had to learn how to cook so I could impress a potential mother-in-law. Deep breath. I had bigger problems at the moment. Like, how was I going to get out of here, go to Jen's house to put my makeup on for the party, and make it back home by curfew? All without making my parents suspicious.

Aamir sauntered to the dining table and plopped himself into a chair. "What's for dinner?"

"Murgir jhol, baba. Your favorite." Mom stirred the spices in the pot. Wisps of coriander, cumin, and cloves wafted around the copper pots that hung on a hook near the stove before settling into my hair and clothes. I recalculated in my head the time I would now need to get ready. Shampooing, drying, and straightening my absurdly curly, long hair added at least another hour to my departure time.

Jen was going to kill me.

With a resigned sigh, I gathered my thick hair into a knot, securing it at the nape of my neck with an elastic band from my wrist. I measured out two parts flour to one part water into a large mixing bowl for the roti, casting angry glances at my mother as she kept one eye on the pot.

At least kneading the dough for the flatbread was cheaper than therapy.

"Mom, I don't really have that much homework to do. I can help out," Aamir said, unfolding his lanky frame from the chair.

"No, no, abbu, you go and relax," Mom said. "Rukhsana will help." I glared furiously at my mother. If I had a dollar for every time I'd been treated like Cinderella in this house, I'd be as rich as

Prince Charming by now. Thankfully, I only had to endure this for a few more months. Then I was out of here.

"Mom, this is ridiculous. He said he wants to help. I really need to go and work on my project with Jen."

Mom waved a dismissive hand. "Aamir is a growing boy." She returned her attention to the simmering murgir jhol on the stove. "He needs to rest so that he can study properly."

Aamir picked up the rolling pin, holding it awkwardly, which was not surprising since he'd never used one before.

"Mom, I can—"

"I said, go upstairs, Aamir." Mom's tone did not invite argument and my brother slowly backed away from the kitchen counter, mouthing a "sorry" to me before he disappeared up the stairs.

I sighed deeply.

"I'm graduating this year, Mom. I think my grades are just as important as Aamir's, even though you don't seem to think so." I pounded the ball of dough relentlessly into the counter. "I don't understand why you always do this."

"Rukhsana, I've told you before. Daughters and sons are not the same. You have the power to honor our family's good reputation. But if you're not careful you could also be the one to stain it. And it is my job to make sure that does not happen." Mom reduced the heat on the stovetop and readied a pan for the roti.

I wondered what she would do if I let out the scream that was building inside me. I took several long, deep breaths and recited the mantra I'd been living by lately:

Just hold on for a little bit longer.

Having an outburst would be counterproductive at this point. If I antagonized her, I'd never be able to leave the house tonight. I swallowed the lump in my throat and began to roll out the flatbread, allowing the simple, repetitive act to erase my frustration. Soon enough, a layer of perfectly round rotis covered the plate.

"You're getting much better." Mom grabbed the plate, nodding in approval before tossing one onto the pan to cook.

I held out another plate with the last batch. "Can I go now?"

"You have to eat first, no?" she said, expertly flipping the roti on the pan just as it puffed up.

"I'll just grab something at Jen's."

Mom scooped some rice pudding into a bowl. "Here." She handed me the bowl. "Take this up to Aamir. No need for him to come down when he's working so hard. I'll call him when Daddy gets home."

I took the bowl from her with one last glare and trudged out of the kitchen. Upstairs, I set the food down on the desk in front of Aamir.

"Mom sent this up for you. She didn't want to bother you when you're working so hard."

Aamir looked up from his book. "I'm sorry, Rukhsana. I did try to help," he said. "Mom can be so ridiculous sometimes." He stood and walked over to me.

"Here, you can have some of my rice pudding." He held out a spoonful, just like he used to when we were little and I wouldn't finish my food. Even though he was two years younger, most of the time he acted like a protective older brother. I couldn't help smiling at him as I ate the pudding. He always knew how to make me feel better.

• • •

I washed my hair twice in an attempt to replace the smell of the spices with vanilla and jasmine. After straightening my hair, I pulled out a clean black top from my closet. I never understood why people were always telling me to wear lighter colors. Even though I knew they popped against my brown skin, I was way too comfortable in my dark clothes. I did go all out in bright colors for Bengali functions, though, because even I wasn't immune to the glamor of desi fashion.

I loaded a backpack with my black strappy heels, makeup, and body spray, pulling on a different oversized hoodie and throwing my hair into a messy ponytail. Before heading downstairs, I shoved my cosmic spiral earrings into my jeans pocket.

"Bye, Mom, I'm leaving," I called out.

I didn't wait for her answer as I stepped into the cool Seattle evening. Jen lived just a couple of streets down, so I could walk there in less than five minutes. I felt a tiny pinch of guilt about lying to Mom. If it were up to her I'd never step out of the house. My mother had missed the memo that this was the twenty-first century and I was a senior in high school.

● ● ●

I heard the squeals as soon as I got to Jen's front door.

I had to knock loudly a few times before she opened it, her blue eyes sparkling. "'Bout time," she teased.

"Tell me about it," I said as I entered. "Is that Rachel screaming?"

Jen nodded. "Cody's on the phone. He says he's coming to the party."

"Is Ariana here already?" I slipped off my sneakers and placed them against the wall.

"She just got here. Everyone's upstairs."

Jen's room looked like the aftermath of a tornado. Clothes strewn about on the bed, shoes scattered on the floor, and the top of her dresser was a veritable crime scene. When I took off my hoodie, Rachel whistled at me.

"Does your mom know what you're wearing, young lady?" she asked with mock sternness.

"Are you kidding?" I grinned back at her. "If it were up to her I'd be wearing a burqa whenever I go out."

"But then I wouldn't be able to see your beautiful face," Ariana said as she exited Jen's bathroom.

She was breathtaking, wearing a short blue dress that matched the color of her eyes. We'd been together for six months now, but every time I saw her I still got butterflies. I walked over and kissed her softly on the lips.

"Gross. Get a room, you two," Rachel said with a grin.

"Preferably not mine." Jen rolled her eyes.

"You guys are just jealous because I have the hottest date for the party," I said, making a face at both of them.

"No, Rukhsana," Ariana said overdramatically, her hands on her heart. "*I* have the hottest date to the party." And with that she spun me around into a complicated dip and I promptly fell out of her arms and onto a pile of Jen's laundry on the floor, causing everyone to burst out laughing.

Rachel composed herself first. "Ariana, I think you've been watching too many Bollywood movies with Rukhsana."

"Just practicing my moves for the dance, you know," Ariana said, her eyes full of laughter. "Gotta keep up with this one, right?" she said, gesturing to me.

"Well, make sure you keep practicing," Jen said. "And now that it's *officially* settled that you guys are the cutest couple, can we go? We're already late, thanks to Miss I-Couldn't-Get-Out-Of-Kitchen-Duty here." She grinned at me and Ariana affectionately as we filed out of her room.

• • •

"Have your parents said anything more about letting you drive?" Rachel asked as the car stopped at a red light. Rachel, Jen, and I had been friends since elementary school, so they knew all about my usual family arguments.

"I'm pretty sure my brother will have his license before I do," I said bitterly. "According to my parents, I don't really need to drive since they can take me everywhere I need to go."

"Rukhsana, just remember, before long you and I will be out of here and living it up in sunny California," Ariana said, just as Jen turned onto Caitlin's street.

"Only if I tell my parents that I applied to Caltech. I'm not looking forward to that conversation." Jen's eyes met mine in the rearview mirror and I grimaced.

"Rukhsana, you've only been talking about being a physicist since forever," Jen said, her eyes back on the road. "You have to tell them."

Ariana put her arm around me and squeezed gently.

"Don't worry," she said with a grin. "We'll make a Plan B just in case."

The party was in full swing when we arrived, and Jen and Rachel immediately went off in search of Cody. The patterned bass of some dubstep remix reverberated in my chest as Ariana laced her fingers with mine. We were consumed by the music, and Ariana pulled me into her arms.

"Dance with me," she said.

As we swayed with the rhythm, the rest of the world fell away. She nuzzled my ear and kissed my neck, and my body tingled from head to toe. I had no idea how long we danced together like that or when one song ended and a new one began. All I knew was, this moment in time, this place right here? Pure heaven.

"Wanna get something to drink?" Ariana yelled over the din of the music.

I nodded and we began to make our way to the kitchen, weaving through the thrashing sea of bodies.

Rachel was there, her face slightly flushed and her usually perfect hair a little tousled.

"Umm, guys, you're not going to believe what just happened," she said, grabbing the cup Jen was holding out to her.

"I think we have a pretty good idea, Rachel," I said, grinning at her as I reached over to smooth down her hair.

"Well?" Ariana said. "Are you going to tell us?"

While Rachel gushed about Cody and his make-out skills, I stole a glance at my watch.

Crap. How did it get so late?

If Mom or Dad decided to walk over to Jen's and check up on me, like they did sometimes, I was dead.

"Jen," I said, panic tightening my throat. "I have to get home. Could you drive me, please?"

"Already?" Jen's voice had taken on a whiny tone.

I drew a deep breath. "C'mon, you know what my parents are like. If they find out I'm at a party, I can kiss Caltech goodbye."

"Fine." Jen grabbed her car keys out of her purse and handed them to me. "Just let me go tell Caitlin that I'll be back after I drop you off."

"Okay, I'm going to go change really quick before we head out." I went outside and grabbed my backpack from the back seat of Jen's car before going back in to find the bathroom. I scrubbed my face until there was no trace of my fierce dark red lipstick and black eyeliner. I put on my hoodie and tied my hair back up in a ponytail, hoping Mom wouldn't notice that it wasn't in its usual state of uncontrollable frizz. I doused myself in jasmine body spray just in case. Hopefully she'd be half-asleep when I got back and wouldn't pay attention. Ariana was waiting for me by the front door when I was done reverting back to my mother-approved self. She had that look she got every time I bailed on my friends to make it home before curfew. I quickly kissed her, said my good-byes, and walked out before the guilt pulled me back in.

It was just after eleven, way past my ten thirty curfew, by the time Jen pulled into my driveway.

I entered as quietly as I could but wasn't surprised to see Mom waiting up for me in her favorite recliner in the family room.

"Good, you're back. I was about to wake up Daddy to go over to Jennifer's house and bring you home." She stood and stretched. "Are you hungry? There's still rice pudding left. I saved you some before Aamir finished it all."

I shook my head. "I ate at Jen's house. But don't let Aamir eat the pudding. I'll eat it tomorrow."

She smiled indulgently. "You look tired. Look at those dark circles." She kissed my forehead before tucking my hair behind my ears.

"I'm going to go to sleep now. Good night, Mom," I said as I walked up the stairs.

"Good night, ammu."

My heart hammered in my chest as I unpacked my backpack, stashing my heels in the back of the closet and returning my makeup to the bathroom. I hid the forbidden red lipstick in my junk drawer, making sure it was impossible to find in all the other clutter.

chapter
two

At school on Monday, Rachel, Jen, and I waited for Ariana to come out of band practice.

"So were your parents mad that you came home late on Friday?" Rachel asked. She was wearing her basketball jersey, all ready to leave for a game after lunch.

"No, I don't think my mom realized how late it was," I said.

"I told you it would be fine," Jen said. "You were just panicking for nothing."

I opened my mouth to retort, but then I spotted Ariana coming out of the band room and waved her over. I would have to talk with Jen later. Lately she'd been a little dismissive about my concerns and it was bugging me.

"Hey, guys," Ariana said, a little out of breath after fighting her way through the hallway crowd. "Ready for lunch?"

• • •

When I arrived home from school Dad's dark blue Toyota sat in its usual spot in our driveway. My anxiety took over and I immediately started thinking the worst.

Why is he home so early? Did he and Mom find out about Friday night? I thought I was careful. Did they find out about Ariana?

My legs trembled, threatening to give out at any moment. I found Mom and Dad sitting at the kitchen table. Aamir was there too. How did he always manage to get home before I did? The light coming through the window reflected off the wood veneer on the dining table, casting a soft glow around them.

"Good. Madam is finally home," Mom said, her voice dripping with sarcasm. It was never a good sign when Mom called me that. It meant she thought I was being too clever for my own good. My eyes fell to the pile of opened mail in front of them.

"Rukhsana, what is the meaning of this?" Dad waved a letter in front of my face. I took it from him, my brow furrowed in confusion. As I skimmed the letter, a smile shattered the anxiety that had been building inside me.

Mom threw her hands in the air and shook her head. "Look at your daughter, Ibrahim. Smiling as if she has won the lottery."

"Actually, I kind of did," I said. I couldn't stop smiling. It was an acceptance letter from Caltech stating they'd awarded me a full academic scholarship.

"Why didn't you tell us you were applying?" Dad asked.

"Forget about all that. What makes you think we will let you go?" Mom's voice shook ever so slightly.

Mom had made it abundantly clear more than once that she wasn't going to let me go out of state for college. The last time I'd brought it up hypothetically, she had asked me why I needed to go away from home to get an education. She'd brought up her friend's daughter who attended the University of Washington. If it was good enough for her, then it should be good enough for me.

That was reason 34 of 62,372 I decided not to tell my parents that I'd applied to Caltech. I hadn't expected to get in, much less get a scholarship. At least now she couldn't use money as an excuse.

"I'm getting a full ride." Sheer joy and relief bubbled through every pore in my body. "You don't have to pay for anything."

"But it's in California," Mom said.

Yes, hence the name Caltech.

"California . . ." Dad's voice trailed off as he pondered this concept. "That is very far away." It finally dawned on him. "How will you get there?"

By plane, train, or automobile?

"Rukhsana, why are you talking about such strange things?" Mom said.

Umm, I don't know. Because I want to have a life?

"Mom, it's an amazing opportunity. Mr. Jacobs said a lot of people apply for a scholarship to Caltech. I'm lucky to get one." My voice had risen several octaves and yet Mom looked completely unimpressed.

"Who is this Mr. Jacobs? Is he Bengali? Does he know that we don't send our unmarried girls across the country?"

My counselor, Mr. Jacobs, was not Bengali. I was pretty sure he was from the Midwest. And no, he did not share my parents' views on unmarried girls.

"Mom, you met Mr. Jacobs last year, remember? He's the one who told you Aamir was failing math and science."

"Hey," Aamir protested, his mouth full of samosa. "I didn't fail. Mr. Jacobs just hates me."

"Yup, that's it. It's all Mr. Jacobs's fault," I said in mock agreement. Classic Aamir, always blaming everyone else.

"Aamir is a very intelligent boy," Mom said, raising her hands in anticipation of my usual verbal onslaught. "It's not his fault that his brain cannot wait for everyone else to catch up."

"Zubaida," Dad interjected. "You have to admit, our Rukhsana is also brilliant. Caltech is a very good school."

Mom shook her head and put two more samosas on Aamir's plate.

"Thanks, Dad," I said. "At least someone in this house thinks I can do more than cook." I snagged a couple of samosas before they were all gone.

"Rukhsana, your mother just wants you to be taken care of after you are married. You know how difficult it was for us when your mother and I first moved to this country," Dad said, his eyes glazing over with that faraway look he always got when talking about the past.

I rolled my eyes. "Yes, Daddy, I know. I've heard this story a hundred times before."

He ignored me.

"We arrived here with practically nothing except the clothes on our backs, a small suitcase, and some cash my brother had loaned us." He turned to Mom. "Remember, Zubaida, that first table we bought?" He smiled as their eyes met, heavy with secrets from a time before I existed.

"Yes, how can I forget?" Mom said. "It was blue, a small card table really, but it was all we could afford at the time." She turned to look at me.

"When you came along, Rukhsana, everything changed," she said, her tone softening as she remembered.

Dad touched my cheek gently and I placed my hand over his.

"Suddenly nothing was good enough," Mom said. "Your daddy worked two jobs just so he could buy you everything. But then we talked to your Uncle Maruf."

"It was his idea to start a business of our own," Dad said.

Mom got up to make some chai. I stood, intending to help, but she motioned for me to sit while she continued to reminisce.

"He told us the Bangladeshi community needed a local shop where they could buy hilsa fish and jackfruit and panch phoron," Mom said.

"And he wasn't wrong," Dad chimed in. "The store did well right from the beginning."

They fell quiet for a minute until the sound of water bubbling on the stove broke the silence.

"This is why I am very proud of you, Rukhsana," Dad said. "I never managed to get a degree, but my daughter will."

"That is all good," Mom said. The kettle whistled and she turned off the stove. "But why does she have to go so far away? Let her be brilliant nearby. What is wrong with UW?"

Nothing at all, except it isn't Caltech.

"UW doesn't have a good physics and astronomy program, Mom."

"Imagine"—Dad looked at Mom with a broad smile—"our daughter, a physicist. Or maybe even an astronaut." His eyes glistened with pride.

Mom's eyebrows almost disappeared into her hairline. "What will you do with a degree in astronomy, hanh? Will you climb into a spaceship and fly off to Jupiter?" She shook her head and looked at my dad. "Ibrahim, please talk some sense into your daughter."

What I wouldn't give to be on Jupiter right now.

"Okay, Rukhsana, we'll talk about it," Dad said. "There is still plenty of time."

Mom poured chai into three cups and placed them in front of us.

Dad stood and stretched. "I have some work to finish before dinner," he announced before taking his cup of tea into the study with him.

"Aamir, go upstairs and finish your homework," Mom said, and I braced myself for more lecturing on how it was better for everyone if I didn't go away for college.

"Rukhsana," Mom began as soon as Aamir left the kitchen. "You know I am very proud of you, right?" She took a sip of her tea and looked at me, her eyes filled with concern.

She sighed deeply and her shoulders sagged. "I worry what people will say. If you move away, there is no telling what kind of nasty rumors will fly around."

I sipped slowly at my tea to buy myself some time. "Mom, I can't make important life decisions based on what people might say."

"But that's what your father and I are here for. It is our job to make all the important decisions. That way we can make sure there is nothing for anyone to gossip about."

What would she do if she found out about my relationship with Ariana? I knew I had to come out to my parents at some point. But definitely not before I was eighteen and over a thousand miles away with Ariana in California.

chapter
three

As Ariana's soft lips trailed down the side of my neck, I let out a soft moan. I turned to face her and buried my hands in her hair. Her arms circled my waist, pulling me closer until we blended into each other, a feverish tangle of limbs. The chiming sound of the doorbell startled me and I jumped away from Ariana in a panic.

"Shit." Ariana's face was ashen. "Who could that be?" Her fingers shook as she hastily buttoned up her blouse.

"I don't know. My mom is supposed to be at the dentist—"

"Rukhsana?" I froze. It was Aunty Meena. If she found us like this—

I didn't want to complete that thought.

"Ariana, hurry. You have to hide," I whispered, pulling her toward the pantry. Her eyes widened.

"Are you crazy? I'm not hiding in there," she protested, pulling her arm away. "You realize you're literally forcing me back into the closet."

"Rukhsana, I can see you moving around in there. Open the door," Aunty Meena called out.

"I'm so sorry." I planted a big kiss on Ariana's lips right before shoving her inside. "I'll get rid of her in two minutes, I promise," I said, shutting the door in her face.

I straightened my shirt and ran my fingers through my hair. Taking a deep breath, probably my last, I opened the door with a professionally fake smile plastered on my face.

"Aunty Meena . . . how nice to see you," I lied, waving her into the living room. She floated regally past me, a cacophony of colors with her voluminous silk sari swishing around her ankles. Her floral perfume engulfed me in a suffocating cloud.

"Here, I brought some halwa." Her eyes scanned the living room as she handed me a glass container.

"Thank you, Aunty. You're the best." I ushered her toward the couch.

"Why did you take so long?" she asked, her eyes narrowed suspiciously.

"Sorry, I just got home from school, so I was changing upstairs."

She pursed her lips as she ran her eyes up and down the length of me.

"You've become so dark," she declared. "I keep telling you that you need to stay out of the sun, but you kids nowadays." Her voice trailed off and she shook her head. "You never listen to your elders."

Gulping down my murderous inclinations, I forced a smile. I needed her to leave, but if I rushed her visit she would definitely mention it to Mom and then I'd have to explain myself.

"You look so pretty, Aunty," I gushed. "Is that a new sari? I don't think I've seen this one before." That always did it. Her face relaxed and settled into a self-satisfied sneer.

"Yes, your Uncle Maruf bought it for me on his last trip to Dhaka," she said. "Where is your mother?"

"She had a dentist's appointment and I'm not sure when she'll be back. Would you like a cup of chai?" I regretted the words as soon as they left my mouth.

Maybe she'll say no. *Please please please say no.*

"Yes, I think I'll have a cup," she said, before settling into the love seat. The cushions protested in vain while she wiggled herself into a comfortable position. She adjusted the aanchal of her sari so that the peacocks in the pattern lay right in her lap and looked at me expectantly.

"Well, are you going to just stand there or will you make me some tea?"

"Of course, Aunty. I'll be right back."

I rushed back into the kitchen.

Poor Ariana. This was going to take a lot longer than I thought.

I opened the pantry door quietly and peered inside. Ariana was still alive, sitting cross-legged on the floor and playing with her phone. She raised her head to glare at me.

"I'm so sorry," I whispered, bending down to kiss her quickly on the lips. "I panicked. I'll get rid of her as fast as I can. I promise."

"Rukhsana, do you want me to help you with the chai?" I jumped at the sound of Aunty Meena's voice right behind me.

That woman was a ninja.

"No, no, please relax, Aunty. I've got it," I said, hastily shutting the pantry door.

"Okay, let's see how well your mother has taught you." Aunty settled into a perch on one of the kitchen stools.

I forced my breathing to slow down while I retrieved cups and saucers from the cabinet. I threw a glance at Aunty Meena. She was flipping through a copy of *Femina*, the Indian magazine where she and Mom caught up on all the latest Bollywood gossip.

A hiss from the stove brought me back to the task at hand. The milk had nearly boiled over. I quickly reduced the heat and put in the black tea, fresh ginger, cinnamon, cloves, and cardamom.

The aroma immediately began to fill the room, easing my nerves slightly. When the chai was ready, I placed a cup in front of Aunty.

She blew on it before taking a careful sip. "Very nice, Rukhsana," she said, nodding in approval.

I turned away for just a second to take the saucepan off the heat and when I looked her way again she was at the pantry door.

"Your mom's delicious cumin cookies would go so well with the chai," she said, her hand closing around the handle. My heart was in my mouth.

I quickly jumped in front of her before she could open the door.

"I'll get them, Aunty. They're on the top shelf; you won't be able to reach them." I gave her a very gentle push back toward the kitchen island.

"You're acting very strange today, Rukhsana. What's the matter with you?" she asked, getting back to her perch.

"Nothing, Aunty, I'm fine," I said, opening the pantry door cautiously.

Ariana leaned against the wall, holding out a tin of cookies.

"I'm so sorry," I mouthed, grabbing the tin before closing the door in her face once again.

"Are you sure?" Aunty Meena insisted. "Why are you so jumpy?"

"Just too much coffee, Aunty," I replied quickly, grabbing a plate from the cabinet. I put a few cookies on it and placed it in front of her. "I've had a lot of studying to do these past few days." Hopefully that would satisfy her.

"Good, good. Studying is good," she said, dunking her cookie into the chai before taking a bite. "Nowadays no one wants a daughter-in-law without at least a bachelor's degree."

I bit my tongue.

Yes, that's the reason I work so hard at school. To make sure that I will be a worthy bride for some loser.

Aunty Meena sipped the last of her chai and finally slid off the stool. "Okay, Rukhsana, I have to go now. Your uncle will be home soon and I still have to make dinner. The chai was very good, by the way."

"Thank you, Aunty. Please remember to tell Mom, okay? She thinks I'm useless in the kitchen." I gently ushered her out into the living room before she changed her mind.

"She is just worried that she won't find a good match for you, that's all." Aunty Meena pulled me in for a quick hug before walking out.

I shut the door and slumped against it, heaving a big sigh of relief. That was too close.

I ran back to the kitchen and flung open the pantry door. Ariana sat on the floor, her shirt covered in cookie crumbs.

"Is she gone?" she whispered, standing and brushing off the crumbs.

I nodded, pulling her gently out of the pantry and into my arms.

"I'm so sorry. I panicked and didn't know what to do," I said, chuckling into her hair.

Ariana pulled away and narrowed her eyes at me. "Do you think this is funny?" she demanded. The corners of her mouth twitched, giving her away. We held each other's gaze before breaking into laughter.

"I was terrified she would open the pantry to get the cookies," I said. "I don't know what I would have done if she had caught you in there."

"I thought you were never coming back. I was so glad you had chocolate chip ones in there. I was starving." Ariana found a big crumb clinging to the front of her shirt and popped it into her mouth.

"I'd planned to make us something to eat, but someone decided to distract me, remember?" I teased, pulling her to me. We swiftly picked back up where we'd left off.

"I bet Aunty Meena will mention something to my mom," I said when we took a moment to breathe. "She knew something was up."

Ariana stared at me. "Are you ever planning to tell your parents about me?"

I cringed, not knowing what to say. We'd had this conversation before and it always went the same way.

"Ariana, you know how it is with my family. They'll never understand."

"So, what are you saying? That I'll always be your little secret? Because I'm getting kind of tired of this." She forcefully straightened her skirt.

"Ariana, what do you want me to do? If I tell them they'll kick me out or lock me up or some other crazy shit. I can't take that risk, not with graduation coming up. Things will be much different when we get to Caltech."

I gazed deep into her eyes, willing her to understand. "You know how much you mean to me." I squeezed her hands.

She didn't pull away and I felt a small fluttering of hope. I wrapped my arms around her, hugging her tight.

"I'll tell them," I whispered into her ear. "Soon, I promise. Just not right now. I can't risk it."

She tensed and pulled away from me, her hands slipping out of mine. "Rukhsana, I know how hard it is for you. But you have to understand how it feels to be hidden away. As if I'm something you're ashamed of."

And with that she left. I didn't go after her because I knew it wouldn't matter. She needed time to be alone and I needed to think. What if she was right?

After lying in bed for a few hours, unable to sleep, I grabbed my cell phone off the nightstand.

> Ariana, I'm sorry. Talk to me. Please.

I stared at the screen, willing her reply to pop up. Nothing. Of course she was still mad at me. Who could blame her? Was I ever going to have the courage to face my parents? I thought I had the perfect plan. We would go to Caltech together and be far away from home, so no one in Seattle would know about our relationship. But was that really how I wanted to live my life? In the shadows, hiding away the person I loved?

I checked my phone again. Still nothing.

> Ariana, please don't be mad anymore. You know how much I love you.

A minute ticked by. Then finally, a ping.

> I just need some time. I'm going to sleep now. Good night.

I wanted to cry but the tears wouldn't come. Maybe because I knew I wasn't being fair to Ariana.

As I finally drifted off to sleep, one thought lingered.

She deserved better than this.

chapter
four

I waited by Ariana's locker after school the next day, anxiously twirling a curl of my hair. She hadn't replied to my text this morning and now my stomach was in knots. I scanned the crowded hallway, desperate to find her. Then, from out of the crushing mob, she appeared carrying her violin in her left hand. She wore high-waisted black jeans with a pale yellow sweater and her thick, chestnut hair cascaded down her shoulders. It always reminded me of the betel nuts we'd find strewn around my grandmother's yard back in Bangladesh.

I waved, a slight smile edging up the sides of my mouth. Ariana's face hardened when she saw me, hesitating before continuing toward me.

"Ariana, I'm so sorry about yesterday," I said, grabbing her by the hand as soon as she was beside me. "You were right about everything. I'm going to tell my parents, I swear." I touched her cheek gently, her skin smooth beneath my fingers. "And you're not my little secret. You're everything to me. But I just need a little more time."

She didn't say anything, although her eyes filled up a little. Then she blinked back the tears and nodded.

"I'm sorry too," she said, squeezing my hand. "Look, Rukhsana, I know it's different in your family and I should be more patient. But it's just so hard sometimes." I threw open my arms, wrapping them around her.

"I know it sucks. But I just don't want to give them any reason to stop me from going to Caltech."

"You think they'll ever accept us?"

"I don't know." I fell silent, my shoulders sagging. "Could we go over to your place and talk after school?"

• • •

"So, what are you going to do?" Ariana asked, joining me on the edge of her bed.

"Well, for now, I'd really like it if you came over for dinner and met them."

"What if they don't like me?"

"Come on, Ariana," I said, giving her a quick kiss. "They'll love you. Just like I do." She stiffened for a moment. Then, leaning in, she kissed me back.

"I love you too," she whispered in my ear. She pulled back and looked at me earnestly. "What do you think I should wear?"

I grinned. "You should wear a burqa. My friend Nasreen has one, I think. I could ask to borrow it for you."

"You think you're so funny," Ariana said, making a face at me. "But we can't tell them about us, right?"

"No," I said hastily. "Not yet. But that doesn't mean they can't get to know you as my friend."

She smiled again. "Well, that depends," she said teasingly.

"On what?"

"If you can keep your hands off me," she replied, running her fingers up my arm.

● ● ●

A week later I was nervous and excited all at once. My parents would be meeting Ariana for the first time and I was terrified something would go wrong. It wasn't as though I was going to introduce her as my girlfriend. As far as my parents were concerned, she was just another friend from school. But after months of sneaking around, I would finally bring her home officially. It felt like a tiny step in the right direction.

Mom wasn't home when Ariana and I arrived after school, so we worked on our homework in the kitchen until she came back. Because that's what girls who were friends did. Homework in the kitchen, instead of making out over calculus.

Midway through our next-to-last assignment, Mom came home with sweets from the store and bags of groceries.

"Ariana, I hear you're new to the school," Mom said as she put the groceries away.

"Yes, Mrs. Ali, my family moved here right before the fall semester started." Ariana's voice had a slight tremor.

"I'm glad you can join us for dinner. Have you had much Indian food before?"

"A couple of times and I really liked it." Ariana was quite adventurous when it came to food.

"Good, then I won't have to hold back on the spices too much," Mom said, beaming with satisfaction.

"Okay, Mom, but please don't go too crazy with the chili powder." I didn't want Ariana to run out of here with her mouth on fire.

"Don't worry, ammu. Now go and finish your schoolwork and I'll call you when dinner is ready."

We gathered our books and ran upstairs.

"That was a little scary," Ariana said, slightly out of breath. "But your mom seems super nice," she added quickly.

I nodded. "She's always happy when she can cook for my friends."

We worked on our homework, not daring to share more than a longing glance with each other every so often.

"Rukhsana, dinner is ready," Mom called from downstairs about an hour later.

"Are you ready for the Bengali Inquisition?" I grinned at her terrified expression.

"You can laugh all you want, Rukhsana," Ariana said sternly. "But if I screw up, I still get to go home. What will you do?" she added teasingly.

I peeked my head into Aamir's room to drag him down to dinner with us and found him playing one of his Assassin's Code video games or whatever, as usual.

"Aamir, get up. Mom's calling us down for dinner," I said as he tore his attention away from the screen.

"Is she here?" he said conspiratorially, trying to look over my shoulder.

"Yes, she's here, and stop being so rude. Come and say hi like a normal person."

He jumped up and came to the door.

"Hey, Ariana, how's it going? Today's the big day, right?" He wiggled his eyebrows and grinned knowingly.

"Shut up, Aamir, nothing's happening. Ariana's just over for dinner, that's all. So, don't even think about mentioning it." Aamir shrugged nonchalantly.

"Geez, relax, I get it. I won't say anything. You don't have to be so bossy. I've kept my mouth shut until now, haven't I?" He looked at me with a wounded expression.

His fake hurt feelings were nothing I hadn't dealt with before.

"Just watch it, okay?"

He had a point though. He'd known about Ariana and me for a while now and had never ever said anything to make my parents suspicious. I knew he had my back, but then again, he could be really stupid sometimes.

● ● ●

"So, Ariana, where did you move here from?" Dad asked when we were all seated at the dinner table.

"San Diego. My dad got transferred here back in September," Ariana replied.

"And what line of work is your father in?" I'd warned Ariana that meeting my parents for the first time was more like a job interview than a casual dinner at a friend's house.

"He's in IT," she said.

"And your mother?" Mom asked as she offered Ariana some chicken.

"She's in IT as well." Ariana poured a spoonful of chicken curry over her rice. When Mom continued to hold the dish in front of her, she took another spoonful.

"That must be nice, to work in the same field," Mom said, satisfied that Ariana had enough food on her plate. No one came to our house for a meal and left without a food baby.

We all watched intently as Ariana took a tentative bite, expecting her to combust spontaneously. But she seemed fine, only reaching for her glass of water after finishing half of her food.

I had to give her props for not getting up and running out the door. I could bet she'd never eaten a meal under such intense scrutiny. I'd feel sorry for her, but I had to admit I was having too much fun.

"Wow," Aamir said after she had only about a third of the food left on her plate. "I'm impressed. You can really handle the heat."

Ariana smiled at him. "We tend to eat out a lot. And my parents like their food spicy too."

"Then we must have them over for dinner soon," Mom said, smiling broadly. I knew she was already planning the menu in her head.

"Yes, they would love that," Ariana said. I stretched out my foot under the table to touch hers, but she didn't seem to notice. Aamir, on the other hand, gave me a weird look. I quickly withdrew my leg and shoveled some food into my mouth.

"And what are your plans after graduation?" Dad asked Ariana as he took a second helping.

"Well, I'm thinking of going back to California for college," she said. "All my old friends are still there, and my parents plan to move back there eventually."

"What field do you want to study?" Mom asked as she spooned more rice and curry on Ariana's plate.

"Computer science. I am my parents' daughter, after all," Ariana said, worriedly eyeing the food on her plate. I looked at Aamir, trying not to laugh. Ariana was too preoccupied with fielding my parents' interrogation to notice.

"Good, good," Dad said thoughtfully. It looked like both my parents approved of Ariana. I relaxed my shoulders a little. This was going better than I'd hoped.

"Has Rukhsana told you she is also planning to go to California for college?" Mom said.

I nearly choked on a piece of chicken and gulped down some water to compose myself. "Wait, I am?"

"Yes, it will be nice for you to have a friend while you are there," Dad said. "Maybe you can even live together."

What is happening right now?

Ariana nodded calmly and smiled. "Yes, she's mentioned it a few times."

Mom stood to clear the plates and Ariana and I helped, while Aamir slinked off as usual.

For once, I didn't care because not only did I have my girlfriend by my side—even if my parents didn't know that's who she was to me—I was going to Caltech.

chapter five

A family friend had invited us to his daughter's wedding. In true Bengali fashion, everyone even remotely known to the bride's family was invited. As we walked into the lavishly decorated wedding hall, I looked around to find my friends. There had to be at least a thousand people here, all dressed to the hilt.

"There you are, Rukhsana." The shrill voice belonged to Nasreen, a Bengali girl my age. Our parents were friends so we saw each other frequently at dinner parties. She was draped in a purple sari, shot with silver thread and gorgeously intricate embroidered flowers. A heavy silver necklace with matching earrings adorned her neck, and she wore sets of two dozen silver and purple bangles on each arm.

"Nasreen, how are you? You look beautiful. It's been way too long."

"I'm fine. Oh my God, I love your sari. That dark blue chiffon is gorgeous on you. And that necklace. I bet you Irfan won't be able to keep his eyes off you."

"Irfan? How do you know him?" Irfan was the son of one of Uncle Maruf's friends and was known as somewhat of a prodigy in the Bengali community. Although I'd never officially met him, I'd

38

heard about him through the grapevine. Mainly because my mom and Aunty Meena were hoping to snag him for me. Apparently he was good husband material, because all the aunties with young daughters were aquiver.

"Please, Rukhsana, you think your mom is the only one looking? My mother heard he just got promoted to VP of marketing at his firm. She went into nuclear launch mode when she heard your aunty was talking you up to his mom."

Sounded like this Irfan was the Mr. Darcy of Seattle's Bangladeshi community.

"Seriously? What's so special about this guy?" Not that I was interested, but it didn't mean I couldn't enjoy the turf war about to ensue. Who needed Bollywood when we had the real-life drama right here in Seattle?

Nasreen shook her head. "I don't know and I don't really care. I already have a boyfriend, Salim, remember? But I did get this new sari out of it."

She nudged me. "Look, that's him over there."

My eyes followed to where she pointed. All I saw were over-dressed older women wearing far too much gold. I had to wait a moment before I spotted him. He was standing in the middle of all those women, smiling and charming them. No wonder they were trying to snag him for their daughters. From where I stood I couldn't make out much of his appearance, other than being tall. For a Bengali, that meant five foot seven or so. We were a vertically challenged people. What we lacked in height we made up with our love for food, poetry, and music.

To my horror, Irfan caught my eye while I was checking him out. He leaned forward to say something to one of the aunties surrounding him. I quickly looked away before one of them saw me and came over to scratch my eyes out. Nasreen had lost interest and was texting on her phone, so I grabbed her by the arm and pulled her away with me toward the bathroom.

"What's going on? What did I miss?" Nasreen said, tucking her phone back in her bra.

"I think he saw me looking, that's all."

"Soooo," she said suggestively. "What do you think?"

"I don't see what the big deal is. But it's hilarious how the aunties are all over him."

Just then, Aunty Meena descended upon us and Nasreen made a quick escape.

"Rukhsana, you are looking very beautiful. This dark blue color is looking very good on your skin." She nodded appreciatively as she checked out my gold choker and the teardrop-shaped earrings.

"Thank you, Aunty. You look very nice too," I murmured.

"Nice, shice . . . I am an old woman. These weddings are for you young people. Where else will you find your husbands?"

Oh, I don't know . . . college, the internet? Apparently, it is a truth universally acknowledged that a single Bengali girl of marrying age must be in want of a husband.

She scanned the crowd and then froze, having spotted her prey. I followed her gaze only to find myself staring directly at him. Irfan. The Boy Wonder. He looked back with smug amusement, clearly used to girls and women fawning over him.

I would have loved to burst his bubble, but obviously, I couldn't risk exposing myself. I could just imagine the panic and chaos. This would become ground zero for the lesbian plague. So, I smiled demurely back at him as Aunty Meena did her best handiwork.

"Irfan . . . there you are, my darling boy," she crooned.

"Aunty Meena, you look breathtaking in that sari. Maruf Uncle is a very lucky man." I nearly gagged. He laid it on very thick, but

I had to admit he was good. Aunty Meena's face looked like a gulab jamun that had been left in syrup for too long.

"Oh, Irfan . . . you naughty boy. Don't let your uncle hear you saying such things. He gets very jealous, you know." Aunty Meena fanned herself with the aanchal of her sari.

As I tried to stop from howling with laughter, Irfan winked at me. The guy was pure evil.

"Irfan, have you met my niece, Rukhsana?" Aunty Meena asked, once she regained her composure. "She is graduating this year and going to Caltech in the fall." Clearly, word had gotten out. Mom certainly hadn't wasted any time in laying the groundwork. She knew having a daughter in Caltech would make her look better in the Bengali community. And no doubt give her an added advantage when the marriage proposals started coming.

We exchanged greetings and then, luckily for me, another group of mothers swarmed Irfan. I left Aunty Meena in the thick of it to find my parents.

"Rukhsana, come and say hello." I turned to see who was speaking and saw Mrs. Rahim standing by the gifts table. She was the local Bengali teacher my parents had sent me to for a few years to learn how to speak and write Bengali fluently. Thanks to her, I spoke it well enough to pass scrutiny from even the most critical relative I came across at family functions.

"Mr. and Mrs. Ali, you must be looking for a groom for Rukhsana, no?" she said as Mom and Dad joined us. She was also a self-appointed matchmaker, always keeping her eyes and ears open for potential Bengali sons and daughters of marriageable age.

"No, Mrs. Rahim, Rukhsana will be going to university to study physics and astronomy. So, we will not be looking for a husband until she is finished." I smiled at my dad gratefully as Mrs. Rahim scrunched up her eyebrows at this foreign notion.

"That is very good, Rukhsana. Congratulations." She smiled at me, her mouth at odds with her eyes. She turned to Dad again.

"But, Ibrahim Bhai, aren't you worried that Rukhsana will be too old by the time she's finished?"

Mom had been standing silently next to Dad during the exchange, but now I saw a vein throbbing visibly on her forehead.

"Mrs. Rahim, how is your daughter?" Mom interjected, saving Dad the trouble of answering. "I was so sad to hear about Shabnam's situation. It must be difficult for you to see her like this. A divorced woman with no job. It's a good thing she has you."

Mom could throw shade with the best of them. Mrs. Rahim mumbled something about food and slinked away, no doubt to find another unsuspecting parent.

• • •

"Who does that Mrs. Rahim think she is?" Mom fumed on our way home from the wedding. "Telling us what to do with our own daughter."

"Zubaida, why do you care what she says?" Dad said soothingly, but it did little to calm her.

My feet hurt from standing around in high heels for so long and I kicked them off as I relaxed in the back seat of my dad's Toyota.

"These are the kinds of things I'm worried about," Mom said, still riled up. "This is why I don't want you to go so far away, Rukhsana." She turned a little to look at me in the back seat. "Who knows what rumors these busybodies will start when you're gone?"

"Let them say whatever they want," Dad said. "We know our Rukhsana will finish her degree and come back to us. Then there will be plenty of time to find a nice boy and she will get married." He looked at me in the rearview mirror and I was grateful for the cover of darkness.

"You're home late. How was it?" Aamir asked when I passed by his room. He stretched lazily, one hand still clutching his video game controller.

"It was fine," I said dismissively. "Is that thing welded to your hand or something?"

He stuck his tongue out at me. "Any cute girls at the wedding?"

"Maybe you should have come with us instead of pretending you had too much homework," I said.

"Nah, it's not worth it." He shrugged.

"Well, you missed out. The food was great and there were a lot of pretty girls. Nasreen's sister was asking about you," I teased.

"You're such a liar," he said, turning his attention back to his game. "The last time I saw her, she wouldn't even look at me."

I plopped myself on the edge of his bed with a dramatic sigh.

Aamir turned to me with a knowing look on his face. Despite Mom's blatant favoritism, which he took full advantage of, Aamir always knew when something was bothering me.

"What's wrong?" he asked, putting the controller down.

When I didn't reply immediately, he rolled his eyes.

"C'mon, you know you're going to tell me sooner or later, so just tell me what's going on." For someone whose mission in life was to annoy me, Aamir was surprisingly insightful when it really mattered.

"It's nothing . . . Just, at the wedding, Mom got so upset at Mrs. Rahim because she made some stupid comment about me going to Caltech. I'm so scared of how she'll react when she finds out about Ariana and me."

"Wait," Aamir said, turning his chair all the way around until he was facing me. "I thought the plan was not to tell her until you two are in California."

"It was, but lately it's been so hard." Tears of frustration pooled in my eyes and I dabbed at them angrily with the aanchal of my sari. "For Ariana, especially. It really hurts her that I haven't told Mom and Dad yet. I've tried to explain it to her, but she just doesn't know how bad it could get. She thinks they'll just get mad and ground me or something."

Aamir snorted. "Yeah, right. That would be nice. Of course they're going to freak out. And they wouldn't let you go to Caltech, that's for sure."

Aamir looked at me with such a serious expression on his face. I felt guilty for burdening him with my problems.

"Rukhsana, I know I always give you a hard time, but you have to listen to me. Please don't tell them anything yet. I know it's difficult with Ariana right now, but she'll just have to understand."

He drew me in for a hug and that's when I knew he was really worried for me. Aamir was not the hugging type.

"I won't say anything yet, I promise," I said in what I hoped was a reassuring tone.

He was absolutely right. I couldn't let my mom or Mrs. Rahim or even Ariana push me into making a huge mistake. It was my future, my whole life that would change if my parents stopped me from going to Caltech. I couldn't risk it.

I got up and planted a big, wet kiss on Aamir's forehead. He scrunched up his face in disgust, but I knew he was faking it.

"Will you be okay?" he asked, wiping his forehead with the sleeve of his shirt.

I nodded, walking to the door. "I think so. I just have to figure things out with Ariana."

I heard footsteps coming up the stairs.

"Get into bed," I whispered to Aamir, stepping out and shutting his door quickly before my parents figured out that he was still awake.

Back in my room, I took a selfie and sent it to Ariana, wishing she could see me dressed up like this. I didn't expect her to be up this late, but a few seconds later there was a ping.

You're gorgeous, babe. How did I get so lucky?

I smiled as I texted her back.

I'm pretty sure I'm the lucky one.

chapter
six

I waited in line at this new French fry place in the mall called Franken-Fries, looking over the menu. They were known for their monstrous culinary creations, combining ingredients that should never work together, but somehow magically do. I decided on the sriracha and peanut butter fries, but before I could order I felt Ariana's hand slip into mine and her lips on my cheek.

I froze instantly, fear making my arms go numb. We were in public, at the mall, and there were at least a hundred people who could have seen us. A hundred people who would tell a hundred more, and by the time I got home, my parents would have heard that I was making out with a girl in the food court.

These thoughts were crashing around in my head like waves, and I didn't realize until it was too late that Ariana had noticed. She had felt the way I stiffened at her touch and drew away. It was not going to be easy to make her understand just how terrified I was of what would happen if anyone in my community found out. How it would ruin my family, but mostly how it would ruin my entire life.

I ran after Ariana as she made her way to the restrooms, but by the time I got there she had already locked herself in one of the small family bathrooms. I waited by the exit, feeling powerless as a wave of guilt washed over me.

Just then my cell phone pinged. It was Rachel, wondering where Ariana and I were.

I saw her and Jen across the food court and flagged them down. We found a table near the restrooms so I would see Ariana when she came out.

"Hey! Where's Ariana?" Jen asked as soon as we sat down.

"She got pissed at me and ran into the bathroom." I told them what happened and they didn't even try to hide their disapproval.

"I don't know why you can't just tell your parents," Jen said, her eyebrows knitted together in irritation. "I mean, it's the twenty-first century, I think your parents will get over it."

"Yeah," Rachel chimed in. "I mean, what's the worst they'll do? Ground you?"

I pushed back a hysterical laugh as I listened to them. They really had no idea.

"C'mon, you guys, you've known my parents for years. You know how strict they are. They won't just ground me, they'll probably lock me away, and I could definitely kiss Caltech goodbye."

My shoulders sagged at the thought of giving up everything I'd dreamed about since I was little.

"Okay, honestly, Rukhsana, I think you're exaggerating a little," Rachel said. "I mean, yes, of course your parents will be pissed, and yes, they'll probably threaten you with all kinds of things, but do you really think they'll go that far?"

They both looked at me as if I was crazy and I wondered, as I had many times lately, if they really knew me at all. Sometimes it felt as though all they saw was the Rukhsana who went to school with them and hung out and went to parties. They couldn't see the Rukhsana who was torn up inside because she had to lie to her family all the time, had to pretend to be something she wasn't. And even Ariana. How could she not get what I was going through? It had been so much easier for her. Yes, her parents had been shocked initially when she came out to them, but they had attended counseling sessions together and seemed to be in a good place now.

If my parents found out it would tear our family apart. I was sure of it. I looked up just then to see Ariana walk out of the restroom, and I quickly went to her.

"Ariana, I'm so sorry. You know I didn't mean it like that."

She refused to look at me, but at least she wasn't walking away.

"Ariana . . ." I didn't even know what to say anymore. It felt like we were having the same fight over and over again.

She sighed then and looked at me, tears pooling in her eyes, and my heart broke a little. I was doing this to her and I couldn't bear it.

"Rukhsana, you keep saying that you didn't mean it like that. So why don't you explain it to me, then? How did you mean it exactly when you shied away from me, like I'm contagious or something?"

I felt the frustration rise in me like bile.

"Do you think I have a choice? Do you think I don't want to hold your hand or kiss you when we're out together? I've told you this before, Ariana. Maybe you don't get just how serious this is for me. Any one of my mom's friends or relatives could have seen us! How long do you think it would be before they tell my parents? Do you have any idea what would happen?" My eyes were filling with tears too, from the strain of not being able to yell the way I wanted to and because I could see that I wasn't getting through to her.

Jen and Rachel came up to us and I just stood there, not knowing what else to do.

"Ariana, are you okay?" Rachel put her arm around Ariana's shoulder and squeezed it gently. "Do you want to get some frozen yogurt?"

Ariana nodded as she blew her nose. Jen looked at me.

"Do you want to come too?" she said, looking from me to Ariana.

I looked at Ariana but she wouldn't meet my eyes. My shoulders slumped.

"No, it's okay, you guys go ahead. I'm just going to go home."

They both shrugged sympathetically, but it was clear they were relieved I'd opted not to come. I made my way home on the bus, and by the time I got there I had decided. I was going to tell my mom. I didn't even care about the consequences anymore. If it was going to cost me my relationship with Ariana to keep this secret, then it wasn't worth it. I'd figure out a way to go to Caltech. It wasn't as though I needed them to pay for any of it, and once I was eighteen they couldn't really stop me short of physically locking me up. My life was not an Indian drama serial. This was Seattle in the twenty-first century. Things like that didn't happen. I wouldn't let them.

Determined to talk to my mom as soon as I could get her alone, I walked in the front door to see Aunty Meena sitting on the couch with my mom next to her.

The day just kept getting better.

"Assalaam alaikum, Aunty Meena," I said, bending to kiss her cheek. Today she had decided it was a day for Shalimar. Not that I didn't love the scent of vanilla, jasmine, and rose, but Aunty Meena did not have a light touch when it came to perfume.

"Rukhsana, can you please make some chai?" Mom said. "And bring some of those laddoos Daddy got yesterday."

I nodded and walked to the kitchen. There was no way I was going to be able to talk to Mom today, not with Aunty Meena in the house. She'd probably end up staying for dinner. As I made the chai and put the laddoos on a plate, I heard the doorbell ring. A few seconds later I heard Uncle Maruf's hearty laugh and then he was in the kitchen carrying a box from my favorite Indian sweet shop.

"Rukhsana, ammu, how are you? I haven't seen you for quite some time now."

I walked over to give him a hug and he handed me the box of sweets.

"Your favorite, rasmalai," he said with a big grin.

"Thank you, Maruf Uncle. You're the best."

His grin became even bigger. "Your Aunty Meena says the same thing when I bring her gifts." He chuckled at his own joke and I marveled at Aunty Meena's good fortune.

He sat down on one of the stools at the kitchen island.

"So, tell me, ammu, what are your plans now? Meena just told me today that you got a full scholarship to Caltech?"

I nodded, a big smile on my face as I transferred the rasmalai into one of my mom's pretty serving bowls from Dhaka.

"Mashallah. That is wonderful, but we must celebrate properly. This is a great accomplishment, Rukhsana. I'm very proud of you."

I gave him another quick hug before we walked back to the living room with the tray of chai and sweets.

Aunty Meena was regaling Mom with some gossip as usual, so I left to go to my room, using homework as an excuse. Tonight was not the night for confessions. I'd have to figure out how to get Mom in a good mood and tackle this another day.

I sat on my bed, my calculus book open in front of me, but I could not focus on derivatives. I replayed the conversation with Ariana, Rachel, and Jen in the food court, and it stung to realize that they all thought I had any control over this situation. They could at least try to understand what I was going through. Was it really that bad to keep everything under wraps for a couple more months? Then we'd be free to hold hands and kiss in public as much as we wanted. The chances that someone who knew me might see me with my girlfriend in California were close to nil.

• • •

Later at dinner, the conversation was entertaining as it always was when Uncle Maruf and Aunty Meena were together. He was the perfect antidote to her toxic personality.

"Zubaida, did you hear about Nafeesa's son in Florida?" Aunty Meena asked over dessert.

"I heard he got married and has a son now, isn't that right?" Mom said as she poured chai and handed a cup to my dad.

"Yes, yes, but did you know he married a gori? Now he is too embarrassed to bring his wife and son to Seattle to meet his family."

"How do you know of all this, Meena?" Uncle Maruf said between bites of laddoo.

"Oof, you don't understand these things, Maruf. I just know," Aunty Meena said with a dismissive wave of her hand.

"You should start up a fortune-telling business, Meena," Uncle Maruf said, his face completely serious. Dad suddenly had to closely inspect something in his bowl of rasmalai while I tried not to choke on the food in my mouth.

"You think you are very funny, Maruf, hanh?" Aunty Meena sniffed a little. "But when have I been wrong? Tell him, Zubaida. Am I not always right about these things?"

Mom nodded in silent support, quietly sipping her chai.

"Remember when I said that Fatima's son was gay. That time also you laughed at me, Maruf, remember? But I was right, wasn't I? Now he is living with some boy on the other side of the country. His poor parents can't show their faces anywhere."

"I don't understand why they are so ashamed," Uncle Maruf said. "After all, their son is doing very well. He has a master's degree and he has a good job from what I hear. So what if he is gay. That is not the end of the world. Nowadays even in Bangladesh there are activists fighting for the rights of gay people. Times are changing and we have to change with them." He put his cup down. "Meena, we cannot only think about what people will say all the time."

I could have kissed my uncle. But Aunty Meena was not thrilled at being called out.

"Yes, yes, it is very easy to be open-minded when it is other people's children. Wait until someone in your own family does something like that. Then we'll see how fine you are."

Uncle Maruf said nothing in response, obviously realizing there was no reasoning with her.

"I am so happy that my Rukhsana isn't like that," Mom said, raising her hands in prayer position. "By the grace of Allah, she is a normal girl."

Dad shook his head sympathetically. "I can't imagine how I would show my face anywhere if I was in their shoes. Poor Fatima and Ilyas."

Sometimes I found it hard to believe that I was related to my parents. I wished Aamir was home, so at least I could exchange looks with him. But he was happily away at a friend's house for the night and thus did not have to witness my parents' blatant display of homophobia. How could I ever tell them? Maybe if Ariana heard some of the things they were saying, she'd actually believe me. But of course, that would never happen.

My plan to tell my mom was rapidly disintegrating. But I had to wonder what benevolent being was looking out for me. If Aunty Meena hadn't shown up tonight, I would totally have told my mom. And the proverbial shit would have hit the fan. I was angry at myself because I had almost let my friends convince me that their way of dealing with this was better. I'd have to be much more careful if I was going to get through the next few months without raising any suspicion.

I stood, pushing back my chair and grabbing my plate. "I have a lot of homework to catch up on, so I'm going to go upstairs, if that's okay?"

I waited for Mom to ask me to help clear the table, but she didn't.

"Okay, ammu, I'll save some rasmalai for you in case you get hungry later."

Who are you and what have you done with my mother?

But I didn't want to jinx it, so I quickly gave hugs and escaped to my room. I sat on my bed and was about to call Ariana, but she beat me to it.

"Rukhsana, can we talk?" Her voice sounded small and my heart sank a little.

"Yes, of course. Look, Ariana—"

"I'm sorry, Rukhsana. I overreacted today at the mall. I was being selfish."

My eyes filled with tears and suddenly I wanted nothing more than to hold her in my arms.

"No, I'm the one who should be sorry. It's my fault you keep getting hurt. But I just don't know what to do." The tears were rolling down my face now, plopping dramatically onto the cover of my physics textbook.

"No, Rukhsana, I feel like I'm just making things harder for you." Ariana's voice shook and I knew she was crying too. "I know what you're dealing with, and even though I don't fully get it, I should at least be supportive. And I haven't been doing that very well lately."

I didn't say anything in response.

"Rukhsana . . . are you there?"

I sighed deeply, all the anger and frustration of the whole day rushing out of me.

"You know, when I came home today, I was going to tell my mom everything."

"What happened?" Ariana's voice sounded slightly panicked.

"My aunt and uncle came over and I didn't get the chance. They started talking and I got really angry. But I couldn't say anything."

"What were they saying exactly?"

"My aunt is such a gossip, sometimes I really hate her. She was talking about some Bengali couple who have a gay son. And she was saying how they can't show their faces anywhere. Like that's the worst thing that could happen to parents. And I realized she'd be talking about me and my parents the same way to someone else once they found out."

"That's awful." Ariana sighed deeply into the phone.

"Ariana, can I be completely honest with you?"

She didn't say anything, so I continued.

"I hate that I have to hide this part of me from everybody. I love you so much. I wish I could shout it from the rooftops. But my reality is that I can't do any of that. And try as I might, there's not much I can do to change it."

"I never asked you to change anything," Ariana said. "But you can't get mad at me because my feelings get hurt. I can't pretend that this doesn't affect me too."

"Of course, I get that. But what I'm saying is that I'm not willing to risk our relationship by telling my parents every time your feelings get hurt. I feel awful, knowing that I'm the one hurting you. But I'll feel a whole lot worse if I can't be with you at all."

"Look, I don't want to fight anymore and I can't stay mad at you. Let's just get through the next couple of months and then we won't have to worry about all this anymore."

I could kiss her.

chapter
seven

My last class of the day was physics. I was fluent in this language and loved how absolute everything was, this world of vectors and straightforward laws. My dream was to one day work at NASA. I knew it was a long shot, but I liked a challenge. It all started in seventh grade, when we had to do a research project on notable women in science. I did mine on Madhulika Guhathakurta, an astrophysicist who worked at NASA, and ever since then I was hooked. I'd always been fascinated by metaphysics and the more I read about this accomplished woman, the more I realized that I wanted to follow a similar path. And now, if my mom didn't ruin everything, I would soon be on my way to realizing my dream.

I went home, and after I'd finished my homework, I walked over to Ariana's house to meet up with her, Jen, and Rachel to go to a movie. When I arrived, I heard voices coming from the backyard. I figured I would just go through the back entrance like always but I hesitated. It sounded like Ariana and her mom were arguing. About me.

I considered leaving but found myself unable to move, listening.

"Mom, you're being ridiculous," Ariana was saying.

"Really?" her mother said. "You don't think there's anything duplicitous about a girl who lives a secret life behind her parents' backs?"

"You don't know them. They're very strict. They wouldn't understand. But you've met Rukhsana. She's nothing like them."

I'd met her mom a couple of times when Ariana and I hung out at her place. She'd been welcoming and friendly, but I sensed a hesitation behind her smile. I'd encountered this before, usually when I went to some of my white friends' houses. There was a slight wariness in their parents' demeanor, as if they couldn't be sure that I wasn't going to suddenly scream "Allahu akbar!" and blow them to smithereens. It was disconcerting, but I'd sort of grown used to it over the years. I was the brown Muslim friend and therefore had to be regarded with some suspicion, at least initially.

So, when I heard her saying these things about me, I sort of got it. I mean, I'd be suspicious too if, say, Aamir was going out with someone who was lying to their parents about everything. And I really couldn't expect them to understand my situation.

"Ariana, I'm just trying to protect you. I hope you understand that. Rukhsana is a great girl, but her family is not like ours. Those people are different. You see it on the news, don't you?"

I'd heard enough. Not waiting for Ariana to reply, I turned and walked away. When I got home, I went straight up to my room, just wanting to be alone. I was angry and felt guilty for being angry. What right did I have to be upset at what her mom was saying, when my parents said things that were way worse?

I grabbed my headphones and collapsed onto my bed, burrito-ing myself with my blanket. I began to relax as the soothing vocals of Sam Smith's "Pray" filled the silence, the lyrics echoing in my head like stolen thoughts. The pounding slowed and I closed my eyes, losing myself in the melody. I must have dozed off, because the next thing I knew Mom was shaking me gently.

"Rukhsana, Ariana is here. She said you were supposed to meet up with her an hour ago."

I blinked at the late-afternoon sun filtering in through the lacy curtains and sat up slowly.

"She's here?" I hated napping during the day because I was always disoriented after.

"Yes, ammu." Mom put a hand on my forehead, frowning a little. "Are you feeling okay?"

"Yes, I'm fine, Mom." I stood and made my way to the bathroom. I splashed some cold water on my face and felt a bit better.

Mom was still sitting on the edge of my bed.

"Do you want me to tell her you're not feeling well?"

"No, it's okay. I'll go down. We were supposed to go to a movie."

We went down together and Mom went into the kitchen. Ariana was waiting for me in the living room.

"Rukhsana, where were you?" Ariana's brow was furrowed. "I thought you were going to meet me at my place."

"I had a headache." I couldn't decide if I wanted to tell her yet.

"Are you feeling better now? We don't have to go to the movie if you don't want to. I'll tell Jen and Rachel."

She pulled her phone out and sent off a quick text.

"You know what, why don't you go ahead with them," I said. "I think I just need to go to sleep early today."

Ariana wasn't buying it.

"Are you sure you're okay? We can just stay here and talk."

I quickly glanced over my shoulder to see Mom right there in the kitchen. We most definitely could not stay here and talk. Ariana nodded wordlessly.

"We can go over to my house. My mom's out running errands."

That was the last place I wanted to go right now.

"I think I kind of want to be alone." I realized I did want her to know something was up. Otherwise I'd just spend the entire evening obsessing over what I'd heard.

"Rukhsana, could you please just tell me what's going on?" Ariana pleaded.

This was awkward.

"I heard you. Earlier."

"What do you mean?"

"I came by. Before, to go to the movie."

I saw the realization dawn by the way her face fell.

"How much did you hear?" she asked quietly.

"I don't know. Enough? I knocked on the door and then I heard you in the backyard."

"Why didn't you say something?" Ariana's face was flushed.

"Honestly, I didn't know what to do. That's why I left."

Ariana reached for my hand and pulled me down on the couch.

"I'm so sorry, Rukhsana. I never wanted you to hear that. My mom's being really weird about us all of a sudden."

"Why? Did something happen?"

Ariana shook her head. "I'm not sure. She was fine when I first told her. But recently she's been all over me. About Muslims and stuff on the news, you know?"

Mom popped her head in, startling us both. Ariana dropped my hand as if it were on fire. "Do you two want anything to drink? Some chai maybe?"

"No, thank you, Mrs. Ali," Ariana said.

I shook my head. "We're good, Mom."

"Okay, but let me know if you change your mind." Mom disappeared back into the kitchen.

I took a deep breath and exhaled. That was close.

"So anyway, I think that's why my mom's suddenly on my case," Ariana continued.

I looked down at my hands. What could I even say? The only bright side to this that I could see was that maybe now Ariana could understand what I was dealing with as far as my parents were concerned.

"Say something, Rukhsana," Ariana said softly. I looked at her then and a wave of affection rushed over me. I wanted so badly to kiss her, but of course I couldn't with Mom a few feet away. I squeezed her hands and I knew she understood what I wanted to say. She smiled tremulously, her eyes a little moist, and I almost gave in.

Ariana gave me a quick hug and I walked her to the door.

After she left I went into the kitchen to grab a glass of water and some Tylenol for my headache. Mom was there getting things ready for dinner.

"You didn't go out?" she said, tying her hair into a knot at the nape of her neck. "I thought you were going to a movie?" She began chopping onions, her hands fast but steady with the knife.

"I changed my mind. I have a headache." I grabbed a glass from the cabinet and turned on the faucet. I waited for the water to be absolutely cold before I filled my glass.

"Maybe you're coming down with something." She finished chopping the onions and started on the carrots next.

"Maybe," I said noncommittally.

Mom stopped chopping midway with the knife hovering menacingly above the carrots. She held me with a scrutinizing look.

"Are you sure there's nothing else going on?"

"Like what?" I pretended I wasn't terrified of what she might have seen or heard while Ariana was here.

"I don't know, ammu. I'm just saying that you can talk to me if something is bothering you." She resumed her chopping and the staccato sound filled the kitchen.

My heart was racing and I struggled to find the words that would convince her that there was nothing untoward going on. I wanted nothing more than to succumb to the desire to just lay my head on her shoulder and tell her everything. And to let her tell me that she would make everything better. But I couldn't be sure that this wasn't a test. I couldn't be sure that she hadn't heard some or all of my exchange with Ariana in the living room.

"There's nothing bothering me, Mom. Just a bad headache. I'm getting my period soon, so that's probably why." Hoping desperately that she would let it go, I put the Tylenol in my mouth, swallowed it with a big gulp of water, and went up to my room.

● ● ●

Jen pulled me aside after chemistry.

"What happened to you last night? Ariana said you weren't feeling well."

"Yeah, it was just a headache," I mumbled.

Jen stared at me for a second. "Are you seriously trying to blow me off right now?"

A pang of guilt stabbed at me. Jen was my best friend and deserved better.

"I'm sorry, I just don't know if I can talk about it."

Jen put her hands on her hips and gave me her most severe I-know-what's-best-for-you look.

"Hey, Rukhsana, it's me, remember? Best friend since elementary school? You can tell me anything."

I couldn't help smiling. Jen did always know how to make me feel better.

"I overheard Ariana arguing with her mom yesterday when I went over there."

"About what?" Jen pulled me over to a corner by the wall, out of earshot from all the students milling about.

"About me and her. And that I'm Muslim and she's worried something will happen."

"Did she just realize you're Muslim? I mean, she must have known that from the beginning, right?"

"Well, yes, but I think it's all the hiding and the secrecy that she has a problem with." I wondered if Ariana had been talking to her about that. She must have told her mom how much it bothered her that I had to keep our relationship a secret from my family.

"I guess I kind of get that though," Jen said. She touched my arm gently. "I know it's really hard for you, but I'd be upset too if my boyfriend had to pretend we weren't together. Especially if we were serious about each other."

"I don't know what to do. It's going to be so weird talking to her mom, now that I know how she really feels. I guess it was nice thinking that at least someone was okay with our relationship."

Jen threw an arm around my shoulder. "It's going to be okay, Rukhsana. You and Ariana will figure it out. And once you're both at Caltech, things will be a lot easier."

I squeezed her arm. I hoped she was right.

chapter
eight

The tantalizing smells of my mother's cooking welcomed me as I walked into the kitchen.

"Mom, whatever you're making smells amazing." I dropped my backpack, walking over to give her a quick hug while she stirred something creamy in a large pot.

My parents were hosting one of their regular Friday dinner parties tonight and they always went all out to impress.

"I'm making coconut shrimp curry," Mom said, gesturing for me to get the cilantro that sat chopped and ready in a small bowl on the counter. I handed it to her and grabbed one of the cauliflower-and-potato pakodas that were resting on newspaper soaking up excess oil.

"Rukhsana, please take a plate and sit and eat like a human being." I handed her a small plate and she put some pakodas on it, adding a dollop of date-and-tamarind chutney on the side before handing it back to me. I dunked a pakoda in the sauce and savored the tangy, sweet crunchiness before I could speak again.

"Who's coming tonight, Mom?" I popped another piece into my mouth.

"The usual . . . Aunty Meena and Maruf Uncle, Iftekar Uncle and Sheila Aunty. And Samira Aunty said she might come too." Mom transferred the curry into a serving dish and put it in the oven to keep warm. "Sheila said Nasreen is coming too," she added.

"Oh good," I said, licking the last bit of chutney off my fingers. "I haven't seen her since the wedding."

"Ammu, can you make the raita, please? Daddy says you've learned to make it just like him. I still have to finish up the daal and the vegetable curry."

"Sure, I'll make it, but then I have to go upstairs to take a shower before everyone gets here."

"Just put it in the fridge before you go up." Mom gave the daal a stir before turning off the flame.

I opened the fridge and took out a tub of yogurt, some carrots, and two cucumbers.

"Do you think Aunty Meena will sing tonight?" I asked Mom, grating the vegetables.

"If we accompany her, then yes. Otherwise, she will not sing on her own." Mom added sliced onions to a pan of hot oil and a few seconds later, they were happily sizzling away.

"What should I wear? The pink shalwar kameez or the blue one?"

"I think the blue one. You haven't worn that yet, tai na?" I nodded, whisking the yogurt in a bowl before adding a pinch of black salt and sugar to it.

The pan on the stove sputtered as Mom added mustard seed to it.

After finishing the yogurt salad, I went up to shower and change. When I got upstairs, Aamir stepped out of the bathroom and pulled me into his room.

"Hey, do you know if Nasreen's sister is coming?" he asked while he dried his hair with a towel.

"No, I don't think so. And anyway, you said she doesn't even know you exist," I reminded him.

He stuck out his tongue at me. "That doesn't mean I'm not going to try."

"Well, good luck to you." I turned to leave.

"Do you know Mom asked me if you have a boyfriend?" Aamir said and I stopped in my tracks.

"Are you serious?" We grinned at each other. "What did you tell her?"

"Lucky for me I didn't have to lie," he said, pulling a T-shirt over his head. "You know how bad I am at lying, right?"

I snorted. "Yeah, right. Anyway, hurry up and go downstairs or Mom's going to start freaking out."

I showered and dressed in a blue chiffon tunic and loose pants that gathered at my ankles, making the outfit super comfy for sitting on the floor. I knew that's where I would end up later in the evening when the singing began.

Our guests began arriving soon after I went back downstairs. Dad was back from work, helping Mom put the finishing touches on the sumptuous meal she had prepared. The doorbell rang and as people started filing in, Aamir set up more chairs in the living room. Nasreen arrived with her family and we went to the kitchen to start making chai for everyone.

"Have you told your parents about Salim yet?" I asked as I put a pot of milk on the stove.

"No, I'm waiting for him to tell his parents first." Nasreen pulled out the cups and saucers from the cabinet and began arranging them on my mom's silver tray.

"Do you think they'll agree?" Nasreen's parents were probably the most liberal among our family friends. And Salim was the right sort of guy. He was Muslim, Bangladeshi, and educated. Everything Bengali parents would want for their daughter.

"I don't know. He says his parents are really conservative and don't approve of love marriage," Nasreen said, putting plates of cumin biscuits and cauliflower pakodas on another tray.

"Don't you wish everyone had parents like Rashida's?" I said.

"I know, right? She's going out with a white boy and her parents are so cool about the whole thing."

"I met her at the mall the other day and we were talking about it. Apparently her parents told her she could go out with anyone as long as she was treated with respect."

Nasreen shook her head. "I wish Salim's parents were more like that."

"What are you going to do if they say no?" The milk had started to boil, so I added the tea leaves, cloves, cardamom, cinnamon, ginger, and sugar. A delicious aroma filled the kitchen as we talked.

"Honestly? I'm not sure. Sometimes I don't think he's strong enough to stand up to his parents. That's why I'm not saying anything to my parents yet."

"I'm sure it will all work out, Nas." I squeezed her hand gently before pouring the chai and taking it into the living room with Nasreen following close behind.

After dinner, while everyone sat down with more cups of chai, Dad pulled out the harmonium for Mom and the tabla for himself.

"Zuby Apa, I've been waiting to hear you play for so long," Maruf Uncle called out, clapping enthusiastically.

"Meena, you have to accompany me. Otherwise it is not fair." Mom waved Aunty Meena over to the center of the living room, where they sat on large cushions.

As Mom coaxed beautiful notes out of her instrument, Dad kept the beat with the tabla and Aunty Meena began to sing. A hushed silence came over the room. It was impossible not to feel mesmerized by her rich voice as she sang a popular song by Rabindranath Tagore.

"I can't believe Aunty Meena can sing like that," Nasreen whispered in my ear. "She's usually such a witch."

I couldn't stop myself from snorting, which earned me a glare from Mom.

"That has to be why Uncle Maruf stays with her," I whispered. "She probably sings to him every night."

Nasreen made a face as the song ended and we all clapped, cheering for more. As the evening wore on and I watched everyone enjoying themselves, I couldn't help but wonder about the dichotomy of it all. These same friendly people I'd known since childhood would likely turn on me if they ever found out about my relationship with Ariana.

chapter
nine

"Ariana, what are you getting?"

We stood in line at Starbucks, and as usual, Ariana was having a hard time deciding what she wanted. It was Saturday morning and the line grew longer by the minute.

"I think I'll have a venti chai latte with skim milk."

"Are you serious?" I couldn't believe my girlfriend was ordering this whitest of white drink. "Have you learned nothing about chai after being with me all this time?" I said, laughing.

"What's wrong with my drink? I love a good chai latte." Ariana pouted.

"OMG, I will make you a proper cup of chai when you come over next time." I glared at her in mock frustration.

"Okay, but could you just grab me one for now? I'll find us a table."

I'd evaded Mom this morning and told Dad I had to meet with my study group. He nodded absentmindedly as he read his daily newspaper. Since Mom didn't believe in Starbucks, I was safe here.

After ordering our drinks, I found Ariana at a table for two tucked away in the corner. She looked incredibly hot with her glasses on and her nose scrunched up, poring over her English textbook. In jeans and a hoodie, with her hair in a messy ponytail, she looked like the cutest little nerd. Against my better judgment, I leaned over and kissed her quickly on the mouth as I put our coffees down. She looked up at me and smiled, then rose up a little out of her seat to kiss me back.

Slipping into the chair beside her, I took out my book and fished out my pen and highlighter. I was a couple of paragraphs into the short story our teacher had assigned when I looked up to ask Ariana how far she'd gotten. And I froze.

Irfan. Standing in the line. Shit. How long had he been here? Had he seen us?

He stood there looking in our general direction. I moved my body as discreetly as I could, so that my back faced him.

"Ariana, we have to leave."

"Huh?" She looked up from her work. "What? Why? We just got here."

"There's this guy over there. No, don't look," I hissed as she turned her head in his direction.

"What guy?" she whispered.

"This guy, my family knows him. I think he just saw us."

It took a few seconds, but then Ariana's eyes widened in understanding. "Are you sure he saw us?"

"No. I'm not. But we need to leave. Now."

• • •

I couldn't focus on anything, going over the morning's events again and again until my head hurt. I took turns kicking myself for being so cavalier about kissing Ariana and cursing Irfan for choosing my Starbucks to get his coffee.

I grabbed my cell phone off the nightstand.

> Are you awake? I can't sleep.

I waited a few seconds.

> Ariana? Are you there?

Are you okay?

Finally, a reply.

> Not really. I'm freaking out.

Why?

Was she serious right now?

> Because of this morning.

I think you're worrying too much. He probably didn't even see us.

Easy for her to say. I'm the one who'd be in deep shit if my parents found out.

I'm going to try and get some sleep now. Good night.

> Good night babe.

• • •

I eyed the phone in the living room with trepidation. It was Sunday morning and everyone was home. My palms were sweaty as I waited for the call that would signal the end of my life as I knew it. Irfan had probably told Aunty Meena already and she must be plotting the best way to ruin my life. Irfan must have wondered why I hadn't flirted with him at the wedding like every other female in his vicinity. It wouldn't be long before he put two and two together. It would all make sense to him now. The only reason a girl wouldn't be interested in him had to be that she was a lesbian. I had to do something, I couldn't just sit around waiting for a phone call.

Mom came into the kitchen and began to pull ingredients out of the fridge to cook lunch. I walked away into the living room before she could enlist me to help. I was just about to chew my nails off when the phone rang. I jumped up and ran to the kitchen, almost knocking Mom to the ground as she picked up the phone. She glared as she frantically gestured at me to watch the stove while she stepped into the family room to talk to whoever was on the other end of the line. I tried to think of a way to get out of this. I couldn't hear what she was saying, so I turned back to the stove just in time to stop the daal from boiling over.

"Rukhsana, that was Aunty Meena," Mom said, coming back into the kitchen. She pushed me gently out of the way as she checked the pot. "She's coming over for chai in a little bit."

So, this was it. He certainly hadn't wasted any time telling her. I had to think fast to come up with an excuse, anything to explain why I was kissing a girl. I could say it wasn't me he had seen, that he was mistaken, but I didn't know if Mom would buy that. On the other hand, would she even believe that I was gay? That seemed even more far-fetched, but maybe I could get out of this somehow.

● ● ●

Half an hour later, I sat facing Mom and Aunty Meena, my life flashing before my eyes. If Mom and Dad found out, they would probably ground me for the rest of my life, or worse, make me go to UW.

"Rukhsana, Aunty says Nani is not doing too well."

The words didn't make sense right away. Slowly, my brain registered what she was saying. They didn't know about Ariana and me.

But then it sunk in. My grandmother in Bangladesh was sick. Suddenly, I came back to life.

"Is it serious? Is she in the hospital? I spoke to Shaila last week, she didn't mention anything."

"Don't worry, ammu, it is nothing very serious. Just old age, so we are a little bit worried, you know?" said Aunty Meena. "Don't think about it too much. She is always asking about you and Aamir."

I was relieved that my Nani was fine, but as I listened to them talking about her, I couldn't shake the uneasy feeling that this thing with Irfan wasn't over yet.

• • •

Weekends were always the busiest at my parents' grocery store where I helped out sometimes, as Bengali families stocked up on hilsa fish, rice, daal, and other food items that they couldn't find in the local grocery store.

It was Sunday, a week after the near catastrophe with Irfan, and customers milled about the store, while children ran around the big, clear plastic containers that housed pulses of all kinds, as well as bulk dry kidney beans and chickpeas. Gunny bags of rice sat neatly arranged in pyramids, threatening to topple over every time a customer grabbed one. Along one wall, a refrigerated glass display case hummed along while brightly colored sweets soaked blissfully in a sugary syrup. I could see at least twenty different varieties of the sweetmeats that Bengalis were famous for all over the Indian subcontinent. On top of the case were several trays piled high with bright orange jalebis, the deep-fried, syrupy swirls of goodness that I'd been craving all day.

When the checkout clerk went on his break, things slowed down a little, so I busied myself by refilling some of the bulk containers of ground spices while keeping an eye on the checkout counter.

I had just finished topping off the whole red chilies when the bell above the door jingled. I turned to look through the shelves and my heart skipped a beat. It was Irfan. I ducked behind a mound of gourds, grateful that the vegetable I detested was finally doing me some good.

What's the deal with this guy? Is he stalking me?

It had to be some weird coincidence that he showed up here only a week after he'd seen me with Ariana. No. It couldn't be. I was sure he had come for me. Or maybe his mom wanted some mustard oil for her fish curry. Debating whether to confront him or continue hiding out among the gourds, I watched as he placed a bag of rice and several packets of lentils in his basket. But then a customer wanted to know where she could find jaggery and I pointed her in the right direction. By the time I resumed my spying position, Irfan was nowhere to be seen.

Great, now where did he go? Could he have left the store already?

I was still crouching behind the gourds, craning my neck to try and see if I could spot him, when someone tapped me on the shoulder. I turned so quickly that I knocked over a few of the gourds on the top of the mound. I stared helplessly as they fell to the ground with a loud thud.

"Umm, are you okay?" Irfan's eyes twinkled.

"Yes, of course," I said hastily. "I was just checking if there were any bad ones in this pile." I bent to pick up the runaway gourds closest to me, replacing them carefully on top of the mound. Irfan immediately began to help, retrieving a couple that had rolled under the shelves. As I attempted to arrange them in a neat pyramid, my mind was racing.

Why is he here?

"Hey, I was wondering if there's someplace we could go and talk?" he said after the last of the errant gourds were back in their pile. "After you're finished here, of course," he added with a smile.

I scrutinized his face, trying to find a hint of malice or something equally evil. But either he was really good at masking his true feelings or I was totally off base. But then again, this could not be a coincidence. I guess there was only one way to find out.

"Sure. There's a Starbucks nearby. I could meet you there in an hour." I would take him back to the scene of the crime and put an end to this.

"That sounds good. I'll go and get us a table." He went to the counter. The checkout clerk was back from his break and I watched as Irfan paid for his items, offered one last look at me, and left the store.

I took a deep breath and finished restocking, all the while trying to decide how I would find out what his intentions were. Or if he had even seen us that day.

• • •

I spotted Irfan sitting at a corner table by the window, sipping his coffee. I walked over to him and hung my purse on the back of the chair across from him. He jumped up as soon as he saw me.

"I'm sorry, I didn't know what you like to drink—"

"That's fine, I'll just grab a coffee—"

"No, please, just tell me what you'd like. I insist."

I gave up, knowing there was no point in arguing.

"I'll just take a latte, then. Thanks."

He went off to get my drink and I sat down wondering what I'd gotten myself into. He seemed so nice and normal, it was becoming hard to imagine that he was plotting anything evil. But I knew I shouldn't let my guard down.

He returned a few minutes later and placed a steaming cup in front of me. He opened his mouth as if to say something, but then took a sip of his coffee instead.

Finally, I couldn't take the awkwardness any longer.

"So, what did you want to talk about?"

"I saw you here last Saturday with your"—he cleared his throat again—"girlfriend."

I didn't say anything. I struggled to keep my face neutral. I didn't want to give him the satisfaction of knowing I was terrified.

"I just wanted you to know that you don't have to worry about anything," he was saying. "I haven't told anyone. And I'm not going to."

I hadn't realized I was holding my breath. I released it slowly. The knot in my stomach unfurled a little.

"When I saw you at the wedding the other night with Aunty Meena, I didn't realize you were, umm—"

If he was so uncomfortable with the word, I wasn't going to make it any easier for him. Labels weren't my thing, which was ironic because in our community, labels were everything. The thinking went: You didn't really know someone unless you knew where they were born, what village in the motherland their parents and grandparents hailed from, and so on. Watching my relatives meet someone new exhausted me. They only did it to feel some sort of connection to people, but I just never felt comfortable under such scrutiny.

So now I let Irfan squirm for a bit before I answered.

"Gay? Yes, I am. And no, my parents don't know, but if you think you have something to hold over me, well, you don't. I'm planning to tell them myself, so—"

I stopped. What was he smiling about?

"Hey, I told you already, I'm not going to say anything to anyone," he said, holding his hands up in mock self-defense. "If you give me a chance, I can explain."

"The stage is yours," I said with a dramatic wave of my hand.

"So," he began hesitantly, "here's the thing. I'm kind of in a relationship with someone myself."

Wait, is he gay too?

Oh, please please please.

I could just see Aunty Meena's face. It would be priceless.

"So, who is it . . . Anyone I know?" The Bangladeshi community in Seattle was fairly large, but it wasn't uncommon to run into the same people at events. Also, my dad was big on socializing with people from the homeland, so he made it a point to invite any new families over for dinner when they arrived. As a result, we knew most families, if not directly, then at least by association.

"Her name's Sara. She goes to UW," he said. "She's not Bengali," he added quietly.

There it was. The silver lining in the black cloud that had been hovering over me for the last week.

"Is it serious?" It had to be, for him to go to all this trouble. But I wanted to hear it from him.

"We've been together for over a year now. But you know Aunty Meena and my mom have been on me to get married, and I'm running out of excuses."

A wave of compassion struck me.

"Have you tried to talk to your parents?" They seemed like nice enough people when I'd met them at the wedding. But that didn't mean anything when it came to a situation like this.

He shook his head. "It's no use . . . They wouldn't agree to a love marriage. Especially not to a white girl." I knew he was right. If they found out they would probably just force him to get married to a nice Bengali girl, someone they picked out for him.

"What about her family? Maybe they can help?"

"Her family isn't too keen on it either. They don't want their daughter marrying a Muslim. I mean, I've met them and they're really decent, but I think deep inside they're not too sure that I won't blow something up."

I gave him a wry smile. "Sadly, I'm familiar with that particular sentiment."

Irfan shook his head. "I don't know what to do. I love her so much, but I just don't see a way that it could work."

"So why did you want to meet with me? I'm happy to help you, but to be quite honest, I'm not sure what I can do."

"I was hoping maybe if you and Sara could become friends, then you could introduce her to Aunty Meena. And then after some time, I could bring it up with my parents."

He smiled disarmingly. "I really don't want to lose her, but I don't want to hurt my parents either."

So, we were in the same boat. Although my parents were totally unreasonable as far as I was concerned, I did believe that all their rules came from a place of love. They had just been raised with a different set of beliefs.

"Okay," I said after a while. "I'll do it."

"Thank you! And I promise I will help you with whatever you need. You saw how much Aunty Meena likes me, didn't you?"

It occurred to me then that he was on my side. It was nice, having someone in my corner. He hadn't made the usual crude gay jokes and he didn't even seem shocked. It was sad that this was a relief. I'd come here half expecting to meet a homophobic misogynist, but instead I found a really nice guy.

"You know, when I saw you that morning I was terrified that you'd seen us and would tell Aunty Meena."

He smiled at me again, his dark eyes crinkling at the edges. I could see how girls might find him attractive. From what I could see, he had a toned body and his skin was just the right shade of brown, dark enough to make white girls swoon and light enough to make him good marriage material. At least, as far as all the matchmaking aunties were concerned.

We sat in mutual silence for a while. Darkness had set in and my parents were likely wondering where I was by now.

"Irfan, I have to get home. It's getting late."

"Of course," he said, pushing back his chair as he got up. "Rukhsana, thanks for doing this. You don't know how much it means to me."

"Look, we'll figure this out," I said, standing up to leave. "Now, when am I going to meet this girlfriend of yours?"

"We could go for lunch next week if you're free. I know she'd love to meet you too."

chapter
ten

"I hear we're in a similar mess." Sara's brown eyes shone as she smiled at me. A lavender blouse and dark jeans set off her brunette hair and light complexion.

We were at my favorite sushi restaurant and had just finished ordering.

"I guess you could say that." I pointed my chin at Irfan. "He isn't sure how to tell his parents about you two."

"Can you blame me?" Irfan said. "It's bad enough that they won't let up about the whole marriage thing. I don't want to give them any reason to speed things up."

"And what do you think about all this?" I tried taking a sip of my green tea but it was still too hot.

"To be honest, I was kind of pissed at first," Sara said. "I mean, I don't get why he can't just tell his parents. He's not a child."

"I may as well be," Irfan said bitterly. "At least when it comes to this."

"Well, I have an idea, if you're interested. I don't know if it'll work, but it's the only thing I can think of right now."

"Okay, let's hear it," Sara said, leaning forward. "Should I be taking notes?"

I grinned. "Not right now, but you might want to at some point." I took a sip of my tea before I began.

"I thought you could start by coming over to my place a few times and giving my parents a chance to get to know you."

"Won't they be suspicious if I start showing up all the time?" Sara asked.

I shook my head. "I'll tell my mom we met at school when you came to talk about UW and that you're trying to convince me to go there."

Sara let out a sigh of relief. "That's not even a complete lie. I love UW."

"There you go," I said. "Mom's going to love you, and when the time comes we'll tell her about you guys."

Irfan and Sara exchanged a glance that made me miss Ariana. She was going to like them, and I couldn't wait for them all to meet.

Our food came just then and we ate while I told them all about my predicament.

"What can we do to help?" Irfan asked as we were finishing up.

It was hard to believe that less than forty-eight hours ago I thought he was going to spill my secret. But there still wasn't anything they could do to help me at this point.

● ● ●

Sara came over to hang out the following Tuesday. Mom wasn't there when she came, so I took the opportunity to show her a few things.

"I'm going to teach you how to make chai," I said.

"I love chai tea," she said as she watched me pour milk into a saucepan. While we waited for it to boil, I told her that chai was the Urdu word for tea.

"Gotcha," she said. "So, I've really been asking for tea-tea all this time?"

"Pretty much," I said with a grin. "Actually, in Bengali we call it cha, but in Hindi and Urdu it's chai. People here are more familiar with chai, so we just got used to saying that."

"I have so many questions about that," Sara said. "One of these days you're going to have to tell me all about the differences. I feel like I don't know enough about the region."

"I will, but one thing at a time," I said with a smile.

I showed her how much ginger, cardamom, cloves, and cinnamon to add to the tea leaves, and when it was ready, we each poured ourselves a cup. Mom had left some singharas on the counter, so I served her those as well.

"I thought these were samosas," she said, understandably confused.

"That's what they call them in India, but in Bangladesh these are called singharas. Our samosas are crispy and the outer part is thinner." She eagerly took a bite and I felt bad for not warning her. She coughed as soon as the morsel went down her throat and her eyes watered. I had a glass of milk handy and she gulped it down gratefully.

After her tongue stopped burning and she could speak again, I thought it was time to introduce her to Bengali people's favorite obsession when it came to food.

"Here's the thing, Sara," I began. "If you want Irfan's family to like you, there's only one surefire way to go about it. You must learn all about fish. And rice."

Sara looked at me in bewilderment. If I hadn't grown up listening to endless complaining about the lack of varieties of rice and freshwater fish here in the US, I would have thought it was weird too.

Her eyes began to glaze over by the time I was halfway down

the list, so I decided she'd had enough for one visit. When my mother came home, she was surprised to find Sara there.

"It's nice to meet you, Sara," Mom said after I made the introductions. "I hope you can stay for dinner."

Sara looked at me in a panic, probably reliving the burn of the singhara.

"You can stay, right, Sara?" I smiled like the villain that I was. Irfan would thank me later.

"Of course, yes, I'd love to stay. Thank you so much." She glared at me as soon as Mom turned away to start dinner. "If I die tonight, you'd better have a good place to hide from Irfan," she whispered coolly, but I saw the twinkle in her eyes.

I grinned. "Don't worry, it'll be fine."

Luckily, Mom made a simple meal of daal, roti, and chicken curry. I'd be lying if I said I didn't enjoy watching Sara tentatively bite a piece of chicken as if it might bite her back. Fortunately, she seemed to make it through the meal with most of her gastric lining intact.

Dad had to work late but Aamir came home just in time for dinner, so it was just the four of us at the table.

"So, Sara, how do you know our Rukhsana?" Mom asked as she put some more chicken curry on Sara's plate. I'd forgotten to warn her that we Bengalis liked to force-feed our guests.

"I met her in school when I came to talk about my university," Sara replied, woefully eyeing her plate. "I go to UW. I was just telling her how much I love it there."

Aamir perked up suddenly. "Mom, weren't you saying Rukhsana should go there too?"

I glared at my brother.

Mom pounced on this opportunity immediately.

"Yes, that is what I've been telling you, Rukhsana."

She walked over to the stove and began to make fresh rotis.

"And if you go to UW, you can still live at home," Aamir said helpfully.

Why is he still speaking?

I kicked at him under the table, but he moved his leg just in time and grinned at me.

Mom brought the rotis to the table and spooned some more daal and chicken curry onto Sara's plate. When she went to check on the rice pudding simmering on the stove, Sara frantically gestured at me to do something. But I didn't know how to stop Mom when she went into supreme hostess mode. I looked to Aamir and surreptitiously spooned the excess food onto his plate. For once, I was glad that my brother was an equal opportunity pig. By the time Mom came back to the table, Aamir had claimed the rest of the rotis.

"See, Rukhsana," she said to me, jabbing a spoon in my direction. "Sara says UW is great."

She gave the rice pudding one last stir before she spooned some into small glass bowls.

"And you are living at home?" she asked as she placed some pudding in front of Sara.

"Yes, it's much easier. My parents thought it would save some money, and to be honest, I'm glad I don't have to do laundry." I wanted to kick Sara under the table too, but alas I was cursed with short legs.

"Money, laundry . . . all good things. Why do you want to go and live in those dirty dorm rooms?" I was pretty sure Mom had never set foot in a dorm room of any kind.

Dad came home then and spent the rest of the evening asking all the important life questions while Sara wondered what she had signed up for. I'd been so busy experimenting with Sara's ability to handle spicy food, I'd forgotten to give her a heads-up about my parents' interrogation methods.

chapter
eleven

My eighteenth birthday was still months away, but it seemed to have triggered some sort of bat signal for potential suitors from the arranged marriage network, which was basically a bunch of Bengali aunties who didn't know how to mind their own business and had way too much time on their hands. Visitors showed up on random days, most of them unannounced. I received a constant stream of proposals, even from places as far as Bangladesh and New Zealand.

I came home one day to find Aunty Samira in the living room drinking chai with Mom. There was a stack of papers on the coffee table along with an assortment of Bengali sweets. Rasgullahs, sandesh, and gulab jamuns, arranged in tiny pyramids in my grandmother's silver bowls, all vied for my attention. I gave Aunty Samira a hug before snagging a couple of pieces of sandesh and grabbing a seat across from them.

"Rukhsana, I haven't seen you for a long time," Aunty Samira said. "I was just telling your mother about my friend's nephew in Australia."

I took a bite of my sandesh, savoring the creamy sweetness, while I waited to hear about the latest prospect.

"Actually, I have known the family for many years. They are looking for a very traditional girl for their son."

And they think I'm a good candidate? I must be doing a better job at fooling them than I thought.

"He wants someone who can cook Bengali food and will look after the household properly. Of course, it's a joint family, so you will never be alone."

Great. A fish-loving, rice-obsessed chauvinist? My dream spouse. And as a bonus I'd get to spend every minute under his parents' scrutiny.

I shoved the last bit of sandesh in my mouth to avoid answering her. Thankfully, Dad walked in at that very moment.

Aunty Samira repeated her pitch to him and handed him a sheet from the stack on the table. Mom passed me one as well with a glint in her eye. I took it from her and nearly burst out laughing. It was a resume with a grainy black-and-white picture in the bottom right corner. I had to look closely to make out any features through the pixelation. I arranged my face into a blank expression before handing it back to Aunty Samira.

Does she really think this will work?

"Rukhsana is going away to university in the fall," Dad said. I could have hugged him. "She will get married only after she has completed her education."

The stunned expression on Aunty Samira's face was priceless. Since my parents had accepted that I was going to Caltech, they had been lording it over everyone. My standing in the marriage market had gone up overnight, and my parents interpreted that as a legitimate source of pride.

●　●　●

Ariana came over a few hours later so we could study for our calculus test together. When Mom came into the kitchen to start dinner, we went up to my room. I closed the door and turned to Ariana.

We'd been super careful not to give anything away while we were at my house, but she looked at me with such tenderness, I couldn't help it. I leaned over and kissed her gently. My lips traveled to her earlobe and she gasped with pleasure when I nibbled gently. She took my face in her hands and pressed her lips to mine, kissing me fervently. I was so engrossed in the kiss that I didn't hear the door open. I didn't notice anything until I heard my mother's voice.

"Rukhsana," she said sharply. "Eita ki hocche?" Ariana and I jumped apart and then froze. Both of us. My body was incapable of movement. I couldn't speak. But that didn't stop the avalanche of thoughts in my head.

STUPID. How could I be so stupid? So reckless that I didn't even lock the door like I usually do. My blood ran cold. How long had she been standing there?

Slowly, feeling returned to my body and I grabbed her hand.

"Mom, please. Sit down. Please don't be angry. I didn't mean for you to find out like this." Two fat tears dropped onto my forearm. Where did they come from? I touched my face and it was wet. She looked at the two teardrops and then to me.

She opened her mouth to say something, but no sound came out. She glared at Ariana, who sat as still as a statue, her eyes wide, her hand trembling.

The slap came so fast I didn't even realize my mom had moved. The sharp sound of her hand connecting with Ariana's cheek brought me back to my senses. I looked at her in horror, the imprint of my mother's hand blooming red on Ariana's cheek almost instantly.

"Mom. Don't. She didn't do anything wrong." My head throbbed with anger and fear.

Mom looked just as shocked as I was, but she regained her composure almost instantly.

"Get out." Each word was like a punch in the gut. Her voice sounded unfamiliar, so cold and filled with rage. "Get out of my house right now. And don't you dare come near my daughter again."

Ariana stood and before I could stop her, she hurried down the stairs and out of our house. I had to stop myself from running after her. But I knew without a doubt that I had to stay here and face my mom.

• • •

"Mom, please." Fifteen minutes of begging and she wouldn't even look at me. Searching for something on her face, a flicker of understanding, I found nothing.

In a few minutes, my father would come up the stairs, wondering where we were. Maybe he had seen Ariana running out of the house in tears. No. He couldn't have, otherwise he'd be up here already.

"Mom. Please, you have to talk to me." Nothing.

When she finally looked at me my heart went cold. Her look was empty, detached, as if I was a stranger. I had to make this right.

"Mom, I love you. Please . . ." I touched her arm.

She flicked it away and stood. "Don't. Touch. Me." Her voice was hard and cold.

I stared at her, not knowing what to do or say. "Mom, I—"

"You disgust me." She spat out the words, her teeth clenched. "You're sick." And then she turned away and walked out of my room.

I could feel my heart wrenching inside my chest. It hurt so much that I couldn't breathe.

I had imagined this scene, this exact moment, over and over in my mind. The look of hurt on my parents' faces, and the yelling, telling me I was too young, that I couldn't possibly know what I wanted. But not this. I had never pictured this.

My mind went back to the summer before high school. I had just turned thirteen and Mom made me sit down for the talk. Not the talk about the birds and the bees. In our culture, the birds and the bees did not get together. Neither did boys and girls until they got married.

"Rukhsana, now you are no longer a little girl," Mom had said. "You are a young woman, so you have to be aware of many things. Most importantly, you are a young Muslim woman. Everyone in our community will be watching to see if you do something bad. Do you remember Aunty Nargis? Her daughter ran off with a white boy. Her parents had to sell their house and move to Toronto where no one knows them."

"But what's so bad about marrying a white boy? Nowadays, it's not such a big deal."

"Rukhsana," Mom said sharply, "I'm warning you. Don't get any ideas like that, okay? We are giving you a lot of freedom, but that doesn't mean that we won't take it away. Remember, boys want only one thing. It is up to you to protect it."

Her threat had been very effective. I was careful not to cross the lines. Until I started feeling things. Until Ariana came into my life.

Is she telling my dad right now?

My dad, who was usually all hugs and affection, would look at me and feel sickened by who I was. A wave of nausea hit me and I grabbed the trash can just in time to release the contents of my stomach. My hands shook uncontrollably as I wiped my mouth with a tissue.

What should I do now?

I had to talk to them and try to explain. I stood up and waited for the trembling to subside. Then I took a deep breath and walked downstairs into the living room. Mom and Dad's hushed voices carried over to me as I stood on the last step, contemplating what I should say.

They turned when I walked into the room. Their faces were ravaged. I had done this to them. Mom's cheeks were wet with tears. Dad looked at me and I couldn't tell what he was thinking. Maybe it was better I didn't know.

I tried to speak but my throat was closing and I had to force the words out.

"Mom, Dad, can we please talk about this?" For a second, I thought maybe they would smile and tell me that everything was going to be alright, that we would get through this and that they loved me, no matter what. But it was just a trick of my mind, the memories of another time when they said that to make all the hurt go away. Not today. Today, I only saw two people I had disappointed so much that maybe there was no coming back from this.

"I meant to tell you. I just didn't know how. I'm so sorry."

Mom wouldn't look at me, but Dad sighed deeply.

"It's our fault. We should never have given you so much freedom." He looked at Mom, who had started sobbing quietly.

"Mom, I'm sorry." I bit my lip. "Please stop crying."

"Look at what you are doing to your mother. Is this why we gave you everything that you wanted? So that you could repay us with this? I don't even know what to call it."

"It's a disease. That's what you call it," Mom said quietly. "I will take her to that doctor that Saira told me about. Her son went through the same thing. Now he's fine."

What the hell was she talking about? A conversion therapy program?

"Mom, I'm not sick. Please, just try to understand. This is how I feel; it's not some disease or something. You know that."

"You don't need to tell me what I know," she said. At least she was looking at me again. "Your dad is right. It's our fault. I should have never let you have so many American friends. This is what happens. They are too freethinking. And now you are becoming like them."

"But not in our house," Dad added forcefully. "All this nonsense is going to stop right now. Do you want to see your own parents become the laughingstock of the community?"

Are they for real?

Of course they were. This was classic guilt-tripping. They thought they could guilt me into not being gay anymore. At this point they would probably be overjoyed if I told them I was pregnant. Anything was better than this. A daughter who is a lesbian? How could they ever show their faces in public again?

I had to be patient, to give them time to get used to the idea. They were from another time, a different place where this was considered a sin, even a crime. But something in me raged at the thought that I should feel ashamed of who I was. And so I kept barreling forward.

"Dad. I'm gay. I'm sorry that I didn't tell you, but I can't change who I am." The words just tumbled out on their own; I could do nothing to stop them. And judging by their faces, they were as stunned at the outburst as I was.

Mom burst into tears again and Dad shook his head.

"What is this rubbish you are saying?" His voice rose an octave and I could see he was trying hard to control his anger.

"Have you lost your mind? Speaking to your parents like this?" Mom placed a hand on Dad's arm as if she could stop him if he really wanted to hit me.

"Go to your room and stay there. I can't look at you right now." His voice had gone quiet, but their anger triggered something in me. I should have just walked away and given him a chance to cool down. But I didn't.

"Well, you'll have to look at me, because we need to talk about this like adults. You're acting as if I killed somebody."

Why did I just say that? Come on, Rukhsana, stop making it worse.

I knew the second I said that, I'd made a huge mistake.

A vein throbbed on Dad's forehead, threatening to burst.

My face snapped to the right as Dad's hand made contact with my cheek.

I reeled from the shock, my legs turning to lead. My parents had never hit me. Ever. Not even when they caught me at a party in ninth grade or when I brought back a C on a math test. They'd been angry and disappointed, but they had never, ever laid a hand on me.

Now I lifted my eyes to hold Dad's gaze, tears streaming down my face. Mom stood there, unmoving. Probably as stunned as I was.

chapter twelve

I found Aamir standing in the hallway outside his bedroom, his eyes wide and his usual smirk absent.

"What happened? I heard yelling." Of course, with his headphones on, he probably hadn't heard the whole thing.

"Mom caught me and Ariana—"

His eyes hardened and he moved closer to look at my face. Even in the dimmed light of the hallway, he could see the angry redness on my cheek.

"Did Mom hit you?" he demanded, his voice suddenly loud.

"No, it was Dad."

He began to move toward the stairs, but I grabbed his arm to pull him back.

"Please don't say anything. You'll just make it worse."

He shook his head.

"Listen, I need to get out of here for a bit. Can you cover for me?"

He nodded. "Where will you go?"

"I don't know. I have to call Ariana and make sure she's okay. Mom slapped her."

Aamir sucked in a deep breath. "Wow, they're really going hard-core on this."

"I should have been more careful." I shook my head. "This isn't how I planned for them to find out."

Aamir put his hands on my shoulders. "It's not your fault. You do what you need to do. I won't say anything to them now, but promise me you'll tell me if you want me to."

I nodded, wrapping my arms around him as a wave of relief washed over me. I was so glad he was here, willing to stand up for me against our parents. It made me feel less alone, and right now that meant more to me than I could say.

I had no idea where I would go. I quickly checked my face in the mirror. If I went to any of my school friends' houses with the red mark on my cheek, they would tell me to call the cops on Dad. If I went to any of my Bengali friends the gossip mill would run wild. The last thing I needed was more drama. Poor Ariana. She might never forgive me and frankly I couldn't blame her. I called her, but she didn't answer until the fifth ring.

"Ariana, it's me. Are you okay?" *Stupid question. Of course she isn't okay.*

She didn't answer at first, but I could still hear her breathing softly, which was oddly comforting. "I'll be fine. What happened with your parents?" Her voice trembled slightly and my heart ached.

"They freaked out. My dad completely lost it."

"More than your mom?"

I deserved that.

More silence.

"Well, at least it's out in the open now. That's good, right?" She wanted me to say that it was, I could tell, and I didn't have the heart to tell her things would just go downhill from here on.

"Listen, I need to get out of here. I'm going crazy. Is there any way—"

"Just come to my place. My parents are away at a conference for a couple of days."

She didn't have to tell me twice. I grabbed a bag while she continued talking and stuffed a change of clothes and my toothbrush in it. We hung up and I peeked out into the hallway to make sure Mom and Dad weren't there. I tiptoed to the top of the stairs and craned my neck to see if they were still downstairs. No one was there. They must have gone to their room. I walked down as quietly as I could and slipped out the front door.

• • •

When Ariana opened the door, she gasped and pulled me inside, my heart pounding in my chest.

"Rukhsana, your face. Did she slap you too?" She touched my cheek gently, but I still winced.

"No, this is my dad's handiwork." I dropped my bag on a chair by the entrance. "I've never seen him so angry."

Ariana's eyes were puffy from crying, but at least my mom's handprint was fading from her cheek. Anger twisted my insides as I looked at her. She didn't deserve any of this.

"Can I ask you something?" I spoke softly, pulling her hand into mine.

She nodded. "Anything."

"You can tell me if you want to break up. I get it. I mean, I wouldn't blame you or be mad or—"

Ariana pressed her lips to mine. She kissed me with such tenderness, I didn't need an answer. Neither one of us needed words as we walked up the stairs, still holding hands. She didn't say anything while she unbuttoned my shirt or as my hands reached out to pull her T-shirt over her head. By unspoken agreement we lay down on her bed, the sheets cool and smooth against my skin. I kissed her lips, the ticklish spot on her neck, her tanned shoulders. She kissed me in response, gently at first, but then with more urgency, as she blazed a trail of kisses down my neck. I gave in to her touch, allowing the waves of bliss to wash over me.

I didn't remember falling asleep, but when the sunrise peeked through the window of Ariana's room I opened my eyes to find her arm lying across my stomach. It felt so good, just being here like this.

The buzzing of my cell phone brought me back to reality. I grabbed it off the nightstand.

Mom and Dad are awake. Are you coming back soon?

I checked the time. Somehow it was already 6:17 a.m.

Shit. I had to get home before Mom and Dad noticed I was gone or I'd be dead.

Ariana stirred.

"What time is it?" she asked, her voice full of sleep.

"It's already past six." I bent to kiss a spot on her shoulder and she pulled me toward her and kissed me on the mouth. The memory of last night was still fresh.

"I have to go. My brother's starting to panic."

Ariana nodded. "See you at school."

I kissed her quickly on the lips and grabbed my bag. "We'll talk later, I promise. I love you."

"I love you too."

One last kiss and then I left, making my way back home as quickly as I could.

Aamir must have been waiting by the door because he opened it just as I walked up the last step.

"Hurry," he said, pulling me inside. "Dad left early and Mom's in the shower. She hasn't come down yet."

I gave him a quick hug.

"Are you okay?" he asked, concern making his face look serious. A wave of guilt swept over me. Annoying as he could be sometimes, I liked it better when he was just his carefree self.

"I'll be fine, Aamir, don't worry too much."

I ran up to my room to get ready for school. The redness on my cheek had faded, but not enough to fool Jen and Rachel. They would know something was up. A little bit of concealer and some eye makeup later, I was ready.

I stuck my head out the door to make sure I didn't run into Mom in the hallway. It was all clear. I tiptoed downstairs and saw her at the kitchen sink. I went straight out the door before she saw me. The cold, crisp air on the walk to school rejuvenated me.

Ariana was already by her locker when I got there, and her face lit up when she saw me coming. It was all I could do not to go running into her arms.

"Hey, you," I said, reaching out to stroke her forearm.

"Hey, yourself." We shared a secret smile.

"What are we talking about?" Rachel's voice came from behind me. Jen was with her too.

"My mom caught us in my room yesterday," I said quietly.

Jen and Rachel stared at us with identically stunned expressions.

"What did she do?" Rachel said.

"Exactly what I was scared of," I said. "She freaked out. Completely."

"Did your parents say anything this morning?" Ariana said.

I shook my head. "I didn't see them at all."

"Maybe you should lay low for a bit," Jen said. "Just until things cool off."

I agreed. But this was going to be tricky. Now that my parents knew, I was sure they would keep an even closer eye on me. And then there was the possibility that I was never going to Caltech.

chapter thirteen

There was an eerie calm at home over the next week. Dad and I avoided each other, and Mom only talked to me when she had to. I was fine with this because the pace at school had picked up majorly and I had little time for drama.

"Rukhsana," Dad called out to me a few days later as I added another layer of mascara to my eyelashes. We were going to a dinner my parents had organized with some friends.

Lately, Dad and I had agreed on an unspoken truce of sorts. Well, he had started talking to me about things like my chores or my schedule, which was better than uncomfortable silence.

"I'll be down in a second, Dad."

He stood in the living room holding out a box wrapped in shiny purple paper with a white bow on top. He handed it to me without saying a word.

"What is it?" I felt a tiny little flutter of hope as I took it from him.

"Open it. Mom and I wanted you to have it."

Impatiently, I tore at the paper and found a maroon velvet jewelry box with Bengali script printed on top.

They must have bought it on our trip to Bangladesh a few years ago.

I opened it to reveal a beautiful gold pendant on a chain nestled inside. The pendant was in the shape of an oval with Arabic script engraved on it.

"It's to keep you on the right path wherever you are." Tears threatened to spill over as I reached out to hug him, and he held me tight as he stroked my hair the way he used to when I was little. I hadn't noticed Mom standing there until she sniffled a little. She came over and I hugged her tightly as she kissed the top of my head.

"Let's go or we'll be late," Mom said, smoothing down the front of her sari. The moment was over.

● ● ●

"How is Sara?" I asked Irfan over Manchurian chicken and fried rice. "I'm sorry, but with everything that happened I couldn't really invite her over."

We were at Chili House, "Home of the Best Indian Chinese Food," where we'd met up with some other families. Of course, Aunty Meena was there along with Irfan and his family. I wasn't sure if it was because of my own skills or Aunty Meena's, but I found myself sitting next to Irfan during dinner. I'd just finished telling him everything that had happened, and he was horrified. It was good that my parents were giving us some space too, because I definitely did not want them knowing what we were up to.

He speared a piece of chicken with his fork as he shook his head, still in disbelief.

"Don't worry about us. You have your own stuff to deal with."

"Yes, I sure do," I said and then leaned a little closer. "Also, I think my mom would prefer if I didn't bring home any white girls. She thinks they're the reason I turned lesbian."

Irfan choked a little on his chicken as he tried not to laugh out loud. It wouldn't be nice to encourage Aunty Meena or my parents. There was already a lot of head bobbing going on at the far end of the table, and if we kept going they might marry us right here and now at Chili House.

"So, what's the plan?" I asked after we'd finished most of our meal. "For you and Sara? You should just tell your parents. How bad do you think it'll be?"

"You know what . . . you've inspired me," Irfan said with a grin. "I think I'll give it a shot. If it doesn't work out then you and I can get married and Ariana and Sara can just move in with us."

I laughed out loud at that, and it felt good.

• • •

"I noticed that you and Irfan were getting along just fine," Dad said as we drove out of the crowded parking lot. I rolled my eyes in the darkness. Great. I knew I should have been less friendly around Irfan. Clearly, I'd given my parents the wrong idea.

"Yes, Dad, he's a great guy." I should have stopped, but of course I didn't. "But that doesn't change anything."

Dad didn't say anything and kept his eyes on the road.

"Rukhsana, you have to think about us too," said Mom. "What are we supposed to tell all our relatives back in Bangladesh? That we let you run around and now you're a lesbian? Chhee. How can I even utter this word to them?"

"Mom, why do you have to worry about what everyone else says? You know I haven't done anything wrong. I can't help who I like."

"What do you mean you can't help it? Of course you can help it. You think your father and I had a choice when we were young?" Her voice reverberated loudly in the compact interior of the car.

"Mom, that was a different time," I protested. "It's not the same now. Even in Bangladesh, people are making their own decisions about whom they marry."

"Yes, you're right, Rukhsana," Dad said patiently. "It is different and that's why we gave you so much freedom. Have we ever pushed arranged marriage on you? No."

"We let you have whatever friends you wanted, but this is too much," Mom concluded. "You are asking us to accept something that is completely against our beliefs." She shook her head. "I should have been much more strict with you. Now I am paying the price."

I balled up my fists to keep from punching something. Was there even a point to this conversation?

"I don't know what kind of jaadu-tona this girl has done on you. Couldn't she cast her spells on some other girl? Why does it have to be my daughter?"

The rest of the drive home passed in bitter silence. When we got home, I stomped up the stairs and slammed my door.

chapter fourteen

I walked into the house, but there was no one downstairs. It had been a couple of days since the last fight, but things were far from okay. Happy to avoid the awkwardness that was my life these days, I went upstairs. As I passed my parents' bedroom I could hear them talking in hushed voices. Curious, I knocked and walked in. An open suitcase sat on the bed, while another was on the floor. Dad knelt beside it, putting clothes in. Mom sat on the edge of her bed crying. I rushed to her side and threw my arms around her.

"Mom, what's going on? Where are you going?"

Dad stood and came over to us. "Tanveer Mama called. Nani is quite sick, so we have to fly to Dhaka."

Tanveer Mama was Mom's younger brother and lived with my grandmother in Bangladesh.

"Did he say what happened? What are the doctors saying?" The worst thoughts crossed my mind. I couldn't lose my nani.

"We will all fly there tomorrow," Dad said. "Uncle Maruf is helping us with the tickets, and he'll drop us off at the airport tomorrow morning. We'll be there the day after tomorrow. He got us the earliest flight he could find."

It would still take us around twenty-seven hours to get there. I wished I could hear Nani's voice right now.

"Is she at the hospital or at home? Can I call her?"

"No, Rukhsana," Mom said. "She's still at home, but the doctors have given her a mild sedative to let her rest. Why don't you go and start packing?"

"What about Aamir?" He'd be devastated when he found out.

"Aamir isn't going," Mom said, and I stared at her in disbelief.

"What do you mean he's not going?"

"He can't afford to miss school," Dad said. "He's not doing that well and we don't want him to fall behind. Besides, we will only be gone for a week or two at the most."

Aamir was not going to be happy about this.

"He can stay here on his own. Aunty Meena or Uncle Maruf can check in on him while we're away." Mom stood and rearranged the clothes in her suitcase before shutting it.

I left them to go up to Aamir's room. He sat at his desk staring at his laptop.

"Hey," I said, walking over and sitting down on the edge of his bed. "You heard about Nani?"

He nodded. "Mom says I can't go. She's worried I'll fall even more behind in school."

"Of course she is. God forbid that she should worry about my classes," I said bitterly. I would have felt a lot better about this if he were coming too, knowing we were all together. It felt weird not going as a family.

"Listen, Rukhsana, be careful when you're over there, okay?" Aamir looked at me intently and a strange sensation unfurled in my stomach.

"What do you mean?" I said. "We're just going to Nani's house."

"No, I know, but I'm just worried, now that Mom and Dad know about you and Ariana—"

"Did they say something?" The uneasy feeling grew stronger.

"Not to me, but it's just the timing of everything. Don't you think it's a little bit suspicious?" Aamir furrowed his brow.

"They wouldn't lie about Nani like that, would they? Besides, Aunty Meena was here a couple of weeks ago telling Mom that Nani wasn't feeling well and really wanted us to visit. That was before they found out about me." But I couldn't shake the thought that Aamir might be right. Maybe Nani being sick was just an excuse to get me there. I was sure my parents thought they could guilt me out of being gay, if only they could get me away from all the lesbians.

I shrugged. "You know what? If they think they're being so clever, I can play along. At least I get a vacation out of it and I'll get to see Nani and Shaila."

I loved my cousin Shaila and hadn't seen her since we visited Dhaka when I was fourteen, but we talked pretty regularly. She was only a couple of years older than me, and we were more like sisters than cousins.

Aamir nodded. "I guess you're right. But still be careful. It's not the same over there, you know. For gay people, I mean. It's dangerous."

I hugged him tightly. I hated that he wasn't coming and that he was worried about me.

"Don't worry so much. I can take care of myself." I kissed the top of his head before returning to my room.

I sat at my desk and began emailing my teachers to let them know I'd be gone. Halfway through my third email, tears blurred my vision. I grabbed a box of tissues off my nightstand and dabbed my eyes. If anything happened to Nani before we got there, I would be devastated. Just the thought made the tears start again.

My maternal grandmother lived with my uncle and his family in Bangladesh. Although we tried to visit every few years, it became harder once I started high school. She always lamented the fact that half her family lived so far away. Once, when I was seven and we had just spent a month with her, the day before we left, Nani had taken my hand.

"Rukhsana, I had a dream about you last night," she'd said, wrapping a string of jasmine flowers around my small wrist. "Do you want to know?" I nodded and she pulled me onto her lap.

"In my dream, you were a little spring bird. You only came to visit in the spring, when the new leaves came in and the champa flowers bloomed. And no matter how many fancy seeds I collected or how many sweet treats I got for you, you always flew away."

"Did you miss me when I was gone?" I asked, playing with the golden tassel at the end of her braid.

"Yes, I did. I sang to you, so that you would find your way back to me. And you always did."

"Can you sing for me now?"

And then she sang for me, sweet melodies about birds and flowers while I braided strings of jasmine in her greying hair.

Now, as I finished up the emails and began to pack, tears ran down my face as memories of her filled my head. I placed the locket from my parents carefully in my purse and packed the half-finished scarf I was knitting for Nani. Taking one last look around, I zipped up my travel bag and placed it by my bed.

I called Ariana to tell her what was happening.

"I'm so sorry, Rukhsana," she said. "Is there anything I can do?"

"No, but thank you. I'm just freaking out right now. My parents won't tell me exactly what's wrong and I'm really scared that it's bad."

"You can't think like that. It will all be fine, you'll see."

• • •

A day and a half later, we landed in Dhaka. After hours of sitting in the cramped airplane seat, it was a relief to stretch my legs.

Once we got through customs and immigration, I scanned the arrivals lobby for Tanveer Mama. I spotted him as Dad pulled the last of our suitcases off the carousel. As we finally stepped out of the building to find the driver and car, the humidity and heat hit me like a tsunami.

Within moments, my blouse stuck to me and sweat ran down my back. Throngs of people milled about everywhere.

My grandmother's house was only a half hour's drive away from the airport, but last time it had taken us over three hours to get there. It was like being stuck in the world's biggest marathon. Only in slow motion.

"Tanveer, is the traffic getting worse or was it always like this?" Dad asked my uncle.

"Ibrahim Bhai, you all have been living abroad for too many years. Things are getting worse every day. Just last month they held a strike. Nobody could go out, no work, nothing."

My uncle turned to look at me in the back seat. "Rukhsana, let me tell you one thing. You are lucky that you are not living here. Shaila couldn't go to her university classes for the last few days, and she is having exams next week. But what to do? I cannot allow her to go with all this going on."

"How is Shaila? She must be upset about Nani too. I haven't spoken to her for a couple of weeks."

"She's doing okay," said Tanveer Mama. "Very excited to see you again."

We moved at a snail's pace in the heavy traffic, our driver weaving expertly in and out through the dense maze. Rickshaw bells competed with honking cars and bellowing truck horns. People, adults and children, jostled one another as they made their way to whatever destination lay in wait at the end of the long and narrow sidewalks.

At one street corner a thin little girl came up to my window. A few strands of jasmine were wrapped around her skinny wrist and more hung from her fingers.

"Flowers, madam?" She stuck a bony arm through the open car window. She couldn't have been older than seven or eight. "Very nice smell," she said in Bengali.

She glanced at our suitcases jammed into the trunk of the car. "Will you buy some? Only three dollars."

Mom was already fishing around in her purse for her wad of Bangladeshi takas and handed me a five-hundred-taka bill. When I put it in the little girl's outstretched hand, her eyes widened. She threw the strand of nearly dead jasmine flowers on my lap and scampered away to the next car with a big smile on her tiny face.

Outside on the sidewalk a vendor had set up a stand and was deep-frying jalebis. My mouth watered at the thought of the gooey, crunchy sweet treats melting in my mouth.

Tanveer Mama noticed me staring at the stand and told the driver to stop the car. He jumped out, and minutes later, there was a paper bag full of piping hot jalebis in my hands. The rest of the ride didn't seem as bad after that.

My grandmother's house came into view at the end of a long, winding driveway with betel nut trees standing to attention on either side like sentries. High brick walls surrounded the entire compound, and a black steel gate granted entry from the street. Hers was the only large detached house on this street. All around her, tall apartment buildings had risen as people from surrounding towns and villages flocked to the capital over the years in search of work. But despite exorbitant offers from real estate developers, my grandmother had staunchly refused to sell her property, and so it stood out prominently among the more modern structures that filled the city blocks.

When our car pulled up in front of the house, I jumped out. A slender older woman in a dark blue sari and grey hair waited by the main door holding a plate of sweets in her hands. Rokeya. She was my grandmother's cook and had been with the family since my mom was a young girl. I ran over to embrace her and she held my face in her hands as she simultaneously tried to feed me sweets and scold me for how skinny I'd become.

"How is your daughter? And her two girls?" I asked her in Bengali. Rokeya's daughter worked in a garments factory on the outskirts of Dhaka and raised her two daughters alone after her husband kicked her out for giving birth to two girls but no boy.

"They are growing up," Rokeya replied, putting another piece of milky sweetness in my mouth.

"Did they like the dresses I sent for them?"

"Yes, and the books and school supplies. You are spoiling them."

We all went inside and I looked around, taking in all the things I loved about this old house my grandmother had inherited when her husband died. The marble floors in the entry and the stairway were cool under my bare feet as I ran up to my grandmother's room. I knocked on the door.

"Nani?" I heard a faint reply and entered. She was propped up on the four-poster bed, looking like a porcelain doll as she smiled and held her arms out. I rushed to her side and enveloped her petite frame, worn by age.

"You came back, my little spring bird." She cupped my face in her tiny hands and examined it. "You look too thin," she admonished. "I have asked Rokeya to make all your favorites. I want to be able to squeeze your cheeks."

"Nani, you have to get better quickly now that I'm here." I hugged her tightly again.

Mom was right behind me and I left them to spend time together while I washed up. Then I went to find Shaila and saw her walking in the front door.

"Rukhsana, I can't believe you're really here," she said as we hugged. I stepped back to look at her. We both had the same round faces with high cheekbones, but where my nose was too big for my liking, hers was pert and just the right size for her face. And unlike me with my unruly long curls, she wore her thick hair in a braid.

"Have you been up to see Dadi yet?"

"Yes, I have. And my nani is still better than your dadi," I teased, thinking back to my first visit to Dhaka as a five-year-old.

Shaila grinned. "Remember how angry you got because I called her Dadi? You wouldn't stop crying."

"Well, I thought you were calling her the wrong name on purpose. I didn't like you very much," I said playfully.

"And I thought you were dumb because you didn't know the right names of our relatives." Shaila scooted away from me in mock fear.

"How was I supposed to know you all have so many different names for everybody? Your mom's mother is Nani but your dad's mother is Dadi? It was very confusing." I tried to look sad, but Shaila was just laughing at me.

She pulled me into the living room and we sat down on one of the sofas by the French doors that led out onto the spacious lawn. The lace curtains fluttered in the small breeze that blew in from the lake behind the house. I stood up to look outside.

There used to be a swing that my uncle had hung on a mango tree branch a long time ago. The swing was made of jute rope fashioned into a chair. I would clamber into it in the afternoons while everyone else was asleep except Rokeya, who would sing old Bengali folk songs to me while I swung back and forth in the shade. *Is it still there?*

Shaila came to stand beside me. "Do you want to check out the garden?"

I nodded and followed her out through the French doors.

Tall jackfruit trees lined the perimeter of the garden, interspersed with tall palm trees and the occasional mango tree. Vines of bougainvillea climbed over the walls, their blooms bursting with purple. We walked to the koi pond at the end of the garden. There, hanging from a low branch of a mango tree, was the swing. I marveled at how I could have ever fit in it. It was so small, yet it held a wealth of happy memories for me.

Shaila watched me with a bemused expression as I walked over to the trunk and examined the bark. It was still there, my initials carved in my five-year-old scrawl. After I'd done it I couldn't stop wondering if the tree had felt pain. Nani always said that all living creatures felt love, hunger, and pain. Even trees. So, every time I went outside I would make sure to run my fingers gently across the spot. I did the same now and Shaila shook her head.

"You were always a weird one, you know?" She smiled at me. "But that's why I always loved you so much."

We walked back inside with our arms around each other's waists just like when we were little. I was glad some things never changed.

chapter
fifteen

I woke up groggy but ravenous. Something in the air here made me hungry all the time. Or maybe it was because the food here was so good. I joined Dad, Tanveer Mama, and Shaila for breakfast.

"Shaila, can we go out and get phoochka?"

"Thanks for ruining the surprise," Shaila said, pretending to glare at me. "I have a whole day planned for us tomorrow."

"You're the best, Shaila," I said, leaning over to kiss her on the cheek.

Afterward, I went to see my grandmother in her room. I found her there with Mom, just finishing their breakfast.

"Nani, you look so much better already," I said, bending to kiss her cheek. "See what happens when I visit?" I snuggled up beside her. Mom frowned at me.

"Rukhsana, get off the bed," she said, swatting my behind. Nani glared at her daughter in mock anger and pretended to protect me from her.

"Zubaida . . . you are always too strict with her. She can lie down with me whenever she wants. Her place is here, right next to my heart." She pulled me closer, surprisingly strong all of a sudden. Mom grumbled something about spoiled grandchildren as she shook her head and walked out the door.

"How are you? Any boyfriend?" Nani asked, her eyes twinkling.

"No, Nani. No boyfriend. I'm too busy with school and work." I hated lying to her.

Maybe it was wishful thinking, but I felt like she would actually understand if I told her about Ariana. *Who am I kidding? She'd probably have a heart attack if I told her I was gay.* She was from another generation; there was only so much she could handle.

So, I had to be content lying to her and hoping she would never find out I wasn't the good Bengali girl she thought I was. At least she was happy to have me here. We talked about the orphanage where she volunteered and how she missed going there these days.

"I've been too tired to go out much, but I am hoping we can go together in a few days. They would love to see you again."

"The doctor said you have to rest, Nani. We'll go when you're better."

"What doctor? I'm fine, I'm just old and old people get tired. You'll understand when you are my age."

She didn't even remember the doctor. Maybe it was for the best; she seemed happier this way.

That afternoon a whole bunch of my cousins came over to visit and I was so happy to see them again. We caught up, playing Carom late into the night, and I realized how much I'd missed that.

• • •

The next day was Pohela Boishakh, the Bengali New Year. My past visits had never coincided with the middle of April, so it promised to be an exciting day. This was a huge celebration in Bangladesh. There were going to be marches, art shows, and musical extravaganzas. And food, lots of mouthwatering Bengali street food.

Mom had given us permission to spend the day enjoying the festivities, so I came down dressed in a cream-colored kurta and jeans. I wanted to be comfortable for a whole day out. Traditionally I should have worn a sari, preferably white with a red border, but I knew it would become cumbersome later in the day, since I didn't really wear saris that often.

After a breakfast of daal poori and eggs, Shaila and I got into the back of Tanveer Mama's Honda and were driven to Ramna Park, where the Boishakhi Mela was taking place. The fairgrounds were teeming with people, families with children, all milling about as they checked out the various vendors selling everything from vibrant, colored glass bangles to slippers and toys. Interspersed between those stalls were stands holding a tantalizing array of street food, everything from the ubiquitous jhal moori to young coconut and mango slices dusted with salt, sugar, and chili powder.

Shaila and I bought two paper cones of jhal moori and I savored the explosion of spice and tartness as I took my first mouthful of the savory puffed rice mixed with green chilies, onions, peanuts, and mustard oil. Even the potential threat of spending the night on the toilet did not dissuade me from enjoying all of it.

I looked around the fair while we ate and spotted a bangles vendor. I waited impatiently for Shaila to finish her jhal moori before dragging her over to try some on.

I ended up buying six dozen glass bangles, some in gorgeous hues to match my saris and shalwar suits at home and some to bring back for Ariana, Jen, Rachel, and Sara. I was obsessed with them, even though my dresser at home had no room for more.

Shaila was amused at my enthusiasm and tried to steer me away from the bangle stalls for the rest of the fair.

All the food stalls were making me hungry again and I soon got tired of looking around.

"Shaila, let's get some phoochka," I said, pointing to a stall just ahead of us. Hollow spheres of thin, deep-fried dough were arranged in a pyramid. We ordered a plate each and my mouth watered as I watched the man fill the phoochka with spiced potatoes and arrange them on a plate. Then he filled two little bowls, one with spiced tamarind water and the other with a green chili and mint sauce.

"I've missed this so much," I said, spooning the sauces into the crispy shells before popping one in my mouth. There was an explosion of sweet, tangy, and spicy goodness, and I closed my eyes to savor it. There was nothing better.

"I wish I could take a picture of your face right now, Rukhsana," Shaila said with a grin, a little tamarind juice dribbling down her hand and onto her plate.

"A thousand pictures wouldn't do justice to how amazing this is."

"You want to order more, don't you?" Shaila said, signaling the man for two more plates.

After we finished eating, we decided to check out the parade.

"There's some really cool art on display," Shaila told me as we made our way through the dense crowd. "And the Dhaka Art College students have really cool pieces for sale. I have a feeling you'll love them."

She was right. There were stunning owl and tiger masks in striking colors. I just had to get some for my bedroom. I bought one for Aamir too. He could thank me later.

By late afternoon, we were exhausted from the heat and the crowds and I was ready to go home. But I still had to get a new SIM card so I could call Ariana, and I asked Shaila to make a quick stop for that.

When we got home, it was getting dark. I ran to my room before Mom could intercept me, and locked the door. The last thing I needed was for anyone to come barging in while I was talking to Ariana.

"Hello?" Ariana answered on the first ring.

"Hey, it's me. It's so good to hear your voice," I said.

"I miss you so much." She sounded so close, it made me want to reach out and hold her. "How's your grandmother?"

"She's actually not that sick. I think they were just trying to guilt us into visiting."

"Wow, that's a bit manipulative, isn't it?" Ariana said. "Well, at least you get to see her."

"I'm so glad I came. To be honest, I don't know how many good years she has left."

"Then I'm glad too. But when are you coming home?"

"We're only here for two weeks and then I'll be back."

"Well, I'm going to miss you every single day. I love you so much."

"I love you too."

"Have you gone shopping at all?" Ariana asked.

"No, but I got some cool stuff when I went to the Bengali New Year festival," I said, getting comfortable on my bed.

"What kind of stuff?" Ariana said.

"Well, I got some glass bangles for you. Remember the ones on my dresser at home that you liked? They're just like that but in blue and silver."

"Aw, you remembered. I can't wait to try them on," Ariana said.

"They'll go great with your blue dress."

"Yes, they will. Maybe I'll wear it to the Spring Fling."

My friends and I had been excited for the senior dance for months now. It was coming up next month and I couldn't wait to go.

"My cousin Shaila and I are going shopping tomorrow. Maybe I'll find something cute to wear to it."

"Have you had a chance to see any of your other cousins yet?" Ariana said. She knew all about my huge family here. At last count, there were twenty-six cousins and thirteen nieces and nephews.

"Yes, I have. But only some of them and it was great to catch up."

"That sounds like fun. You haven't seen them for a few years, right?"

"Yes, and two of them got married in the meantime. It's so weird, you know, because they're just a couple of years older than us. And one of them is already pregnant."

I reached over to the nightstand, where Rokeya had left a cup of chai. It was still warm enough.

"I can't imagine being married right now. There's still so much I want to do," Ariana said.

"I know, right? But her in-laws are really sweet," I said. "They're insisting that she should finish her degree and they'll help with the baby."

"That's nice of them," Ariana said. "I still don't know if I could do something like that though."

"Me either. You know what else though? My cousins and I played Carom last night."

"Okay, I have no idea what that is," Ariana said.

"It's this really cool game we used to play when I was little. There's a square board with pockets in all four corners and you have to slide discs into them using a bigger, heavier disc."

"Sounds a little like air hockey?" Ariana said.

"I guess. It's really fun, I'll have to show you when I get back. I think my parents have a board somewhere in the garage."

"I'd love that." She sighed loudly. "I really miss you, you know."

"I miss you too. I wish you could be here with me." It had only been a couple of days, and two weeks would fly by, but it was almost unbearable to be away from her.

• • •

Several cast-iron pots sat crowded on the burners, bubbling away as Rokeya chopped vegetables.

"What's the occasion?" I asked her in my American-accented Bengali. Rokeya always got a kick out of the way I spoke the language.

"Some guests are coming for tea," she replied with a grin. "Your mother told me to prepare some special dishes."

"Can I help?" I rolled up the sleeves of my kameez and tied my hair up in a knot. "I don't want you to do all of it alone."

"You want to help?" Rokeya smiled. "It will be a big help if you don't burn any of the food."

I laughed at the memory of the last time I'd tried to assist in the kitchen. I had somehow managed to burn most of the dishes I touched.

"Okay, I won't touch anything, I promise."

"You should stay out of the kitchen anyway; otherwise you'll smell like garam masala." This was true, so I made a hasty exit, running into Mom on my way out.

"Rukhsana, go and get ready. The guests will be here soon." She carried an empty tray in one hand.

"Who's coming? Do I know them?" I thought I'd seen most of my relatives in the past week.

"No, they're some friends of your dad," Mom said. "They just wanted to see him and meet you."

"Sounds fun," I said. "I'll go get ready, then."

"I put out a nice shalwar kameez for you to wear," she called out as I walked up the stairs.

A gorgeous deep blue silk outfit with intricate embroidery lay on my bed. I thought it was a little too much for afternoon tea, but whatever. If it made Mom happy, I didn't mind wearing it. After a quick shower, I put on some makeup to complement my clothes. I even straightened my curly hair until it was smooth and silky. I took my time, because even though my mom said our guests would be here soon, according to Bengali Standard Time that could mean anywhere between two to three hours.

By the time I came downstairs, all the food had already been set out on the buffet, with gleaming white-and-gold plates on the side. There were pooris with spiced potatoes, samosas, chicken rolls, freshly cut mangoes, and an assortment of sweets. Quite the feast for just an afternoon tea. I was about to snag a samosa when the doorbell chimed. I glanced regretfully at my plate but decided I could always pig out after the guests left.

Asif Uncle, Dad's friend from college, walked in first, followed closely by his wife, Rita Aunty, and their daughter, Neera, and son, Minhas.

"Hello, ammu, you must be Rukhsana," Rita Aunty said, enveloping me in a hug. "Your father has told us so much about you." She turned to Dad. "But, Ibrahim Bhai, you didn't tell us she was so beautiful."

Mom and Dad beamed proudly.

"Yes, she is very brilliant also. She just got a scholarship to Caltech," Dad said.

Heat rose to my cheeks as they continued to gush.

The love fest went on throughout the evening. By the time they left my ego had swollen to the size of a watermelon.

Back in my room, I couldn't find my cell phone anywhere. Thinking I must have left it on the coffee table in the living room, I headed back down. I was halfway down the stairs when I heard Mom and Dad. It sounded like they were arguing.

"Zubaida, this is not the right way," Dad said. "We cannot do this. At least we should tell her."

"If we tell her then what do you think will happen?" Mom's voice floated up.

"Zuby, please be reasonable. Things are not the way they were when you were her age."

"All this nonsense is the reason we are in this mess," Mom said accusingly. "I always told you, don't give her so much freedom. But you never listened."

"I want her to have all the opportunities we didn't get. You told me yourself you wished that you had been able to attend college. How can you deny her this?"

What are they talking about?

It sounded like it was about Caltech, but there was something else going on too. Aamir's words from the night before we left echoed in my head, and I couldn't help but wonder if I should have taken his warning a bit more seriously.

"Yes, yes. I know what I said. But she has forgotten we are still Muslims. Just because we are living there doesn't mean that she can forget all our values and just carry on like that. Ibrahim, what do you think will happen if someone finds out? We will not be able to show our faces anywhere, here or in Seattle." She lowered her voice. "How do you think your family will feel when they find out their granddaughter is a lesbian? People get killed for these kinds of things here."

That must have convinced Dad because he didn't say anything more after that. I didn't want them to know that I'd heard them, so when I heard footsteps coming, I hurried back to my room. Ariana would have to wait.

chapter
sixteen

"I don't understand all these parents sending their children away to college," Nusrat Mami said between mouthfuls of rice and eggplant curry. "My Shaila is going to Dhaka University and is doing perfectly fine."

Shaila's mother was in full bitch mode. Our two weeks were almost up and I had hoped that this visit would pass without drama created by my aunt.

"Yes, Nusrat, but since we moved to the US, our Rukhsana has many more options. We have to consider those at least."

Funny how Mom was fine with me going away to college when she wanted to show up Nusrat Mami, just not when it was actually about me. That was interesting. I filed this little tidbit away for a later time.

"No, no, of course, you are all *Americans* now, so you want to have many options for everything." She spat out a bay leaf and put it on the edge of her plate.

"Tanveer," she said, turning to her husband. "Do you remember our first trip to the US?"

He grunted as he helped himself to some more rice.

"We went to the grocery store," she continued. "And, my God, I have never seen so many varieties of potato chips in my life. Why does anybody need so many choices? It was very confusing. And so many different types of cereal and bread. It's too much."

Shaila and I made eye contact across the table and she grimaced. We were used to this feud between our mothers. Her mom resented Tanveer Mama because he refused to leave Nani and get a place of their own, while Mom felt guilty for leaving and making a life for herself far away from her family.

"Well, sometimes it's good to have choices. After all, nobody is forcing anyone to choose. You can pick what you want," Mom said as she made a mound of her rice, used her finger to make a crater on top, and then poured daal over it. Using her right hand, she made a little ball and popped it in her mouth. I'd never mastered the art of eating with my hands. I always got the food all over my fingers and made a mess. Mom somehow made it look easy.

"Yes, it's good to have choices. But not all of us are so lucky." Nusrat Mami looked pointedly at my uncle. "Some of us are more concerned about duty."

Mom's nostrils flared a little and she pursed her lips.

"Nusrat, I have told you many times, if you don't want to look after Ma then let us take her to Seattle. We are happy to take care of her."

"You think Ma wants to leave everything and go off to Seattle?" My aunt was not going to take this lying down.

"Well, it's better than feeling unwanted, I'm sure." Mom set her glass down with a little more force than necessary.

"What do you mean?" Nusrat Mami looked quite upset now.

"I'm just saying that she is still the head of this household. It might be better for you to remember that," Mom said with finality.

"Tanveer, are you going to let your sister talk to me like that?" she asked indignantly.

"Zubaida Apa, please." Tanveer Mama looked up from deboning the fish on his plate. "How many times must we have this same argument?"

A deep red color crept into Mom's cheeks. She took a deep breath. "I am not interested in arguing with anyone. But you will treat me with respect." That last part was aimed at Tanveer Mama with a withering look.

"After everything I have done for this family Zubaida Apa, you just come here whenever you feel like and you think you know what it's like? All the difficulties we face? We don't tell you any of it, because what's the point? You cannot help from there."

"What do you mean we cannot help? If you tell us of course we can help."

Dad took a sip of water and cleared his throat loudly.

"Let us all calm down now," he said in a placating tone. "We are all doing the best we can. We shouldn't ruin this time together."

Mom sniffed imperiously and Nusrat Mami pursed her lips. After a few minutes, they both got up and left. Rokeya came in to clear the table and we all dispersed.

Shaila and I went to her room to talk about what happened.

"Wow, that was intense," I said. "I don't remember it being so bad the last time we were here."

"Tell me about it," said Shaila, shaking her head. "You'd think after all these years they would have moved past it."

"Do they really think Mom and Dad abandoned Nani?"

"Well, I think my mom resents that they're stuck here. I've overheard them talking about it." Shaila picked at the hem of her kameez. "I'm getting out of here as soon as I can."

"Really?" I said. "Wait. Is there anyone special?"

Shaila wordlessly stared at her feet.

"Oh my God! You have a boyfriend, don't you?" I yelled, jumping up.

"Shhhh, sit down, Rukhsana." Shaila pulled me back down. "Someone will hear you."

"Okay, okay. But there is someone, right?" I continued in an exaggerated whisper. "I can't believe you didn't tell me." I pinched her arm and she swatted my hand away.

"I'm trying to tell you now, if you'll shut up for a second."

"But I want to know everything. Who is it? Is it someone I know?"

"How could it possibly be someone you know?" Shaila glared at me.

Then she smiled shyly. "His name's Alam. We took the same economics class in first year."

"First year? So, this has been going on for over a year and you never told me?" Now it was my turn to glare at her.

"Hey, it's been really hard to keep it a secret. You have no idea." Shaila's mouth turned down a little at the corners. "If my parents ever found out they'd kill me."

"Why? He's Bengali, right? And going to university? So, then what's the problem?"

"Are you kidding? My mom wants me to marry someone with money so she can brag to all her stupid ladies from the club. Alam is smart and kind and funny, but he doesn't have money."

"So what? He'll have money someday. You'll both make it work."

But Shaila was shaking her head. "There's no point. Once I graduate in two years, Mom will find me a suitable groom and expect me to marry him."

"But then what about Alam?" I'd never met him, but if Shaila loved him then I was sure he was a great guy. And she couldn't just let her mom marry her off to some stranger.

"Rukhsana, when we started going out we knew this was a possibility. That's just how it is here."

That was ridiculous.

"But won't you at least try?" Maybe her parents would understand.

"If I tell them then they'll never let me out of the house. I won't get to finish my degree or see Alam ever again."

"Would they really do that?" I'd never liked Nusrat Mami, but Tanveer Mama was always kind and sweet. And he doted on Shaila. He wouldn't want his only daughter to be in an unhappy marriage, would he?

"You have no idea, Rukhsana. They watch my every move as it is. The only time I feel free is when I'm at school."

Shaila had no idea just how much I understood what she was going through.

chapter
seventeen

"Tell me everything that I've missed!" I was in the study using Uncle Tanveer's computer to Skype with Ariana. It was late Sunday night here, so Ariana was just waking up in the morning. The sight of her with tousled hair, her eyes still heavy with sleep, made my heart ache. I missed her so much and even though I could see and hear her, she still seemed out of reach.

"Oh my God, you're not going to believe the drama that's been happening here," she said, perking up.

"What? Hurry up and tell me."

"Well, remember how you and I were saying that Cody couldn't be trusted? Well, he cheated on Rachel."

"Are you serious? What a slimebag."

"Right? Jen was so mad, she wanted to say something to him, but Rachel wouldn't let her."

"That's because Rachel is too nice. I wish I was there. I could have convinced her to get back at him somehow." I was fuming now, remembering how excited Rachel had been when Cody had asked her out. "How is she? I think I should call her after this."

"That's a good idea. She'll be so happy to talk to you." Ariana's shoulders sagged and suddenly I felt really sad that I was so far away from her and all my friends.

"I can't wait for you to get back," she said.

"Me too. But it's only a few more days now and then I'll be home. I'll message you when I'm able to Skype again, okay?"

"Okay. Love you and come back soon." Ariana blew me a kiss, but I wished it was the real thing.

"Love you too. I'm coming back in three more days, I promise."

I disconnected the call and quickly found Rachel's username in my chat history. It only took two rings before Rachel's face filled the screen.

"Hey! Where have you been?" Rachel's face was puffy from crying and I felt awful for her.

"I'm sorry I haven't called sooner. It's been really hectic here."

"That's okay," Rachel said and she looked so heartbroken I just wanted to reach out and hug my friend very tightly.

"Hey, Ariana just told me about Cody. I'm so sorry."

"It was bound to happen," she said. "Cody's always been a player. I should've known better."

"Hi, Rukhsana." Jen's face popped up on the screen and I squealed.

"You guys, I miss you so much."

"When are you coming back?" Jen said.

"I wish I could come back right now. I feel like I'm missing everything."

"You are. We're plotting to get back at Cody for being such a douche canoe," Jen said, her eyes narrowed.

"Good. He doesn't deserve you anyway, Rachel." I'd never liked Cody.

"Rachel here has decided to be all mature about it," Jen said with a grimace. "She won't let me do anything."

"Well, he's probably not worth the trouble anyway, right, Rachel?"

Rachel nodded, her eyes welling up. "So, when are you getting back?"

"Three more days," I replied. "We'll all go to the Spring Fling together. I'm so excited."

Jen put her arm around Rachel's shoulder. "And we'll have a girls' night as soon as you're back. You, Ariana, Rachel, and me. With mani-pedis and movies. And ice cream and popcorn. And pizza. With pineapple!"

This elicited a smile from Rachel. We usually just squashed her weird pizza topping requests.

"Yes! And it's your turn to choose the movie this time, Rachel, okay?" I added.

"Anything but *Princess Diaries* again," Jen chimed in. "I love Julie Andrews as much as the next person, but we've already watched it a dozen times. Can't we at least change it up with some *Sound of Music* and *Mary Poppins* every now and then?"

Rachel gave a watery smile. "I guess you'll have to wait and see!"

We ended the call after a few more minutes and I sat staring at the computer screen for a moment, thinking how weird it felt being here and there at the same time. It was as if there were two parts of me, but they would never fit together.

My head was throbbing, so I went downstairs to beg Rokeya for a cup of chai. Of course, I could make it myself, but that would send Rokeya into a tizzy and also get her in trouble if Nusrat Mami saw that she was letting me do her work. I found this ridiculous and disgusting on so many levels, but the last thing I wanted was to make things more difficult for Rokeya, who had been with my grandmother forever. As it turned out, I ran into Nusrat Mami in the hallway wearing a very brightly colored kaftan. She looked noticeably smug, and I wondered what plot was brewing in that evil genius mind of hers. But she looked happy to see me. Or maybe she was relieved that we'd be gone soon. At least that feeling was mutual.

"I hear you have big shopping plans for the next couple of weeks," she said.

"I don't think so, Aunty. We're leaving this week."

"Oh, so your parents haven't told you? I thought you knew." Her eyes widened, feigning innocence.

"Told me what?"

"That you're not leaving until—"

"Until what?" I could feel a knot forming in my stomach.

"I think you should ask them. I don't want to get in the middle of anything." And with that she turned around and flounced off in her ridiculous kaftan.

By the time I found my parents in the living room, I was ready to explode.

Mom and Dad looked up in surprise as I burst into the room.

"What is Nusrat Mami talking about?" I sputtered. "She says we're not leaving this week."

Dad recovered first.

"Rukhsana, please don't shout," he said in an infuriatingly calm voice. "This is no way to talk to your parents."

I took a deep breath and counted to three. And then to ten.

"Okay," I said when I finally felt calm enough. "Can you please explain what she's talking about?"

"Nusrat is always sticking her nose where it doesn't belong," said Mom irritably. "Always stirring up trouble."

"So, we *are* leaving, then?"

"Ammu, it's nothing to worry about. We just wanted to stay an extra week to see some old friends Daddy and I haven't seen for many years. They were away but are coming back in a few days. We just couldn't leave without seeing them." She smiled reassuringly at me.

"I'm missing a lot of school and this is my final semester." I felt my anger dissipate a little. I could understand why they'd want to stay a few extra days to see old friends. A trip like this wasn't cheap, so we couldn't just come whenever we wanted.

"Rukhsana, it will be fine. You will catch up in no time."

It wasn't as if I had a choice.

"Fine, but we have to leave right after you've met your friends. I can't afford to lose my scholarship."

"Don't worry. Obviously, we are also concerned about your schoolwork. After all, we are your parents and we will do what's best for you." Mom stood up, signaling the end of the discussion. I went off to find Shaila so I could vent to her.

• • •

"Seriously, another week?" Ariana said when I called her the next day to give her the bad news. "I'm dying here without you."

"I'm sorry, babe. There was nothing I could do." I hated feeling so powerless, but more than that I hated letting her down.

"Why do you have to stay longer anyway?" Ariana said irritably.

"It's just some old friends my parents haven't seen in years."

"I feel like I haven't seen you in years. Seriously, it's been almost two whole weeks."

"Well, what do you want me to do? It's not like we come here all the time." I rubbed my temples, feeling a full headache coming on.

"Anyway, I have a lot of homework to do now, so . . ." Ariana said.

"I guess I'll talk to you later, then." I hung up.

chapter eighteen

"Rukhsana, my friend Sharmin and her family have come back from their Europe trip," Mom said the next morning as I was getting ready for the day.

Finally some good news. Maybe now we can finally go home.

"I've invited them for dinner tonight. Why don't you wear that new magenta shalwar suit I bought you from Mannaf and Sons last week?"

"Sure, whatever." I just wanted this dinner over with so we could leave.

Sharmin Aunty was Mom's friend from high school and they hadn't seen each other in twenty years. They had recently reconnected through a mutual friend and were overjoyed to see each other. Her husband, Rupon, owned an import-export business of some sort, and their son, Ashraf, was visiting from Silicon Valley, where he worked in the IT sector. Ashraf seemed nice enough but a little dull for my taste. We made polite conversation about his work and where he'd gone to school. I didn't volunteer any information about myself and he didn't ask for any details. They left shortly after dinner, saying that they were still on Europe time.

"Sharmin and I were as thick as thieves when we were your age, Rukhsana. Just like you and Jen and Rachel," Mom said after they left. "Their son was also very nice, wasn't he?"

I shrugged. "He was okay, I guess. A little bit boring." I helped Rokeya clear the table and when she left with a load of dishes, Mom turned to me.

"Sharmin said they are looking for a girl for Ashraf. What do you think?" she said, putting leftovers into small containers.

"I don't know . . . Isn't there some sort of website for that stuff? Like shaadi.com or something?"

Mom finished putting the last of the sweets into a covered glass dish.

"I don't think they would like that. I think she would like somebody whose family they know."

"What about Saira Aunty?" I thought about my Mom's cousin who had visited a couple of days ago. She said she was looking to get her oldest daughter married.

"I think they want someone who is settled in the US."

"When we get back we can ask Aunty Meena. She's sure to know someone who knows someone."

Mom stopped rearranging the food. "I think they are considering you." For a second I thought she was joking. But her face was dead serious.

"But you told them that I'm not interested, right? I mean, I'm going to Caltech in a few months."

"Of course, ammu, no one is talking about right now. She was saying just an engagement for now, then only after you get your degree, the marriage will take place."

She doesn't get it. There isn't going to be any marriage. Not now. Not ever.

"Mom, seriously, didn't you tell her?" She didn't answer but just stared at the pyramid of containers she had made on the table.

131

Just then Dad walked in.

"What's going on?" he asked cheerfully, not reading the room at all. "Are we having sweets?"

Mom glared at him. "Your daughter is being unreasonable as usual. Please talk to her, Ibrahim."

I rolled my eyes, appealing to my dad.

"Dad, Mom wants me to get engaged to her friend's son."

Mom and Dad exchanged a look and he said, "Maybe it is not such a bad idea. This boy is from a good family. They will not stop you from getting your degree, and after college you will be ready to get married anyway." This could not be happening. Too many thoughts swirled around in my head.

"Mom, Dad, you have to know how completely ridiculous this is. I am not going to get engaged to some guy I just met."

"And we are not asking you to. You can get to know him for a little while and then get engaged," Dad said, thinking himself clever.

"Yes, Rukhsana, we are not those kinds of people who don't let their daughters even go out before marriage. We know that things are different for your generation. We are very open-minded," Mom said.

So, they expected me to be grateful that I could go out for dinner with a guy I'd just met before I committed to him for the rest of my life? How very progressive of them. I wanted to point out that they were conveniently forgetting I was gay and currently in a relationship, but I didn't think that would go over well.

But Mom wasn't finished. "Rukhsana, I knew you would be stubborn about this, so I arranged for someone else to come to see you tomorrow evening."

"What?" I had to keep my hands glued to my sides because otherwise I would break something.

"You don't have to like the first boy we find. But you have to pick someone. Otherwise, we are not going back to Seattle. That's it." She threw up her palms, washing her hands of me.

"You've been planning this all along, haven't you?" It all made sense now. The other family. Asking me to get all dressed up. Nani.

"Was Nani even sick? Or was she part of your disgusting plan too?" I glared at Mom and her eyes flashed as she looked back at me.

"Disgusting? You want to talk about disgusting?" she said with clenched teeth. "After what you were doing with that trashy white girl? Under my roof?"

I felt like I'd been punched in the stomach. Every word was a blow, and I staggered back under the attack. Tears stung my eyes and I looked over at Dad. His upper body bent forward.

What is he doing?

Through a haze of tears, I saw him clutch his chest. My brain didn't register, couldn't comprehend what was happening. And then through the fog I heard a scream, a keening sound.

The mist cleared from my eyes and I saw Mom on the floor cradling Dad's head, crying and shouting at me to get help.

chapter
nineteen

Mom, Nusrat Mami, and I had been sitting in the hospital waiting area for the past two hours with no updates about Dad's condition. Neither one of us wanted to say what we were thinking. If anything happened to him, I would never forgive myself. And I knew that she would never forgive me either.

Shaila had gone back home to get us a change of clothes and something to eat. All around me people were in pain. Some moaned, others wept. A young woman, a girl really, sat on the ground with a toddler in her arms. The man with her sat in a chair next to an older woman.

When the toddler slid out of her arms, she got up to catch him. Her belly was large and round as she walked awkwardly after her child. He seemed to be getting away and the mother had no hope of catching up. I got up, quickly ran to catch the little runaway, and brought him back to his mother. She smiled gratefully before returning to her spot on the floor. The entire time the man didn't move from his chair. I shot him a look of disgust, and in return, he leered at me. I pulled my scarf a little closer around me and looked away.

Shaila returned with a few bags and set them down on a chair.

"Zuby Phupi, have a samosa," she said, offering Mom one in a paper napkin.

"I can't eat anything right now, Shaila. Maybe later, okay?" She touched Shaila's cheek gently.

"At least have some chai," Shaila said and poured a cup from the thermos she had.

Mom took the proffered cup and took a sip. Shaila poured me one too and I held the steaming cup in my hands, drawing warmth from it.

I threw a glance at Mom. She looked so small sitting there.

"Mom, it's going to be alright," I said, taking her hand and squeezing it. But she shook her head and pulled her hand out of mine.

"This is all your fault, Rukhsana. If you hadn't been so selfish none of this would have happened."

"Mom, I'm sorry. I didn't mean for any of this to happen." Tears pooled in my eyes and ran down my cheeks.

"What are you crying for? You won't listen to us, so why do you care what happens to Dad? Just go home. I don't want you here anymore." I reeled back in shock. I didn't want to leave. I wanted to stay here with Dad, in case anything did happen.

She looked at me with hard eyes.

"Just go. Please."

I still didn't move.

Shaila stood up and took me gently by the arm.

"Rukhsana, let's go. I'll take you home to get some rest and you can come back later. Zuby Phupi's just upset now, so give her some time. Anyway, there's nothing you can do here."

I allowed her to walk me out to an auto-rickshaw so the driver, Malik, could stay at the hospital for my mother and aunt. While we were stuck in traffic, I looked out from under the canopy of the motorized three-wheeler. Despite the late hour, there were still big crowds outside, going about their daily business. Street vendors were closing up shop, and to my right, a gaunt, bearded old man tried to regain control of his bullock cart as it careened around a bend. Pedestrians scattered to get out of his way, while a traffic control officer blew incessantly on his whistle at an unimpressed public.

By the time we finally got home, darkness had fallen. A full moon peeked through the tall betel nut trees and coconut palms, which looked strangely menacing tonight. Or maybe it was just my state of mind.

I ran upstairs and flung myself on my bed. As I rubbed my tired eyes, my eyeliner came off and stained my fingers. Damn it. I still had all my makeup on from before. I got some wipes and started taking it off, rubbing my skin angrily to rid it of all traces of this horrible day.

Mom's words reverberated in my head.

Had she meant what she said? Does she really think I don't care?

I needed to talk to Ariana, to hear her voice. She would calm me down.

"Rukhsana, I'm so sorry," she said as soon as she answered.

"What are you—"

Then I remembered our last conversation. It seemed so long ago, and a lot had happened since then.

"Are you okay?" Ariana's worried voice came over the phone.

"Yes, I'm okay, but Dad's in the hospital."

"Oh my God, that's awful. What happened?"

"I don't know. We had a big fight and then he just collapsed. And Mom doesn't want me there. She thinks it's all my fault."

Silence.

Is she still there?

Her voice came over the line, sounding distant and thin.

"She must be scared and upset. I'm sure she didn't mean it, Rukhsana. But what did you fight about?"

"You're not going to believe what they did! They actually had a guy come over with his family to meet me."

"What do you mean *meet* you?" Her voice was clearer now.

"Meet me. As in, a potential bride. My brother was right, Ariana. He warned me before we left, but I didn't think my parents would go this far. They lied to me about my grandmother being sick."

"Why would they do something like that?"

"Because they're freaking out about us. They think if they can interest me in a guy I might change my mind about you."

"Can they?" Ariana said softly.

It was a second before I realized what she meant.

"What? No, of course not." I spoke much louder than I meant to.

She didn't say anything for so long I thought she'd hung up.

"Ariana, are you still there?"

Silence.

"Ariana?"

"I'm here."

A sigh of relief escaped me. "Ariana, I'm so sorry. I didn't mean to yell at you."

"You know, Rukhsana, this is really hard for me too. You're all the way over there and your parents are acting so weird. What do you expect me to think?"

Rokeya rushed into the room with the house phone in her hand. "It's Nusrat Mami," she mouthed to me.

"Ariana, I have to go. I'm sorry, I'll try to call you later."

With trembling hands, I took the phone from Rokeya.

"Mami, how is he?"

"The doctor says your father had a panic attack. Nothing more. They ran all sorts of tests and there's nothing wrong with his heart."

I had to sit down. I thanked God that Dad was fine. My hands still shook and I could hear my name called from a distance. Nusrat Mami was still on the other end of the line.

"Rukhsana, are you alright?"

"Yes, Mami. Is Mom . . . Should I come back to the hospital?"

"No, no, we left some time ago and we're almost home. You just stay with your Nani and tell her everything is fine, okay?"

"Yes, okay, I'll tell her right now."

I hung up and waited for my hands to stop shaking. My dad was going to be alright. I took a deep breath and then another. When I felt composed enough, I went to Nani's room and gently opened the door in case she was asleep. Her eyes were closed, so I sat in a chair and wept quietly. I cried for all the hurt I caused and for the pain I felt inside.

Is it all worth it? I could have lost Dad today. It felt as though I'd lost Mom already.

But then I thought about Ariana and I knew I couldn't give up on us. I had to be true to myself and stay strong.

Nani stirred in her bed and opened her eyes. When she saw me, she motioned for me to come closer.

"What is it, Rukhsana? Is your father—?"

I shook my head, wiping my tears with the edge of my scarf. "He's okay, Nani. It was just a panic attack. Nothing serious."

"Then why are you crying? Come here. Put your head right here and tell your nani all about it."

I started crying again, my tears falling on her sari blouse and leaving a wet stain.

"It's all my fault, Nani," I sobbed. "I was arguing and that's when Dad—"

"Fathers and daughters always argue, Rukhsana. There is something more that's bothering you, I can tell."

How would she feel about me if I just told her? Would she look at me with the same disgust as my parents?

I wasn't sure, but I had a feeling she might understand. I hated lying to her.

"Nani, I have to tell you something—"

The door opened and Mom walked in. Her eyes were red and her clothes were crumpled. She motioned for me to come to her.

"How's Dad?"

"You can go and see him, he is resting downstairs. And please, I'm begging you, don't say or do anything to upset him."

"I won't, Mom, I promise," I said quietly, not wanting to argue with her right now.

I went downstairs and found him lying on one of the sofas, his eyes closed. I sat down on an armchair next to him, thinking he was asleep, but then he opened his eyes and saw me there.

"Rukhsana, don't look so worried. You're not getting rid of me that easily." I smiled at him through the tears, so relieved to have him back.

"Daddy, I'm sorry. I didn't mean to make you so upset."

He looked so frail, I was still worried something bad would happen to him.

He smiled at me. "I know you will do the right thing, Rukhsana. I have faith in you."

My heart went cold at his words. He thought that I would do what they wanted. Marry a complete stranger? A man. But if I didn't—I couldn't think about this anymore right now.

"Dad, just get some rest. Do you need anything?"

He shook his head. "Just ask your mom to come down, please?"

I nodded and went upstairs to get Mom. She was deep in conversation with her mother when I told her that Dad wanted to see her. I went to my room to lie down, exhausted from the events of the day.

My parents had always been strict with me about boys and the way I dressed. But nothing this extreme. I'd figured that after the initial shock of finding out I was gay, they would at least think about it. But this? Pushing me to get married? This went against everything they believed. Or maybe I had just chosen to see them differently over the years. It was as if I hardly knew them. All the lies and emotional blackmailing was too much, and my head throbbed from the insanity of it all.

chapter twenty

Ariana hadn't answered her texts or her phone since last night and I was beginning to panic. Our last conversation obviously hadn't gone well, so I knew she was probably hurt and angry. But she'd been hurt and angry with me before and she'd never shut me out like this. After sending the twentieth text, I decided to call Jen and fill her in on everything. She'd be able to help.

Thankfully Jen answered right away.

"Hey, Rukhsana, how are you? Ariana said you're staying another week?"

As soon as I heard Jen's familiar, cheerful voice, I burst into tears.

"Rukhsana, oh my God, what happened?"

It took a moment for me to stop sobbing long enough to speak coherently.

"Jen, everything is such a mess. Ariana's mad at me and my parents—"

"Tell me everything, from the beginning, and we'll sort this out. It's going to be okay, I promise."

Even though I knew it was highly unlikely that Jen could help me out of this mess, I still felt calmer just hearing her voice.

"Jen, my parents exaggerated about my grandmother being sick. The real reason they brought me here is so that they could find me a husband."

There was complete silence from the other end of the line. But it was no surprise that it was taking Jen a moment to process.

"Wow, that's so messed up," she finally said. "Rukhsana, you need to get out of there. Like right now."

Fortunately for Jen, she had yet to come across the kind of messed up that my parents were.

"Yeah, my parents will never let that happen. I tried to talk to them and my dad ended up in the hospital. If I just leave, there's no telling what will happen. I can't take that chance."

"What about Ariana?" Jen said. "Have you talked to her about this? I haven't seen her for a couple of days."

"She's really mad at me. I told her about what happened with my parents. I was talking to her after I got back from the hospital, but then we never finished our conversation and now I can't get a hold of her. She won't answer any of my texts."

"I'll go to her house and make sure she's alright. I just thought she was busy studying for midterms. You know how she gets during exam time."

Ariana had a habit of becoming a hermit when exams came around. None of us would see her for a few days while she buried herself in her notes. But this was different. I knew she must be freaking out about us.

"Jen, I'm really worried. She was so upset the last time we spoke."

"I'm going to check on her right now. I'll let you know how it goes as soon as possible."

"Thanks, Jen. And can you fill in Rachel for me, please? And please, please get Ariana to call me back. Tell her I'm sorry about everything."

"I will. But, Rukhsana, please. You have to get out of there."

"I'll figure something out. I promise."

I felt a little better after hanging up with Jen. But this whole situation was still a mess. I knew I had to do something about it, but now after my dad's panic attack, I was afraid to do anything to upset him. What if he really had a heart attack the next time? How could I forgive myself?

I lay on my bed staring at the ceiling for a while, in disbelief about the turn of events. I wished my brother was here. I knew just talking to him would make me feel better, so I called.

He answered right away.

"Hey, Rukhsana. Are the relatives driving you up the wall yet?"

"Aamir, you were right," I said quietly.

"What do you mean?"

"Mom and Dad want me to get married."

"To whom?"

"Doesn't matter. As long as it's some guy they approve of," I said bitterly.

He sighed and I pictured him sitting in his room at home and I wanted nothing more than to be there right now. Back in my normal life, where everything made sense.

"I was afraid they would do something stupid, but not this. I thought they'd just have some sort of intervention to guilt you into being straight."

"Yeah, I wish," I said with a hollow laugh. "They didn't tell you that Dad went to the hospital, did they?"

"Wait, what? Why was he in the hospital?"

I felt a pang of guilt at breaking the news to him like this, but Dad was fine now.

"He had a panic attack when I told them there was no way I was getting married. But he seems to be okay now."

Aamir let out a sigh of relief.

"Aunty Meena hasn't said anything about this. I guess Mom and Dad don't want all of Seattle to find out about your lesbian ways," he said, his voice dripping with sarcasm.

"You think? It's bad enough that Nusrat Mami will start wondering what's up if I don't pick a guy to marry soon."

"What are they doing? Inviting guys over to check you out?"

"Only one so far. But I know there are going to be more."

"So, what's the plan? How do we get you out of there?" Aamir said in his serious big brother voice.

"That's what I'm trying to work out."

"Can't you tell them that you have to get back or you won't be able to graduate?"

"I've already tried that, but I think at this point they're worried someone will find out about Ariana and me if I'm in Seattle."

"Well, at least try and reason with them," Aamir pleaded. "They've been bragging to everyone about you going to Caltech, so maybe it could work."

I saw a glimmer of hope. My brother was right. I had to at least try to appeal to their reasonable side. If they even had one anymore.

"Hey, Aamir," I said, wanting to reach out across the distance and give my brother a hug.

"Yeah?"

"You know you're the best baby brother a girl could ask for, right?"

"Okay, okay, let's not get all emotional and stuff. I know I'm great and all—"

"Never mind, I'm hanging up now," I said with a grin, picturing him sitting there with a smug expression on his face.

I went off to search for Mom and Dad, finding them in their bedroom, Dad lying on the bed and Mom sitting on the edge of it. They were talking in hushed voices when I entered.

"Dad, how are you feeling now?" I asked, bending down to kiss his forehead.

"I am much better now, ammu," he said. "You know, Rukhsana, it is very painful for us to deal with these kinds of things."

I said nothing.

"When you have children of your own, you will understand how difficult it is to watch them go down a wrong path," Mom said. "But I'm happy that you are seeing things our way now."

It took all the restraint I had to not say what I was thinking right then. That they were delusional if they thought I would agree to any of this. Could they really be this out of touch with reality?

"Actually, I wanted to talk to you about something."

"What is it now?" Mom said.

"You know there's only a couple of months left of school. I've already missed so much, and I'm worried my GPA will drop if I don't go back right away. I might lose my scholarship if I don't keep up my grades."

The words came out in a rush, because if I didn't say it all at once I might lose my nerve. Now I waited for one of them to say something.

"Rukhsana, you are not going back until you are engaged to be married." Mom spoke the words with such finality, I felt the walls closing in on me. They were not going to back down until they had utterly and completely ruined my life.

I needed to get some air. Fighting the urge to scream, I turned around and left the room. I went downstairs, out through the French doors, and into the garden. I didn't stop until I reached the edge of the koi pond. It was only then that I allowed myself to cry. I sat at the water's edge, the red bricks pressing hard against my skin. My reflection stared back at me, broken up only by the koi fish darting around under the rippling surface. The sun was setting and a light breeze scented the air with jasmine.

I didn't know how long I'd been sitting there when Shaila came and sat down quietly beside me.

I turned to her and grabbed her hand, squeezing it gently.

"Shaila, I have to tell you something."

"Anything, Rukhsana. You know I'm here for you."

I wondered if she knew just how much that meant to me right now.

"Mom and Dad want me to get engaged. As soon as possible. That's why they brought me here. They lied to me about Nani being sick, just so they could—"

I turned to her, my eyes full of tears I couldn't afford to shed now. Because I had to stay strong.

"Shaila . . . I can't do this. I have to leave."

Shaila put her arms around me and squeezed tightly, just like she used to when we were little and I was upset.

"Tell me everything. From the beginning," she said.

"Mom caught me making out with my . . . umm . . . my girlfriend," I said, hesitantly lifting my eyes to read the expression on her face.

Shaila pulled back just a little to look at me, her eyes wide.

"You have a girlfriend and I'm just finding out about it now?"

I opened my mouth to explain, but realized I had no excuse. I should have mentioned it when she told me about Alam.

"I'm sorry I didn't tell you before, but things have been really tense at home."

She shook her head.

"I'm just giving you a hard time. I kind of figured something was going on when we were at the hospital, but I didn't want to pry."

"It's been awful, Shaila. They refuse to listen and they're trying to ruin my life."

"Rukhsana, that's not going to happen, okay? Trust me. Zuby Phupi and Ibrahim Phupa love you. They wouldn't want you to be unhappy. This must have been a shock to them and they probably just panicked."

I shook my head.

"You don't understand, Shaila. This isn't like when they caught us watching MTV when we were younger and went on about the evils of pop culture and rock music. This is serious. They're worried someone will find out."

I choked back a sob.

"She said I was disgusting, Shaila. That I was sick."

Tears were rolling down my cheeks now, and Shaila gently wiped them away with the ends of her orna.

"I'm sure she didn't mean it. You know how your mom gets when she's angry."

"This time it's different. She really believes she's right. She won't even try to understand how I feel."

"Then we have to make her understand. Let me talk to her, maybe I can soften her up like I used to. Remember how I saved you from getting into trouble the last time?"

I smiled, but it was more out of bitterness than anything else.

"You mean when I was twelve? Shaila, this is different. This goes against everything she believes."

Shaila didn't say anything and an uneasy churning settled in my gut.

"Shaila, do you think . . . You don't feel the same way, right?"

I knew it was a mistake as soon as the words came out of my mouth. I saw the hurt in Shaila's eyes before she even said anything.

"You really think I'm like that, Rukhsana?" she said softly, her eyes glistening.

I hung my head, unable to look at her. She was my cousin, my sister, and my partner in crime ever since I was five years old. How could I have doubted her?

"I'm sorry, Shaila, I just—"

"You just assumed that because I live here and I pray five times a day that I'm also close-minded and judgmental."

I shook my head, but there was a ring of truth in her words. I did assume that most people who observed the rules of my religion would judge me harshly. That's why I'd never confided in my Bengali friends in Seattle. I'd never really thought about it, but now I wondered. Was I just as judgmental as my parents?

"Rukhsana, I know this is a really horrible situation, but trust me, this happens here too. The difference is that people here have nowhere else to go. They're stuck here. At least you have a way out, but we just have to figure out a plan."

She squeezed my hands again and some of my shame began to fade.

"Shaila, you don't know what it means to me that you understand. It's been really tough on Ariana too. She doesn't get how things are in our culture, you know?"

"Ariana," Shaila said softly. "That's such a pretty name. How long have you been with her?"

"A little over seven months now. She's amazing, Shaila. She's smart and funny. We're supposed to go to Caltech together in the fall, and I thought I would tell Mom and Dad once I was far away from home."

"Well, I can't wait to meet her," Shaila said, standing and pulling me to my feet as well. "But for now, let's figure out how to get you back home."

Shaila went off to say her Maghrib prayer while I went back to my room to ruminate on my situation.

I decided to call Irfan and fill him in on what had happened.

"My God, are you alright?" he said, his voice amplified by shock.

"Yes, for now, but I don't know what I'm going to do if they keep pushing me." I pressed my hands to my eyes. I'd cried more in the past two days than I had in the whole year.

"Do you really think they plan to go through with it? Maybe they hope you'll change your mind." I guess one of us was looking on the bright side.

"Yes, well, that's too bad for them, because it won't happen."

"I know, but come on. Did you really think they would just accept it?"

I didn't know what to think anymore. But I had to talk about something else or my head would explode.

"Irfan, I'm trying to come up with a plan to get home. Can I count on your help?"

"Of course, why are you even asking?" Irfan said. "Whatever you need. Sara and I are here for you. You just tell me what I can do, okay?"

The waterworks threatened to start again. It was hard to believe that just a short while ago, I had thought Irfan was a blackmailing jerk. I couldn't have been more wrong. I made a mental note to adjust my judgy attitude. I'd made that mistake with Shaila as well.

"I will, I promise. How is Sara? Did you figure out what you're going to do yet?"

"Actually, we did. I told my parents."

"So . . . how did that go?" It couldn't have been as bad as my parents' reaction.

"Well, let's just say we were both right. They freaked out and threatened to disown me."

"Seriously? What did you do?"

"I told them I would leave and they would never meet their grandchildren." I could feel him grinning on the other end.

"That was bold. Good move though. Did they fall for it?"

"Of course . . . I knew they wouldn't want to miss out on that. They asked to meet her, and she's coming by this weekend." I was happy for him. Truly happy.

"That's really great. You have to tell me everything after they meet her. I wish I could be there."

"It's all going to work out, Rukhsana," Irfan said. "I know it is. And you know you're not alone."

"I really appreciate it, Irfan. More than you can imagine. And I'll be in touch very soon."

We hung up and I felt a little bit better. Feeling buoyed by the knowledge that I wasn't alone, I began to plan my escape.

chapter
twenty-one

The next morning, I found Mom and Dad talking to each other softly in the living room. When they saw me, they stopped. *What now?*

"Rukhsana, come here, we want to talk to you," Mom said.

This can't be anything good.

I came and sat down across from them.

"Rukhsana, your dad and I have decided that we've handled this poorly."

A flicker of hope.

"We should have told you of our plans. But now that you know, let's just be sensible about it."

And it was snuffed out.

"What are you saying?"

"We want to give you options. We have found some suitable men. You can meet with them and make your own decision."

Why do they look so pleased with themselves? Do they think this is a good solution?

"I'm not getting married," I stated flatly.

"Of course not. We are not unreasonable," said Mom.

Umm, I beg to differ.

"We want you to finish your education, obviously. No boy from a good family would agree unless you had at least a university degree," said Dad.

I thought the degree was supposed to be for my benefit. What else have they been lying about? Everything?

I was about to say I had no intention of ever marrying a guy, so they shouldn't hold their breath. But then I remembered that we'd had this argument already. Why did I expect a different result?

"Okay." *Did I really just say that?*

"Good," Dad said. "Now let Mom and I discuss further and we'll let you know."

His assumption that I would sit around and wait for them to "let me know" about my own life was so ludicrous that I almost laughed out loud. I would have, if I wasn't seething inside. But I reminded myself it didn't matter what they said. I wouldn't be around for any of it. Because I was getting the hell out of here.

I needed to talk to Ariana and let her know what was going on. Hopefully Jen had talked to her and now she would pick up my call. I dialed and this time she answered right away.

"Ariana, where have you been? I was so worried."

"I just needed to be alone for a while and figure things out."

My heart sank.

"Ariana, please don't—"

"Oh my God, Rukhsana, can you let me finish?"

"I'm sorry," I said quietly. "I'm listening."

"I was thinking about what my mother said to me when we started going out. That you come from such a different world and how it would be so hard for us to be together because of that."

When I didn't say anything, she continued.

"And then I started thinking of all the things I love about you. And I realized that you are the way you are because of your differences. And I want to be with you. Even if it's really hard sometimes."

I let out a sigh of relief.

"I thought you'd decided to break up with me," I said.

"I was really scared when you told me that your parents are trying to marry you off."

"I'm really scared too, Ariana. You have no idea how bad things are here. But I have a plan."

"Tell me what I can do to help," she said.

"Just promise me that you won't give up on us. The only thing that is keeping me from freaking out completely is that you'll be there when I come home."

"I could never give up on us, Rukhsana."

• • •

I stuck my head out into the hallway to see if the coast was clear. Mom and Dad's voices floated up the stairs. They must have been eating breakfast already.

I tiptoed quickly to their bedroom and searched for Mom's purse, finding it on a chair by the mirror. I rifled through it, horrified to discover all our passports were gone.

Where the hell are they? Oh right, the safe.

She'd probably stashed them with the cash in the safe. There were two big cupboards in the room. I opened the one closest to me. It was filled with saris on suede hangers and a few men's suits. But no safe.

The second one had a row of shalwar kameez suits and some tunic tops. And, hidden below, a safe. It was open, the key still hanging in the lock, probably because she'd taken money out for Dad's hospital bill.

Our passports were all together bound by a rubber band. I took mine out and placed the rest back in the safe and closed the cupboard. Heart thumping in my chest, I hurried back to my room and buried my passport at the bottom of my purse.

• • •

Downstairs, I found Shaila by the front door.

"Are you ready?" she asked, adjusting her orna over her shoulders.

"Yes, I am. Just let me tell my parents."

I found them in the living room poring over some papers. Probably information on potential grooms.

"Mom, Dad, I'm going shopping with Shaila."

I hadn't seen them both smile in a long time. They must really believe they had gotten through to me.

"Good, good, you two enjoy yourselves. And buy some nice outfits, okay?" Mom said.

An hour later, Malik brought the car to a stop outside an enormous cathedral of a building, completely encased in glass. In the parking lot, hordes of eager shoppers hurried from their luxury cars, through the suffocating heat, and into the cool interior of the mall, while their drivers looked for a shady spot to while away the time.

Across the street from the mall sat a sprawling colony of slums. A group of young, emaciated kids were playing with a nearly deflated ball, no doubt rescued from someone's trash. I couldn't help but feel wrong about shopping for extravagant clothing when those kids had nothing.

"We should be done in a couple of hours, Malik Bhai. Could you please be back by two o'clock?" Shaila asked the driver when he let us out by the entrance.

The heat was unforgiving as we made our way from the car and into the refreshingly air-conditioned interior of the mall. A glass elevator transported shoppers between the seven floors of the main atrium, which, from what I could tell, seemed to offer everything from electronics to herbal medicine.

"How do you ever get used to all of this?" I asked Shaila as we took the elevator to the upper level.

"What, this over-the-top mall?" Shaila grinned at me.

"No, just all the poverty and everything. How do you go around and not let it affect you?" I was still feeling guilty about being in an air-conditioned mall and then going back home to eat amazing food.

"Why do you think it doesn't affect me?" Shaila said. "You'd have to be a monster to not let it affect you. But you also have to live your life. I do what I can, I volunteer, I give clothes and food regularly. But I can't help everyone."

I nodded. I was old enough now to know that this was a much bigger problem, one that required a much bigger solution than just handing out food and clothes to some kids on the street.

"The thing is, Rukhsana, you are upset now because this is a shock to you since you're not surrounded by it every day. And believe it or not, once you're back in Seattle, it won't be long before you get caught up in your own life and forget all about those kids. That's just how it is."

She was right. This was not anything new. It was just new to me, again, even though three years ago I'd seen the same things.

We stepped off the elevator on the seventh floor, where all the clothing stores were.

The displays in the shops were breathtaking. Pyramids of glass bangles in brilliant jewel tones sparkled under the artificial lighting, and mannequins draped in richly embroidered saris stood like sentries at the shop entrances. Although Seattle did have a small selection of shops catering to South Asians, nothing compared to the opulence displayed here.

"Let's go look at some kurtas," Shaila said, pulling me into a dimly lit store. Once my eyes adjusted to the subdued lighting, I found myself surrounded by mannequins dressed in dazzling tunics.

"I love this design," I said, admiring one that was bright blue cotton with black block prints on it.

"It would look great with jeans, don't you think?" Shaila said. "Want to try it on?"

"I don't know if I'd wear it back home though," I said, touching the soft fabric. "I usually wear a sari or shalwar kameez to Bengali functions."

"Just try it on, you can decide later." Shaila signaled one of the employees for assistance.

A few minutes later, I was in the dressing room with several other kurtas that Shaila had picked out, ready for my movie montage moment. For the next half hour, my problems took a back seat as Shaila and I took turns trying on clothes and modeling them for each other. I preened and posed like a Bollywood star, the Hindi music playing in the store acting as our own personal soundtrack, and felt utterly carefree in a way I hadn't for a while now.

"Let's get the one with the heavy embroidery," Shaila said, slightly out of breath from laughing. "We have to bring back at least a couple of outfits to show your mom."

I grimaced at the mention of my mother. It probably would be smart to get something she approved of. I picked out two, thinking that I could give them to Rokeya for one of her daughters later. At least someone should get to enjoy them, especially at my parents' expense. We stopped at another store and picked up several simple cotton saris and children's outfits to give away on our way back.

"Okay, let's go find the travel agency now," I said after we'd paid for our purchases. Shaila had checked to make sure there was one at this mall, and now we made our way there so that I could buy a one-way ticket to Seattle. There was a bounce in my step as we walked in, and a half hour later, I had booked my way home on the earliest flight that wasn't already full. Four more days here, and then I would be back with Ariana.

● ● ●

Back at Nani's house, I went straight to my room and pulled the passport out of my purse. I didn't think it was a good idea to carry it around with me. If my purse got snatched, I'd be stuck here without a passport. I looked for a good hiding place, eventually putting it under my mattress. The chances of Mom looking under there were slim.

That evening Shaila had plans to go to a party at a college friend's house. Surprisingly, her parents were fine with her going, and even more shockingly, my mom readily agreed when Shaila asked if I could go too.

"You're going to have a great time," Shaila said as Malik Bhai drove us there. "I know you love to dance."

"I can't wait to meet your friends," I said, glad that I was going to be able to blow off some steam. "Thanks for letting me tag along." I squeezed Shaila's arm affectionately.

"You're only here for four more days," Shaila said. "I want to make the most of it."

"Is Alam going to be there?" I whispered in her ear as the car came to a stop in front of a large house.

"Maybe," she said with a mysterious grin.

I rolled my eyes at her as we got out of the car.

"Malik Bhai, you can go back home now. We'll call when we're ready to leave. It won't be for at least three hours."

As the car pulled away, we walked into a huge marble foyer with a large winding staircase leading to the second floor. I could hear music blaring from somewhere and smiled excitedly at Shaila when I recognized a song from one of my favorite movies, *Dhoom*.

"This is so cool. I haven't been to a party with Bollywood music in a long time."

"I knew you'd like it," Shaila said. "Now come and meet my friends."

A set of double doors in front of us opened and a few people spilled out into the foyer.

"Shaila, you made it." I turned to see a petite girl with beautiful black hair walking toward us. She hugged Shaila first and then me.

"Rukhsana, this is my friend Tabassum," Shaila said. "Tabassum, this is Rukhsana, my cousin from Seattle."

Tabassum hugged me again. "I'm so happy you could make it, Rukhsana. Please come in. There's tons of food, feel free to help yourself. And then join us on the dance floor."

"Thank you so much for having me. Sorry I'm crashing your party," I said.

"Not at all. Shaila's been talking about you for some time now and I'm so happy to meet you." She turned to Shaila. "Shaila, there's someone special who's been waiting for you to get here," she said in a singsong voice. "Go say hi and then get some food."

She ushered us into a large living room. All the furniture had been pushed against the walls to make room for dancing. One group of people was showing off some serious moves as they danced to "Laila Main Laila," another one of my favorite Bollywood songs. I was mesmerized. This was so different than the desi parties I went to in Seattle. Maybe my parents had found the dullest social circle to hang around in. Here, there were no grown-ups, at least not that I could see. At our parties, the grown-ups always stuck around so all of us young people had to pretend to be aunty-loving teens.

Which we weren't. But this was cool. The music was pulsing through me and my legs were willing me to go and join the group of people on the makeshift dance floor. But Shaila was pulling me in the opposite direction.

"Come and meet Alam," she said, guiding me into the next room. She didn't even have to point him out to me. He was the one whose face lit up the moment we walked in.

"He's really hot," I said, having to speak rather loudly over the music coming from the next room. Unfortunately, the music cut out at that exact moment and the entire room heard my comment. I felt the blood rushing to my cheeks as the other people in the room turned to stare at me. Shaila just shook her head, and when I finally glanced at Alam, he was grinning, looking entirely too pleased with himself. Thankfully the music started up again and people resumed their conversations.

"Alam, this is my cousin Rukhsana," Shaila said.

"It's so nice to finally meet you," Alam said, still beaming. He was dressed casually in a kurta and jeans, his curly hair tousled, but it was his eyes that caught my attention. They were kind eyes and I understood immediately why Shaila was in love with him. She was the kindest person I knew, and at that moment I felt true happiness for her and Alam.

Just then Tabassum joined us.

"Come and dance with us, you guys," she urged, pulling Shaila gently by the arm.

I didn't need to be asked twice, and we all went into the next room to join the fun.

I was a little out of touch with the latest Bollywood hits since Seattle was not exactly a hub for Hindi music, but that didn't stop me from having a blast. After a couple of songs, my throat was parched, and I went off in search of a drink. When I came back, a slow song was playing, and my eyes drifted to Shaila and Alam. They were dancing, their heads close together, completely lost in each other. I was thankful for this time with Shaila, to see her so happy with the one she loved. A sad thought came unbidden to my mind. Once I left, there was a very good possibility that I might not see Shaila or Nani again for a very long time. Shaila's mom would make sure to keep her away from my bad influence. And Nani couldn't exactly get around by herself these days. Tears sprang to my eyes and I quickly left to find some privacy. The last thing I wanted was to ruin this evening for Shaila. I knew that the times she could see Alam were precious and too few. I found a bathroom and splashed cold water on my face. I looked at my reflection in the mirror as I carefully dried my face with a towel. On the outside, I looked exactly the same as I had four weeks ago, before I'd come here. But on the inside, so much had changed that I felt like I was looking at a stranger. I was about to take a step that would irrevocably alter the course of my life. Once I ran away from here there was no turning back. My parents would probably kick me out of the house for ruining their reputations. Many in the Bengali community in Seattle would warn their children to stay away from me. I knew that Irfan and Sara would help me, but I would still lose any semblance of normalcy. What if my parents forbade Aamir from seeing me? He could defy them, but he was just fifteen. There was only so much he could do. Could I bear to live my life without my family, my brother, my community in it?

A knock on the door pulled me out of my thoughts. It was just as well. I really didn't need to have doubts right now. Not when I was this close to getting away.

● ● ●

By the time we got home it was past eleven and the world had not yet imploded. Mom and Dad were in the living room chatting with Tanveer Mama and Nusrat Mami when we walked in. Mom looked relaxed and nothing like she did when I got home late in Seattle. No lectures on the disaster that could befall the family of a Muslim girl who stayed out late at night doing God knows what.

"How was the party? Did you enjoy yourselves?" Mom asked, smiling indulgently.

"Yes, Zuby Phupi, we had a really great time," Shaila said. "Rukhsana got to meet some of my friends too."

"Good, that is very nice." Mom nodded approvingly. "Do you girls want anything to eat?"

"There was a lot of food at the party, Mom," I said. "I think we'll just go to bed now."

Up in my room, Shaila helped me pack. Even though I still had a few days before I left, I wanted to be prepared. The waiting was making me nervous, and I needed to keep myself busy.

"Rukhsana," Shaila said, handing me the mask I got for Aamir. "I was telling Alam about your situation and he offered to drive you to the airport."

"That's so sweet of him. Was he shocked when you told him?"

"A little, but he thinks you're really brave to do what you're doing."

We finished packing the backpack, stuffing it with only the essentials: clothes, my gifts for Ariana and Aamir, toiletries, and of course my hair straightener. I never went anywhere without it.

After Shaila went to her own room, I went to check on Nani.

I assumed she would be asleep by now, so I was surprised to see her prostrated on her prayer mat. When she was done she beckoned me to come in. I helped her up and got her settled in an armchair. Then I made myself comfortable by her feet on the cool tile floor and she put her hand on my head, running her fingers through my hair.

"Your mom told me that they are looking for a husband for you."

I nodded, wondering how my life had taken such a ridiculous turn.

"Are you happy with this decision? I thought you were excited to go to university in September."

"I'm not happy with it at all. Mom and Dad are being completely unreasonable."

"Rukhsana, go to my cupboard and get me my wedding veil. Do you remember where it is?"

I nodded as I stood up and opened the large teak armoire that stood against the wall across from her bed. On the bottom shelf, wrapped in velvet, was my grandmother's wedding veil. It was a deep maroon chiffon shot through with gold thread. As a child I used to play dress up with it whenever I visited Nani. She would put makeup on my face and then draw little decorative dots from my forehead, above my brows, and all the way down to my cheeks with sandalwood paste. Afterward, she'd place the veil on my head and tell me I looked like a real Bengali bride. Then she would dream out loud about dancing at my wedding and all the sweets she would eat.

Now as I handed the veil to her, I felt a pang of guilt because I knew that day would never come. She unwrapped it, motioning for me to move closer to her, and placed it gently on my head. As she leaned back to take a better look, she picked up a silver-framed hand mirror from the small table beside her and turned it toward me so that I could see my reflection.

Dark curls peeked out from under the veil framing my face. For a fleeting moment, I pictured myself as a traditional bride, marrying someone my parents had chosen. But I knew I could never go through with it.

"Why not, my angel? What is so bad that you can't tell me?"

I couldn't look her in the eyes, afraid of the disappointment I would see there.

"Is it a boy?" she asked. "You love him and he is not Bengali?"

I shook my head again.

"Tell me one thing. Are you ashamed of it or just afraid of what I will think?"

I looked at her then. "I'm not ashamed. But I'm afraid you'll be ashamed of me if you know."

"My little spring bird," she said, pulling me into her arms. "If you are not ashamed then it cannot be a bad thing. So why should I be ashamed of you? You are a good girl, my best girl. I will never be ashamed of who you are."

"I do love someone. But it's not a boy." I watched her face carefully, bracing myself for the worst.

She looked confused at first. But she didn't pull away and she didn't take her hand off my face. She just nodded slowly.

"Rukhsana," she finally said. "We are who we are. No one can change that. Just like we cannot change whom we love. I learned that many years ago when I was just a little older than you."

Fat tears rolled down my face as I turned to kiss my grandmother's hands. They were the most loving hands in the world to me. I leaned forward and sobbed into her lap. She stroked my hair until there were no more tears left, and my heart felt lighter than it had in a long time.

"You silly girl. You thought I would be ashamed of you? Never. You can never do anything that will make me feel like that."

"Nani, do you think if you talk to Mom and Dad they would understand?"

I hoped that if her own mother thought it was okay, then maybe Mom would be more likely to accept it.

But Nani shook her head.

"Rukhsana, your mother has always had very strong opinions of right and wrong. She and I did not see eye to eye on many things. No, you must fight this. You cannot allow anyone to change who you are, not even your own parents."

"Nani. There's something else."

"What is it, ammu?" She stroked my hair gently, her hands moving in a familiar rhythm.

"I'm leaving in four days. I can't stay here, otherwise Mom and Dad are going to keep me trapped here until I agree to marry someone."

"Yes, you must leave, then. There is no other way," she said without hesitation. "But if you had left without telling me, it would have broken my heart. I'm happy, Rukhsana, that you have someone who loves you. She must be very special."

"She is, Nani. I wish you could meet her. I think you would really like her."

She closed her eyes and nodded.

"How are you getting home?" she said after a moment. "Do you need anything?"

"No, Nani, I've booked my flight already. I'll contact Shaila once I'm back and she'll let you know. She can show you how to Skype with me." I put my arms around her and we stayed like that for a long time. I tried to be brave for her sake as well as mine. Because, in all honesty, I knew there was a good chance I might never see her again.

"Rukhsana, there is something I want you to have." She pointed to a desk that stood by the window. On top lay a wooden box with vines and flowers engraved along the edges.

I brought the box to her and watched as she pulled out a weathered journal.

"This was my diary when I was a young girl," she said. "I want you to have it. Sometimes when things become too difficult you can read it. I used to write down all my feelings because I couldn't tell anyone. In those days, we had to keep many secrets," she said wistfully.

I looked at the diary in my hands, my fingers brushing across the soft cover, and wanted to ask about her secrets, but when I looked back up she had closed her eyes again. I could tell she was tired, so I helped her get into bed and stayed with her until she fell asleep.

I went back to my room and sat cross-legged on the bed as I opened the diary. It was bound in burgundy velvet and the pages were yellowed with age. Nani's handwriting filled page after page with Bengali script, chronicling her life all those years ago. For once I was glad for the years of Bengali classes my parents insisted I attend. As I began to read, my eyes misted over. The first entry was marked with a date.

August 23, 1965

Today a boy's family came to see me. Ma told me to wear the green-and-gold sari because it made my skin look lighter. She said the groom had dark skin so the family would overlook my dusky complexion. But I overheard Ma and Baba talking in the cowshed. Baba said I was too young, but Ma told him if I was married there would be more food left over for Bhaiya and they could pay for his school. Baba said they were asking for too much dowry. He would have to sell three of his cows to pay for the wedding and another two for the dowry. I was so scared before they came, but the mother was kind. She wanted to see my teeth and she said my breasts were too small. But she wasn't rough like the other woman who came last month. She pulled my lips back so far the skin tore and bled a little. It was a relief when they rejected me. But Ma beat me that night. Each time the cane sliced the skin on my back, I tried to think of Raju. Raju as he smiled at me when no one was watching. Raju as he plucked mangos from the high branches for me. But today, Ma was happy. At dinner, I got a piece of chicken even though Bhaiya wanted it. Ma told him that I would be gone soon enough and then he would have all the chicken he wanted. I'm so tired now, but I will pray to Allah that this family will say yes to the marriage. If the mother was kind maybe the son will be a good man.

A tear broke free and fell on the page. I hastily wiped it away with my orna. My heart was breaking for my poor nani. I pressed my hands to my eyes for a moment and then continued reading.

I haven't written for many weeks. I couldn't, because my mother-in-law is constantly with me. But today she went out to visit her sister who is ill, so I can rest a little bit. My husband has gone to the city for some work. He will not be back until it is dark.

I have been married now for two months. On the day of the wedding, I was so happy because I thought I was going to a nice family. Arif looked very handsome in his white sherwani and turban. Our wedding was very lavish, more than any other one in our small village. But I still heard some of the guests complaining that there was not enough meat in the korma. My mother-in-law gave me a very beautiful red-and-gold sari. I'm sure it must have been very expensive because when I ran my hands over it, the silk was so fine and the gold embroidery so heavy. When they brought me home pride surged through me at the sight of their mansion. Arif and I have our own room and there are two toilets, both inside! This is my home now. But at night, I was very nervous. My monthly bleeding just started this year and Ma told me all women get it because it is Allah's curse on us. She didn't explain to me what I should do on my wedding night. When he walked into our bedroom, I began to sweat and my heart pounded loudly in my chest. Arif said I should not be scared because he knows what to do. He gently took off my sari and all the jewelry. When he started to take off my clothes, I felt very shy, so I moved away. He pulled me back *and continued to undress me. At first, he kissed me and it was nice. But then his hands were touching me everywhere and I pushed him off. That is when he slapped me so hard I could taste blood on the inside of my cheek. He said I could never push him away. That since he is my husband, I have to be with him whenever he wants. After that, I was still as a statue.*

My tears fell freely now and I quickly shut the diary before they stained the ink. I went to my grandmother's room and crawled into bed with her. I needed to be near her. I couldn't imagine what she had endured. How did she live like that for so many years?

My grandfather died before my parents were married, so I'd never met him. Her life must have seemed so long, with no end in sight. This is how I would feel if I married according to my parents' wishes. I knew now why my grandmother had warned me and why she wanted me to get away. She had been through hell and she wanted to spare me the same fate. I held her tight, careful not to wake her.

• • •

I slept listlessly that night and woke up with a pounding headache. I went to look for Shaila and found her putting coconut oil in her hair.

"You look like you could use a good oil massage," she said when she saw me skulking by her door. "Come here and sit. I'll put some in your hair."

My mom used to put coconut oil in my hair when I was little, but once I started school, kids would make fun of the smell. It had been years and I hadn't realized what I'd been missing.

"This feels amazing," I said as Shaila massaged the cool oil into my scalp. I felt the tension draining away immediately.

"Don't you put coconut oil in your hair regularly?" Shaila said with a laugh.

"Are you kidding? I barely have time to wash my hair, dry it, and straighten it before school. It takes too long." Shaila had twisted my hair into a neat, thick braid and I turned to look at her with envy. "Your hair is so pretty and silky. Mine's like jute."

"That's because you don't use oil. If you do, yours will be soft and silky too," Shaila said, gently pushing me to move.

"You should have asked me to do your hair."

"You can do it next time," Shaila said. "Oh, hey, there's an art show at the Alliance Française tonight that I thought would be interesting. What do you think?"

"Sure, that sounds like fun."

We went to our respective bathrooms to wash the oil out of our hair. I'd forgotten how much time and shampoo it took, but I had to admit my hair had never felt softer. After a quick lunch of khichuri, aloor bhorta, and shrimp dopiaza, we took a rickshaw to the art exhibit. My hair dried quickly in the blazing midday sun and I was relieved when we entered the air-conditioned building.

"I used to take French lessons here, while I was waiting for my A Level results," Shaila said. "I came to events here all the time back then but haven't been back since. I forgot how beautiful it was." I snagged a pamphlet as she led me down a hallway to a large room where the exhibit was being held.

This exhibit was by a local artist, Khurram Aziz, who painted scenes from the Mughal palaces of the twelfth century. I was stunned by the sheer beauty of each piece, the bold colors, and the feeling of being transported to another place and time. There were scenes of the king holding darbaar for his subjects and another where the ladies of the harem were bathing in a secluded spot. There was one in particular that mesmerized me. It was of a man and woman sitting on a grass-covered hilltop, gazing into each other's eyes, their bejeweled garb indicating that they were royalty. But it was the look of utter devotion that the artist had managed to capture that drew me in.

"Isn't this breathtaking?" Shaila whispered beside me.

• • •

When we arrived back home, we overheard Mom and Nusrat Mami in the middle of an argument in the living room.

"The family is already rich . . . Why are they asking for so much dowry?" Mom asked as we walked in. They sat on the sofa with an open betel leaf box on the coffee table in front of them. The small containers held the fillings: slivers of areca nut, fennel seeds, rock sugar, and lime paste. Nusrat Mami spread a tiny dab of lime paste on a betel leaf. She added a pinch of the other ingredients, expertly folded the leaf into a triangle, and popped it in her mouth. Mom's lips curled in disgust.

"It is normal to ask for something, Zubaida," Nusrat Mami said after she had chewed for a while. "They probably think you are very rich living in America. You think you have the upper hand here, but you don't. They will all ask for more simply because you are American now."

Mom snorted. "We'll see about that. Half of them are desperate to come to America. Marrying a US citizen is their only chance to get there. They'll realize it soon enough."

It amazed me that I had never known this side of my mother. She discussed my worth as if I was a piece of meat. I couldn't listen to it any longer and went upstairs to check on Nani.

• • •

Her words from the diary had stayed with me all day, and there was so much I needed to know.

I found her prostrate on her prayer mat, just finishing up her Maghrib prayer. I waited by the door until she was done and then walked over to help her to her feet. I got her settled into bed and sat on the edge, close to her.

"How was your day today, ammu?" she asked.

"It was good. Shaila and I went to an art show."

I tried to think of a good way to bring up the diary, but in the end, I realized, there was no easy way to bring up something as horrible as what my nani had been through.

"Nani, I read some of your diary last night," I began.

Her brow wrinkled with concern. "I was thinking that maybe it was a mistake to give it to you. It is from the worst part of my life."

"No, Nani, I'm glad that you trusted me enough to share something so personal with me."

"I thought it might give you strength when you need it most. I can tell that there are difficult times ahead for you." She took my hand in hers. "You must fight. Even when everyone tells you that you must obey and accept."

"If I could obey and accept I wouldn't be in this situation, Nani."

Nani lay back with a sigh.

"That has always been the problem, Rukhsana. We must be the masters of our own destinies. I did not learn that until it was too late. You have to fight to take back control of your life. Sometimes you will hurt the ones you love the most. But in the end, it will always have to be your choice."

I nodded, reaching over to hug her.

"I will fight, Nani. I promise I won't give up."

At dinner that night, Mom talked about some other family who would be coming to check me out. Now that my plans for escape were more concrete, I could pretend this was all fine. It was unreal to witness the ease with which my mom could go on as if nothing was wrong.

I wondered if Dad agreed with her or if he was just going along with her. Either way it didn't matter anymore. Three more days and I would be out of here. Once I was back home in Seattle, they could hardly force me to marry anyone. Until then I just had to keep up appearances and let them believe that I'd warmed up to the idea.

The next day I went along with the whole charade, dressing in one of the new outfits I had bought with Shaila. She suggested I wear a long turquoise tunic paired with loose pants that were gathered at the feet. I thought I looked nice when I looked at myself in the full-length mirror by the window. I had silver earrings that matched the silver embroidery on the front and on the cuffs of the flared sleeves. After Shaila finished doing my makeup, she stepped back to survey her handiwork and smiled appreciatively.

"He's not going to be able to keep his eyes off you," she said with a grin.

"I'm glad you find this funny," I said, glaring at her in mock anger. The only reason we were able to joke about this was because everything had been arranged for me to leave.

When the family arrived, they introduced themselves as the Choudhurys. "This is our son, Sohail," Mr. Choudhury announced rather pompously. "He finished his MBA two years ago from Columbia University and now he is working as a financial consultant."

I arranged my face into a suitably impressed expression as we all settled into the living room.

This visit was actually not as bad as the last one. In fact, I rather liked the whole family. Their son, Sohail, reminded me of Irfan, and I was sure he would make some lucky girl very happy. Unfortunately for him, that girl would not be me.

After dinner, his mother suggested that perhaps we would like to take a walk in the garden. My mom could barely contain herself. I was surprised she didn't push us through the French doors.

We walked through the jasmine-scented garden over to the little koi pond in the far corner. The fronds of the tall coconut trees and date palms swayed in the slight breeze that blew in gently from the lake behind my grandmother's house. We passed the tree where I had carved my initials as a little girl.

"Are these your initials?" he asked, running his fingers over them. "R.A. Rukhsana Ali."

I nodded, suddenly shy.

"So, tell me, Rukhsana Ali," he said. "What should I know about you?"

I looked up at him, his face illuminated by the moonlight. The fullness of his lips softened the lines of his chiseled face.

"Why don't you tell me what you want to know?"

"Well, from what I hear, you've been accepted to Caltech with a full scholarship."

"Yes, I have," I said.

"First of all, congrats on that," he said, bowing with a flourish.

"Thank you." A smile threatened to break free.

"But I'm curious," he continued. "Obviously Caltech is a big deal, so I'm just wondering why you would agree to this meeting?"

He smiled disarmingly, the left corner of his mouth lifting slightly more than the right.

It was a good question, but not one I could answer honestly.

"It's just my parents. They're worried if I go away to university, I'll find a boyfriend and elope or something." This was only partially untrue. Until recently, that had been one of the reasons for my mom's reluctance to let me go to Caltech.

"Understandable," he mused. "So, you're not really interested in any of this?"

How much could I say without getting myself in trouble with my parents? It wasn't worth it. I was leaving in two days, and as long as I just went along everything would be fine.

"No, it's not that. It's just that I have to make sure whoever I agree to marry will not stop me from going to Caltech." That sounded reasonable.

"Of course, that makes complete sense. It's not every day that one gets an opportunity like that."

Suddenly he reached behind me and plucked a rajanigandha from the tree and presented it to me. He seemed to be just as nervous as I was, so I smiled and took the flower from him. I tucked it in my hair, securing it with one of the bobby pins.

"So, tell me more about yourself," he said. "What do you do for fun?"

"I don't really have a lot of free time with school and everything, but I do watch a lot of documentaries."

How lame can I be?

"Documentaries, really?" His eyes lit up. "What kinds do you like?"

"Oh man, so I love watching anything that has to do with the universe, naturally, so shows like *Cosmos* and the NOVA science programs. Also, anything narrated by David Attenborough, like *Planet Earth*. There's just something about his voice that is so equally soothing and compelling."

"Serious question though," he said. "Carl Sagan or Neil deGrasse Tyson?"

"Easy. Carl Sagan," I answered without hesitation.

"Good. You passed the test," he said, a huge grin spread across his face.

"What do you do in your spare time?" I said.

"Well, work keeps me pretty busy. But when I have free time I like to play squash. And cricket."

"Rukhsana, Sohail, bhitore asho." Mom was calling us back inside and I suddenly wished we had more time. Not that it mattered, because I'd be gone soon, but he seemed like a pretty nice guy.

When we rejoined them, the Choudhurys were saying their goodbyes. After they left, I disappeared to my room.

• • •

"Mrs. Choudhury called this morning," Mom said when I finally came down just before noon the next day. I stared at her blankly.

"Sohail's mother," she said with pursed lips. "She wanted to know if we would let you go to dinner with him. He wants to get to know you better before he makes a decision." The frown lines on her forehead deepened.

"What did you tell her?" I didn't really care either way.

"I said yes. What else could I say?" I didn't know what she wanted me to say to that, so I said nothing. We sat in uncomfortable silence for a few minutes.

"I need you to be very careful about what you say to him," she said finally.

I shouldn't tell him I'm a lesbian, then?

"How about you just tell me what you want me to say."

Mom narrowed her eyes slightly at me. "Just don't create any more trouble for me, okay? Do you think you can manage that?"

"Yes, yes, don't worry. I won't say anything to embarrass you." I got up and left the room before I said anything I might regret later.

chapter
twenty-three

Malik Bhai drove me to Arirang House, the Korean restaurant Sohail had suggested for dinner.

"No need for people to see you two alone in the car," Mom had said when she refused to let him pick me up. "If this doesn't work out then I don't want people making lewd comments about you."

But being seen in a restaurant with him was fine? Mom's logic made no sense to me whatsoever.

It was fairly crowded when I got there. Sohail was waiting for me in front of the entrance and we were shown to a table in the corner. We ordered some bulgogi and glass noodles, then sat back and began to talk.

"So, Rukhsana, I have a few serious questions to ask you before I can make a decision on whether to move forward with this arrangement."

He seemed different from the other night, more full of himself, and I did not like it one bit. But all I had to do was get through this dinner and one more day.

"Go ahead," I said as nonchalantly as I could.

"First of all, do you consider yourself a religious person?" he asked after the waiter had brought us our drinks.

"That depends," I said. "What kind of person do you consider to be religious?"

He smiled at my evasiveness.

"You know . . . do you pray five times a day, do you fast during Ramadan, do you abstain from alcohol, et cetera?"

"I used to pray five times a day but it dwindled down over the years, and now I just don't pray at all. I do fast during Ramadan though, and I don't like alcohol."

"But you've tried it?" He watched me closely and I knew I had to be very careful. I didn't want to give him any excuse to say something negative about me to his parents.

"No," I lied. "I just don't like the way people act when they've had it."

He seemed to ponder that for a moment.

"Have you had any boyfriends?"

Now, this I could answer with complete honesty.

"No, never." I surprised myself with my calmness. Normally this line of questioning would make me furious. But right now, this was just a means to an end. If he agreed to marry me, it would get my parents off my back long enough for me to get away. I couldn't think beyond tomorrow at this point.

He smiled at me and I had no idea why.

"You know what, this isn't funny anymore," he said abruptly, stifling a laugh.

What?

"I'm sorry, I was just messing with you." He smiled again, disarmingly.

"What do you mean?" I was totally confused.

"I thought it would be funny if I pretended to be one of those guys. You know, interviewing a potential bride and all?" He was grinning now, in a charmingly boyish way. I didn't know what to make of it.

"Okay, so now you're saying you're not one of those guys?" I didn't share his amusement.

"I'm not, I swear. To be honest, I hate this whole idea of arranged marriage and all, but my parents forced me."

"They forced you to screen women, or they forced you to take me out to dinner?" He was weird, this one.

"No, the dinner was my idea," he said. "I thought we were starting to hit it off the other night, right?"

Right, but I didn't want him to know that yet.

"Okay, so why exactly do you want to get to know me better?" This whole conversation was making my head hurt. I didn't have time for this.

"Because you seem like an interesting person and I like interesting people."

Oh, so now he was hitting on me. It would be so awesome if I could just tell him I was gay.

"And what are you planning to tell your parents, then?" I was genuinely curious.

"Well, I was hoping that if we got to know each other better, we could decide together if getting married was a good idea."

"And your parents would go for that?"

"Well, let's just say, they would have to choose between that or me just refusing to go along with them anymore." So, he intended to play hardball with his parents. I could get on board with that. I didn't know exactly how, but this could give me an advantage.

"Okay." I nodded slowly. "What do I tell my parents?"

Could I trust him not to turn this around and let me take the fall? I couldn't let that happen. All I had to do was let my parents believe I was still willing to listen to them, just long enough for me to get away.

"Just tell them the truth. That we want to spend more time with each other before we make a commitment." He paused when the food came.

"If you want," he continued once the waiter had set everything on the table, "I can tell my parents that this is all coming from me, and then you just have to agree."

"Well, it *is* all coming from you," I said, a little more sharply than I intended. I didn't exactly want to push him away. If this worked, he could buy me valuable time.

"I kind of get the feeling that you're not particularly thrilled with the whole idea either. Or am I wrong?"

Okay, so he was intuitive. I couldn't exactly hold that against him. I decided to go with my gut.

"You're right, I'm not. I just want to get back in time to graduate and go to Caltech in the fall. Marriage isn't part of my plans at all right now."

He smiled and it was just a little too smug for me to let it go.

"If you repeat any of this to your parents or mine, I'll just deny everything."

He laughed and this time it felt real. Maybe he wasn't so bad after all.

"Listen, Rukhsana, you have nothing to worry about. This isn't what I want either, so I want to get out of it as much as you do. No offense."

"None taken," I replied with the first genuine smile I'd given him. "But you know how it is."

He nodded and then we finally dug in. The spicy beef bulgogi was delicious and the glass noodles were the perfect complement.

"Tell me more about yourself," Sohail said, placing his chopsticks in the holder.

"What would you like to know?" I reluctantly put my chopsticks down.

"Anything, you know, like what's your favorite TV show?"

"That's easy. I'm addicted to *Grey's Anatomy* at the moment."

"I've never seen it, but aren't they on like season twenty-seven by this point?" He laughed. "What about *Friends*? I've been bingeing that recently."

"Oh my God, of all the shows on Netflix you chose *Friends*?" I said, playfully serious.

"Isn't it like a classic American sitcom?"

"Technically, yes. It's just SO white."

"True. But it is pretty funny. I've also been watching *One Day at a Time*. Now, that's not white at all. And *Brown Nation*."

"Okay, okay. You get a pass this time," I said with a wink. "And I *love* both those shows."

"Do you keep up with any Hindi shows?" he asked.

"Well, not as much as my mom would like, but I tend to get my fill when my Aunty Meena comes over," I said, laughing. "She keeps us up-to-date with all the latest popular movies and serials. Have you watched *Zindagi Gulzar Hai*?"

"The Pakistani serial?" he said. "Yes, it's so good."

"Fawad Khan is a dream."

It was so nice to spend an hour just talking about perfectly normal things like TV and movies; it was clear that we had a lot in common. Later, as we shared a cup of shaved ice topped with chocolate and nuts, he looked at me pensively. I thought about how much Ariana would have liked him and my heart ached.

"You know, if things were different and you weren't going back to Seattle, I have a feeling we would be good friends," he said solemnly.

"I'll drink to that," I said, raising my glass of water. If he noticed the sadness in my eyes, he made no mention of it.

That night I dreamed about Ariana. We were together the way we used to be back in Seattle. I woke up with my pillow soaked in tears, and as I got ready to face the day, there was one thought that kept me going. Soon I would be back and I would do whatever it took to convince Ariana that I loved her more than anything else in my life. In my heart, I hoped she would forgive me and everything would go back to the way it was.

The next morning, I found Mom in a particularly pleasant mood at breakfast.

"Sohail's mother called again," she said, smiling from ear to ear. "He must have said something nice about you to her, because she thinks he will say yes."

"How delightful," I said.

"Isn't it?" Mom said. Clearly, she didn't know how sarcasm worked. "But she said he still wants to spend some more time with you."

I played with the ends of my scarf.

"I hope he decides soon. Otherwise we are just wasting time."

chapter
twenty-four

That afternoon Shaila and I went out to buy some saris that Mom wanted to gift to the potential groom's family.

"I can't believe this is your last day here," Shaila said as we decided which of the many, many sari shops to enter first.

"I know. I'm really going to miss you, Shaila." My eyes began to water and I turned away, not really wanting to cry here in the mall.

"It's okay. Maybe Alam and I can visit you and Ariana in California," Shaila said. "You could show us around. Wouldn't that be amazing?"

It really would. Maybe it didn't have to be so final after all. I would still have a relationship with Shaila after I moved to California.

We spent a few hours looking at gorgeous jamdhani saris, the handwoven silk and intricate motifs making the selection very difficult. The shopkeeper draped each one on himself so that we could get the full effect of the design. There were ones with floral or geometric patterns, each woven with gold or silver thread. We finally picked out several that Shaila thought would be suitable enough and decided to call it a day.

I sensed something was wrong as soon as we walked back into the house later that evening and I saw Mom in the living room. There was something about the way she sat, completely still, that made me nervous. I motioned to Shaila, asking her to leave. I didn't want to take her down with me.

Mom's face was ashen as she looked at me. She clutched something in her hand. As I got closer, I saw it. My passport. My heart dropped when I saw the little blue book in her hands.

"Why were you hiding your passport under the mattress?"

Why were you snooping in my room? I wanted to shout, but I said nothing.

How much does she know?

"All this time we thought you were coming to your senses. But actually, you were deceiving us."

They would know about deception. They're masters of it.

Dad had been sitting quietly the whole time, but now he stood up.

"Give me your cell phone," he demanded.

I hesitated and he came closer.

"I said, give it to me." His voice was dangerously quiet.

I considered not giving it to him. Would he try to get it from my purse? Or would he have another panic attack? Hating myself for the pang of fear and guilt that pierced my heart, I fished the phone out of my pocket and handed it to him. He looked at it cluelessly for a moment, and then handed it to my mother without a word. She swiped the screen and typed in my password. I wanted to kick myself for not changing it. I'd always told Mom my password when she asked me, because I had never thought I would find myself in this situation. It had never occurred to me to protect myself from her. Now I looked on helplessly as she scrolled through my messages. Then she looked up triumphantly, her face transformed by an evil smirk.

"Look, Ibrahim . . . look at what your clever daughter has done." She passed the phone to him. He read it and looked at me, shaking his head.

"How can you do this to us?" he asked in disbelief. "Did you think of what would happen if anyone found out about this?"

"And you dragged poor Irfan into your mess too?" Mom chimed in. "That nice boy, what will his parents think of us now?"

"Mom, I'm not going to marry someone just because you can't deal with the fact that I'm gay."

That just set her off.

"Keep your voice down," she said through gritted teeth. "Do you want the whole house to know about your—I can't even say it."

"Mom, can you at least try to understand? What you and Dad are doing is ridiculous. You can't force me to marry anyone. Especially not some guy."

They didn't say anything at first.

"Rukhsana, we're worried about you," Mom said eventually. "Do you have any idea what will happen when people find out? We'll become the laughingstock of our community. Is that what you want?"

"Of course not. But why do you care what some narrow-minded people think about us?"

"Because we have to live the rest of our lives among them," Dad said. "Maybe you can go somewhere and start your life over, but what is going to happen to us? We will have nothing. We have a business to run that we worked very hard to build. Who do you think will want to shop there after they find out about you? Our good reputation is all we have."

I stood there, unable to speak, unable to move, watching as my only chance of escape went up in smoke. I never hated my mother as much as I did in that moment. Hated her for every time she made me wish I was a boy, every time she made me feel that I was less than. But most of all I hated what she had done to Dad. She had made him see me through her eyes.

"Did you think I would keep quiet and just let you marry me off?" The delicate thread of self-control I'd been holding on to for so many weeks broke and the hate came spewing out. My mother narrowed her eyes and gave me a hard look.

"You will do exactly as we say, do you understand? Now, go to your room." She pushed me slightly when I didn't move and followed me up the stairs to my bedroom. Without a word, she turned around and left, closing the door behind her. Seconds later, I heard a key turning in the lock. I ran to the door and pushed down the brass handle. It was locked.

This could not be happening. Did she actually think she could just lock me up in a room and that I would agree with her medieval ideas?

Well, she can try. Let's see how she explains to Nusrat Mami why I'm locked in my room.

I sat there fuming at first, angry at myself for being so stupid. I should have kept the passport on me. I should have known Mom would snoop around in my things.

I expected her to come through the door any minute now, smug in her assumption that I had been scared straight.

I remembered storing Nani's diary in the top drawer of my nightstand, so I pulled it out and began to read the next entry.

Today was not a good day. Baba was supposed to bring the rest of my dowry, but instead he came to ask for more time. After he departed, my mother-in-law came to me in the kitchen,

*where I was boiling water for our baths. She
grabbed me by the arm and plunged my left
hand into the pot. I screamed in pain and tried
to pull away but she held my arm tight. It was
so unbearable I thought I was going to faint. She
let it go after a few seconds, but there were
already angry red blisters forming on my fingers
and across the top of my hand. When Arif came
home in the evening, he asked me about my
bandaged hand. I lied and told him I spilled hot
water on it. He sneered and said I was a
clumsy good-for-nothing and if my father didn't
bring the money soon, he would send me back.
I cannot go back. Baba will kill himself from the
shame. I haven't told them about the baby.
But I will tell them tomorrow and maybe then
the beatings will stop for some time. I will pray
to Allah that it is a boy.*

I was sick to my stomach. I'd seen the marks on Nani's hand
when I was little. I'd asked her about them, running my little fingers along the edges of her scars. But she'd said it was just an acci-
dent. Now my heart constricted with pain at the thought of what
they had done to her. I turned back to the diary and continued
reading.

*It has been a week since I told them I am
carrying a child. A week in heaven, without
beatings. Arif has even stopped coming to me at
night because he is afraid he might harm his
unborn son. Mother-in-law brings me fruit every*

day and I get the good pieces of chicken as well. One day she even made goat curry. If they continue to treat me like this then I will have ten children. Today mother-in-law took me to a soothsayer in the village. Everyone says that she can predict whether I will have a boy or girl. Mother-in-law brought saris, sweets, and money for her. I was so happy and relieved when the soothsayer said I would have a boy. She put her hands on my belly, which is getting bigger every day. She said she could feel his soul talking to her. Mother-in-law was very happy too. When Arif came home he brought me a flower and put it in my hair. I haven't felt so happy for a long time.

I closed my eyes for a bit and pressed my head against the pillow. Did Mom know about this diary? Nani had said she wanted me to have it, so maybe nobody else had seen it. Nobody knew the hell she'd lived through. I was exhausted but I couldn't help myself. I had to know what happened next.

It has been a month since I had my baby girl. I am constantly hungry, because the baby is drinking so much milk. I'm not allowed to eat meat and fish anymore. Only rice and daal and sometimes vegetables. Mother-in-law says we cannot waste so much food for a girl. Arif is very angry with me these days. More than usual. He has started to force himself on me almost every night. Yesterday I was feeding

Zubaida and I asked him to let me finish. He punched my breast and Zubaida started crying. I put her on the side until he was done. She cries all the time, and if I cannot keep her quiet, he beats me. I don't say anything because then he might beat her. So, I let him take his anger out on me until he is finished. Sometimes I cry with Zubaida, but nobody can hear me because she cries so loudly.

The pillow on my lap was wet with tears. I hadn't noticed when I'd started crying again. I felt as if I had walked right into the middle of a horror movie. But there were no serial killers or demons in this movie. These were just ordinary people. But they were so cruel and unfeeling they may as well have been monsters. How could anyone do this to another human being? I wasn't naïve and I'd heard my share of horror stories about people who were victims of domestic abuse. I knew it happened in every community, but this was different because it happened to someone so close, someone I loved so much. I'd always thought of Nani as a strong woman, the heart of our family, the one who had held it all together after my grandfather died. But until now I'd had no idea just how strong she really was. It was incredible to me that she had survived.

I couldn't wrap my head around it. She'd lived in fear of beatings and torture at the hands of her husband and mother-in-law for years. But she had obviously stayed, because my uncle was born. Tanveer Mama was around four years younger than my mom. I skimmed the pages until I found mention of a baby boy.

I am with child again. I told Arif and mother-in-law as soon as I knew, because that would mean better days for Zubaida and me. Although I pray that this baby will be a boy, I am not hopeful. It is better that way. They must feel the same way because this time they are not as nice to me as the last. But at least they are not beating me. Zubaida is three and a half now and asking why her baba beats us. I tell her I don't know but that we must be very careful not to make him or her grandmother angry. But she is too young to understand. She wants to play and sing songs, but I must squash her spirit so that she is invisible to them. If they cannot see or hear her, she will be safe. It has been one month since the last time he beat me. But he said if I have a girl again he will bring home a new wife. He won't send me back because I am good at housework. Then he looked at Zubaida and smiled. He says it will be nice to have her in the house when she is a little more grown. I am very afraid of what will happen to my Zubaida. I cannot protect her from what he will do to her.

I snapped the diary shut. I felt dirty inside and couldn't bear to read any more. I needed to be with Nani right now and tell her how I felt. I went to the door and tried the handle. It was still locked. This was stupid. I would not be treated like a prisoner.

"Shaila," I called. "Shaila, are you there?"

Does anyone even know that I'm up here?

"Rokeya." No answer.

I banged on the door. Nothing.

I hammered away again, harder this time, calling out to anyone who would hear me. I went to the window and pushed aside the curtains. The windowpane stuck a little, but I managed to open it. I stuck out my head. The two-story drop was too far. There was no way I could make the jump without breaking something.

There had to be a way out. I went back to the door and pounded on it again. Still nothing. I slumped on the ground and closed my eyes.

The sun was setting when I heard a key turn, so it must have been about an hour later. I got up off the floor and sat on the bed. I would not give her the satisfaction of thinking she had won.

Mom walked in carrying a tray. She put it on the small table by the window and left, locking the door behind her again. I looked longingly at the cup of chai and cumin cookies. But I had no intention of touching any of it. Night fell and I could hear the watchman calling out his warnings. His muffled cries of "Shabdhan" reverberated throughout the room. Strangely, I only now noticed this nightly ritual, even though I'd been sleeping in this room for a few weeks now. It was probably around ten or eleven before the door opened a second time. It was her again with another tray. This time there was chicken curry, daal, and rotis. My stomach betrayed me by rumbling loudly. She threw a glance at the uneaten cookies and full cup.

"Eat something, Rukhsana."

I didn't say anything at first. I didn't even want to look at her. But she walked over and stood in front of me.

"Rukhsana, you're just making things harder for yourself."

"What do you care?" I still refused to look at her, choosing to stare at my feet instead.

"We're only doing this for your own good, Rukhsana. Do you think it brings me any pleasure to treat you this way?"

Finally, I met her gaze. "Then why are you locking me up like this?"

"Because, ammu, you're going down the wrong path. And I can't let you do that."

"Why is it the wrong path, Mom? Because of your beliefs? What about my beliefs?"

"My beliefs are your beliefs. Why do you think that they are different?"

"It's not the same anymore. Even here in Bangladesh, people are marrying whoever they want."

Mom shook her head.

"No. We are Muslims. You are Muslim. Don't forget that. What you are thinking is wrong. I will not allow you to make such a big mistake. Once you are happily married to a nice Bengali boy, then you will thank me."

"I'm never going to marry anyone you pick for me, Mom. You can try all you want. But you can't force me."

"You're still a child, Rukhsana. You don't understand what you're saying."

"I'm not a child. You just treat me like one. I'm going to college in a few months and I can make my own life choices."

Mom scoffed. "You think that you love this girl? How do you know she will not leave you for someone else? Then what? You will come crying to me and then how will I find a husband for you? You will be damaged. No one will marry you."

I pressed my hands against my eyes. It was hopeless. She would never understand. She put her hand on my head, but I jerked away.

"Rukhsana, please . . . try to understand," she pleaded. "Daddy and I only want the best for you."

When I didn't answer, she left the room. I was so hungry I could taste bile, but I would not make this easy for her. I was glad that she felt guilty. She seemed to have forgotten that I was her daughter and could be just as stubborn as she was.

chapter twenty-five

I lost track of time, but I still refused to eat. By the number of meals that were being brought to me, I would guess about two days had passed. But I wasn't counting anymore. There was no point; I'd missed my chance to get away from here. Ariana must be frantic. She had no way of getting in touch with me. I hoped Irfan would figure out that something had gone terribly wrong and would think to call Shaila. I'd given him her number in case of an emergency. And this definitely qualified as an emergency. I was sure that Mom would not let even a hint of this be known outside this house. Already she must have had to come up with some story for Nusrat Mami and Tanveer Mama. I wondered briefly what she would tell them. She couldn't tell them I was gay. A lethargy took over and I just wanted to sleep the time away. I stared listlessly at the ceiling, trying to remember the last time I'd felt normal, just carefree and happy. It should have frightened me, but instead I felt an intense longing to close my eyes and never open them again. It was so much easier this way. I felt nothing, no pain or yearning.

I woke to the sound of a key turning in the lock again. But it wasn't Mom this time. Shaila walked through the door with another tray. She started to put it on the table, saw the stack of untouched trays, and placed it gently on the bed instead before putting her arms around me.

"Rukhsana, how are you doing?" She took my face in her hands and wiped away the tears that had started to roll down my cheeks again. "Please don't cry. I'm so sorry I couldn't help you get away."

Her hair had fallen across her face and I tucked it behind her ears. A gasp escaped me when I saw the purplish bruise on her left cheek.

"My God, Shaila, what did they do to you? I'm so sorry, this is all my fault."

"I'm fine, Rukhsana. But I'm worried about you. Aunty said you're not eating anything."

"I'm not going to eat anything until she lets me out of here. I just want to go home." But I was so hungry and the food on the tray was making my mouth water. The toast and eggs looked delicious and I would do anything to have a sip of the steaming hot cup of chai. But I had to stay strong.

"Please, Rukhsana, have a little bit. Just for me," Shaila pleaded. She picked up the cup of chai and put it to my lips. I took a sip and it was so good. I took the cup from her and drank some more.

"I'm sorry, Rukhsana. I tried to fight for you. But they threatened to punish me too."

"I'm so sorry, Shaila." I touched her cheek, causing her to wince. I felt sick to my stomach.

"Listen, they took my phone, but I have another one they don't know about. I'm going to call Aamir and tell him to let Ariana know what's happening."

I nodded and tried to tell her to call Irfan as well, but the room was spinning and her voice started to fade. My head began to throb and my stomach churned. I probably should have eaten something with the chai. The key turning in the lock was the last sound I heard before my vision went black.

• • •

When I opened my eyes, the room was dark. I tried to sit up but my head was spinning and I fell back onto the pillow. My mom stood at the foot of the bed. I lifted my head to look at her. She wasn't alone. I sat up again, the throbbing in my head quickening. A man wearing a stained and crumpled white kurta stood next to her.

Who the hell is he?

"Mom," I said weakly, running my tongue over my dry lips.

Why does my mouth feel like cotton?

"Rukhsana, I have brought someone who can help you."

"Help me with—"

"He can get rid of it."

"Get rid of what?"

The pounding in my head was stronger now and I could taste something bitter.

"Nusrat Mami thinks that you may have been possessed by a jinn. And I think she might be right."

This had to be a nightmare. Bile churned in my stomach and I fought the urge to throw up.

"What are you talking about?"

"He is a jinn-catcher. He knows how to get it out of you. Then I will have my Rukhsana back."

"Mom, I feel sick. Something's wrong."

"Nothing is wrong, ammu. I just gave you something to help you stay calm."

Confusion clouded my mind. I hadn't eaten in days. When did—

Somewhere through the fog in my brain, realization pushed

through. It must have been the tea. Mom had used Shaila to get me to drink it. Or was Shaila in on it too?

I couldn't think straight anymore. My eyelids felt heavy and I succumbed to the plunging darkness again.

• • •

When I awoke, I heard a strange whispering in my ear. I turned and came face to face with the jinn-catcher. His dark, beady eyes stared into mine as he continued reciting something in Arabic. His teeth had the telltale reddish-brown stains of a betel leaf addict and a metallic tinge marked his breath. My stomach churned again and I fought the urge to throw up in his face. A thick fog clouded my brain and through the haze I heard Mom enter the room. He finished his chanting and gave her a slight nod.

"It's working," he said in Bengali. "But this one is a very strong jinn. She will not go easily."

"Do whatever you have to do, Baba," Mom said to him.

"It will cost you more than I initially thought."

"That's not a problem. I will pay you whatever you need. Just get the jinn out of her."

I felt like I was having an out-of-body experience. I watched myself lying on the bed as I floated above. I saw Mom and the jinn-catcher. I tried to say something but my tongue felt swollen and the words wouldn't come.

"You have to leave now," the jinn-catcher said to Mom. "This next part will be extremely dangerous. The jinn will try to talk to you and persuade you. I can't protect you if you are here."

"I think I should stay." She sounded uncertain.

"I am commanding the jinn to leave your daughter's body immediately. It is not strong enough to resist but it is very clever. It may jump from her body to yours."

So, then my mom would be the lesbian?

That prospect seemed to convince her. As she made a hasty exit, the jinn-catcher resumed his chanting. It rose to a crescendo and then dropped to a whisper as he got closer to my ear.

Through the haze, a flurry of thoughts rushed to the surface as I lay motionless on the bed, unable to move. My entire body felt heavy, but at least my mind seemed to be clearing up.

Two thoughts stood out almost immediately: My parents had completely lost their minds, and I had to come up with a better plan to get out of here.

The jinn-catcher continued with his ritual. He spoke to the jinn, first imploring, then commanding it to leave my body. At one point, he poured water over my head, hands, and feet, never stopping his chant. A few incense sticks burned in a holder on my nightstand. The overwhelmingly sweet smell was nauseating. My head began to hurt again, and just when I thought it would explode, he finally stopped. Mom must have been listening at the door because it opened right at that moment.

"Baba, is it safe to come in?" She peered into the room and came in when he nodded.

"It was very difficult," he said. "This kind of jinn is very stubborn. It might try to come back."

Mom's face contorted with fear.

"Then what shall we do? How can we stop it for good?"

"She must avoid anything that will tempt the jinn. No music or movies. In addition, she must not laugh too much."

"I will take care of all that," Mom said.

She came to me then and put her arms around me. I wanted to recoil from her touch and it took every fiber of self-control I had to accept her embrace. I hated her for what she had put me through, but I knew I couldn't let her see any trace of that. I returned her hug, resting my head on her shoulder. She leaned back, swept the hair back from my face, and looked at me.

"Rukhsana, I knew it wasn't you. I knew my daughter would never be like that." Tears began to fall down her cheeks, tracing the lines of her face.

I said nothing but forced a slight smile back at her, despite feeling entirely numb.

"Come now, get cleaned up and then come downstairs. The whole family is waiting for you. Your daddy is very anxious."

"What did you tell them, Mom?"

"I told them the truth," she said, without hesitation. "I told them you were possessed by a jinn and that is why you were being so disobedient."

And with that she turned to the jinn-catcher. "Come, Baba, I have prepared some biryani for you," she said as she shepherded him out of the room.

chapter
twenty-six

After they both left, I tiptoed to the door to check if it was really unlocked. I jiggled the handle and when the door opened, relief washed over me. My legs trembled from weakness as I walked back to the bed. I sat on the edge thinking about the mess my life had become. There seemed to be no way out of this situation. I had no phone and no access to a computer to let my friends know what was happening. Even if I did, what could they possibly do? They couldn't help me from so far away.

Nani told me to fight for my happiness. And I was going to do just that. I thought about my life in Seattle. I thought about my friends and I thought about my plans for school. That's what I would fight for. I would fight for Ariana when I got back. But first I had to get my life back. I decided to first clean myself up and get something to eat; I couldn't fight anything if I didn't have the strength to get through it. I took a long hot shower and changed into a fresh shalwar kameez.

I opened the door to Nani's room and quietly tiptoed in. She was propped up in bed looking frailer than she had a few days ago, but when she saw me standing there, her face lit up. With a big smile, she held her arms out and I fell into her embrace, feeling truly loved for the first time in a while.

"I tried to talk to Zubaida," Nani said, gently stroking my hair. "But she simply refused to listen to reason."

"I'm okay now, Nani. I will think of some way to leave."

I pulled back a little to look her in the eyes.

"Nani, promise me that you won't worry too much."

She nodded. "It is very difficult not to worry about the ones you love, my little spring bird."

"Nani," I began hesitantly. "How did you do it? All those years. How did you stay strong?"

She closed her eyes and I wondered if, in her mind, she had gone back to that place and time. Maybe I shouldn't have brought it up.

"Sometimes the love you have for others can give you a tremendous amount of strength," she finally said. "It was different in those days. I was just a young girl. What did I have but my good name? If I had left I would have condemned your mother and uncle to a lifetime of shame and ridicule."

I squeezed her hand gently, then raised it to my lips and kissed it.

"Listen to me, Rukhsana," she said. "Your parents will realize that they are wrong. Someday. But you cannot wait for that. There is another heart, your Ariana's heart, that will break if you are not strong enough. You said you love her, more than anything. Well, then you must fight. Even when it's hard. I am here for you. Shaila and Aamir are here for you."

My eyes filled with tears as she spoke and I nodded.

"I promise, Nani. I will fight."

• • •

The whole family had gathered in the living room. Mom hadn't been lying when she said Dad was anxious. He looked as though he'd aged overnight. His hair was more grey than black. Tanveer Mama was smiling and Nusrat Mami looked at me with disdain, as usual. Shaila got up when she saw me and came to hug me.

"I'm so sorry," she whispered. "I didn't know Aunty Zuby had put something in the tea. I would have never let you drink it."

"It's okay, Shaila. I believe you," I replied. "And I'm so sorry about this." I touched her cheek gently. The bruise was turning green and I wondered which one of them had done this to her. They were all here. Everyone except Nani, and for that I was glad. She didn't need to see this whole charade.

At dinner Mom kept a steady stream of topics going, ranging from prospective suitors to shopping for the trousseau, as if everything was back to normal. After dinner, Mom and Dad asked to speak to me alone, so we went up to my room. Someone, Rokeya most likely, had cleaned up. No traces of stale food or cups of drugged tea. It was all gone. As if the last few days had never happened.

"Rukhsana," Dad began, "we are so happy that you are okay now. This was a very difficult time for all of us, but now we can put it behind us and never speak of it again. That is very important, do you understand?"

I understood perfectly.

"Yes, Daddy," I said quietly.

"Now, you heard what the jinn-catcher said, Rukhsana, so we have to be very careful." Mom sat down on the bed next to me.

"I know we said that we would wait for you to be married until after you finish college," Dad said. "But with everything that has happened, we cannot take any chances."

My heart sank, but I was careful not to show any signs of disappointment.

"What are you saying?" My hands felt cold and clammy and my head began to spin.

"You will be married before we go home to Seattle. There is no more time. Sohail's parents might still be interested. I will call his mother today."

So, they're just going to leave me here?

But the mention of Sohail gave me some measure of relief. Of course, he didn't know what had happened yet, but I knew he would help. I nodded silently.

"Word can still get out very easily," Mom cautioned again. "Servants talk, and Nusrat Mami too. God knows she is bursting to tell someone in her ladies' club. Those women are champions of gossip."

"Remember, Rukhsana, we can't take any chances of someone finding out. We will become a laughingstock in our community," said Dad.

I nodded again wordlessly.

"Okay, so now that's settled," said Mom. "You should get some rest. Tomorrow we will go shopping. There is so much to prepare. And then in the afternoon Parveen is coming. She is the best wedding planner in town. Luckily she was able to fit us in on such short notice."

And with that they walked out. I was left to my own devices, which was good because I had a lot to figure out. The last time Sohail and I had spoken, we had both decided he would tell his parents that he would marry me after we'd gotten to know each other. It wouldn't have mattered anyway, because by this time I was supposed to be back in Seattle. But everything was different now. I needed to talk to him, so we could figure this out together. I had no intention of going through with it, but for now, agreeing to marry Sohail was my best bet.

I was getting ready for bed a couple of hours later when Mom came back into my room.

"Mrs. Choudhury is not returning my calls. Who knows what she's heard about you." She narrowed her eyes. "That Nusrat must have already started a rumor about it. That woman does not know how to keep her mouth shut."

My stomach dropped. Sohail had been my last hope.

● ● ●

The following day passed in a blur of activity. I was whisked from store to store as my mom began to assemble my trousseau. I must have tried on at least fifty different outfits, everything from heavily embroidered wedding saris to casual shalwar sets. The amount of money she spent in just one day would have been enough to feed an entire slum colony for a week. Not even having zero prospects could deter my mom from ordering several heavy sets of gold jewelry. I protested after she asked to choose the fifth set.

"Mom, do I really need another one?" I said, taking the necklace she thrust at me while she fussed with my earlobes.

"Do you think I want to give Nusrat a chance to talk behind my back again? Only this morning I overheard her on the phone with one of her card-playing friends from the club."

"Mom," I said fastening the clasp on the nav-ratan choker. The brightly colored gems caught the light as I looked at my reflection in the mirror.

"Yes, ammu, what is it?" She had been very affectionate since the jinn-catcher left. Maybe I was a better actress than I thought?

"I was thinking that I should let my teachers know that I'll be here longer, so I need my phone back. All their contact information is in it."

She looked at my eyes in the mirror. For a second I thought I'd blown it, but then she nodded.

"I have it at home. I'll give it to you when we get back." She looked at me intently for a minute. "But only for a few hours after dinner." My heart sank.

I nodded quickly before she changed her mind.

We shopped some more until I was ready to collapse.

Back at the house, we readied ourselves to meet with Parveen, queen of the local marriage network. Since she had not yet arrived, I decided to try my luck again. "Mom, can I have my phone back, please?" I reminded her, and she studied me for a moment before heading wordlessly up the stairs. I followed her to her bedroom and watched silently as she rummaged in the cupboard. When she handed it to me it was as if I'd been given a lifeline. I went to my room and flung myself on the bed, turning it on to check what I'd missed.

Jen and Rachel had called about a dozen times. The longing to be with my friends was a physical ache. That life seemed so far away, even though it had only been a little over a month.

There were quite a few missed calls from Aamir and Irfan, as well as frantic messages from Sara asking me if I was alright. They must have been worried out of their minds when I didn't show up at the airport.

There was nothing from Ariana. Why hadn't she called even once? I tried to think of what she would have felt when I didn't show up that day as planned. She couldn't possibly think it had been by choice? But a nagging voice in the back of my head told me that maybe she did. She would have felt utterly betrayed. How could she ever believe I would just not show up? My eyes began to sting, but I swallowed the lump in my throat and forced myself to focus.

With the time difference, it was a little too early in the morning, but I was afraid I might not get another chance.

I dialed her number, prepared to tell her everything that had transpired since the last time we spoke. She had to understand. I was sure of it. But she didn't pick up. And I couldn't bring myself to leave a message. What would I even say?

I tried Aamir then, but he didn't pick up.

I called Irfan next. He picked up right away, his voice heavy with sleep.

"Rukhsana . . . are you alright? We've been so worried!"

"I'm sorry I couldn't call earlier . . . My parents took my phone."

"So, they found out about your escape plan? I thought that's what might have happened. Are you alright though otherwise?" he asked again.

"Not exactly. They're forcing me to get married. They locked me up and there was this jinn-catcher—" My voice broke, but I couldn't cry anymore.

"My God. I'm so sorry, Rukhsana, I can't believe they're being so stupid."

I didn't say anything for a while. It was just nice to know he was there, to feel connected. There was no one else who could understand what I was going through.

"I'll talk to Aunty Meena and see if she can do anything."

"No, Irfan, please don't do that. I still have a shot of getting away, but if Mom finds out that I told you she'll freak."

"Okay, but I'm worried about you," he said. "There has to be something I can do?"

"Give me a couple of days, please. I promise I'll call really soon. And please tell Sara what happened."

"I will, and you promise me that you will take care of yourself. If there's anything I can do . . . you know I'm here for you."

"Actually, can you talk to Aamir and tell him I'm alright?"

"Yes, of course, I'll try him a little later."

"Thank you . . . You don't know how much it means to me right now."

We hung up and I called Jen.

"Rukhsana, are you okay?" She sounded frantic. "We've been worried out of our minds. Why didn't you come back last week?"

"They found out about my plan and locked me in my room."

"What the hell?"

"I just got my phone back. Have you talked to Ariana?"

She didn't answer right away.

"Jen?"

"Rukhsana, there's something you should know."

My heart plummeted. I didn't think I could handle any bad news right now.

"What happened? Is it Ariana? Jen, please tell me what happened."

"Nothing, she's okay now. But when you didn't show up . . . she sort of broke down."

"What do you mean?"

"She wasn't in school the day after you were supposed to come back," Jen said. "And when I went to check on her, she said she needed to get away for a few days."

"Where did she go?"

"To their cabin, I think. With her parents. She's coming back tomorrow."

"Did she say anything about me? Why won't she answer any of my calls?"

"I don't know, Rukhsana. I think this has all been really hard for her. I guess when you didn't show up, she didn't know what to think."

"It's not like I had a choice."

"I know, Rukhsana, but you have to understand," Jen said. "There was no news, no way to get hold of you. I guess it was just too much for her. I also think her parents were really worried and didn't want her to talk to you anymore."

I didn't know what to say. I felt awful that I had caused Ariana so much pain, but at the same time I couldn't help but think that she should have known something had happened to prevent me from coming home. But maybe my expectations were too high. Maybe I was being unreasonable and unfair to her.

"Rukhsana, are you okay?" I was so deep in my thoughts, I'd forgotten I was still on the line with Jen.

"Sorry, Jen. Yes, I'm okay now, but could you please tell Ariana to call me? I really need to talk to her right now."

"I will tell her everything. You just work on a way to get back. And, Rukhsana, please be careful. We were really scared for you."

Another call was coming through, and I hung up with Jen.

It was Aamir.

"Rukhsana, my God, are you okay? Irfan Bhai just called and told me. Are Mom and Dad out of their minds?"

Hearing my brother's voice had me crying again.

"I'm okay now," I said between sobs. "I miss you so much." I would give anything for one of Aamir's big hugs, but he was thousands of miles away and I didn't know when I would see him again.

"Rukhsana, I'm getting on the next flight there. This is ridiculous. They can't treat you like this."

"No, Aamir, don't, please. I'm working on another plan. This time it's going to work."

"What's your plan?" Aamir said.

Just then, the door opened and Mom walked into the room, carrying a pile of clothes.

"I have to go," I whispered before hanging up quickly.

"You finished calling all your teachers?" Mom said. She laid out the clothes on the bed.

"Not all of them, it's still early." I looked at the clothes. "Do you want me to wear one of these for Parveen?"

A week ago, I would have scoffed at the lavish outfits Mom had picked out for me, but now I knew better than to antagonize her. I needed to make sure that she didn't take my phone away again. That I had access to the outside world, to my friends, to Ariana. I could not fight my way out of this situation with snark or sarcasm. I would have to be very patient and bide my time.

Mom insisted on helping me get ready, which meant I couldn't call Aamir back like I was planning to do. She picked a pink-and-silver outfit and found matching silver earrings and pink bangles to go with it. Then she helped me with my hair, weaving a string of jasmine flowers into my braid.

I watched her as she hummed an old Bengali folk song, her face serene, and I realized that this was all she ever wanted. A daughter who would follow the rules, grow up, and marry a suitable man. Who she could play dress up with, like she was now. But I was not a doll and I was not who she wanted me to be. That part hurt the most. That she would go to all these lengths to prove she was right, but not even try to understand who I really was and what made me happy.

chapter
twenty-seven

According to Mom, Parveen was the most sought after arranged marriage consultant in Dhaka. She was a matchmaker, a wedding planner, and a fortune-teller all rolled into one. At least, that's what I expected her business card to say. Rumor had it if a prospective bride made a bad impression on her, then she was doomed to spinsterhood.

Now, sitting on my grandmother's couch, she didn't look that intimidating at all. She had a birdlike appearance, a sharp, beaklike nose and thin arms that ended in the skinniest hands I'd ever seen.

"Rukhsana, your mother tells me that you've won a scholarship to Caltech. That's very impressive. It will look really good on your profile should I choose to accept you as a client."

Mom's paying her to find me a husband and she hasn't yet decided if she wants to take me on?

I managed to keep a straight face, but it was a struggle.

"Yes, I'm starting there in the fall."

"I see. But of course, that is, only if your future in-laws agree."

"What do you mean?" I shot a panicked look in Mom's direction. She shook her head ever so slightly, a warning imperceptible to anyone but me.

"Well, there's a chance that they may not want their daughter-in-law to spend all her time in school. It's up to them to decide," Parveen said matter-of-factly.

"Yes, yes, of course, we understand," said Mom hastily. "Rukhsana knows that, don't you, ammu?"

I was about to retort but stopped myself. Instead, I nodded.

"Good. So, there is a lot of work to do. First of all, you need a makeover," she said.

Ouch.

"We need to do something about your complexion," she murmured, her gaunt hands gliding over my face as I tried not to pull away. Next, she curled a lock of my hair around her bony fingers and studied it.

"Hmmm." She frowned.

What the hell? The witch doesn't like my hair? I half expected her to open my mouth and check the condition of my teeth.

She turned to Mom. "Twice a week she must apply a paste of turmeric and chickpea flour. On the other days, she must apply a paste of Multani clay and water."

My mother nodded as Parveen continued.

Wow, Mom might actually be intimidated by her.

"Now, about your diet," she continued, her hawkish eyes falling on me again. "No more sweets. No more rich foods." She counted off on her fingers. "A diet of only fruits and vegetables. Rice and fish twice a week only."

Is she for real?

"No going out in the sun at all. We don't want your skin to get even darker."

"We will follow all your instructions, Parveen, do not worry." My mom was clearly very impressed with the woman, and I had a sinking feeling the next few days were going to be hell for me.

"I will come back in one week to see how it is going. Then I will make my decision."

Mom looked at me after Parveen had left.

"So that went well, don't you think?" She picked up the tea tray and placed it on the dining room table.

I rolled my eyes when she wasn't looking. She really didn't want to know what I thought.

"We should get started on your treatments right away." Mom signaled to Rokeya to clear the table. "Your skin will be glowing soon enough!"

Lucky me. I'm getting a husband and *good skin.*

Over the next two days, I underwent a humiliating amount of waxing, scrubbing, and general torture as Mom took me to a beauty salon and told them that money was no object. On the upside, my skin had never been so soft. With my complexion taken care of, Mom's beauty team moved to my hair. Apparently, it required multiple henna and hot oil treatments. If I wasn't so pissed off at why I was going through all this, I might've actually enjoyed the pampering.

It was demeaning to do all this so some stranger could judge and reject me. The whole thing was a sham. But there was nothing I could do about it.

• • •

"I need to get hold of Sohail," I said to Shaila when Mom finally left us alone for the first time in a couple of days. I'd snuck some sweets in a napkin earlier when no one was looking and now I laid them out between us. Shaila looked on in amusement as I popped a piece of sandesh in my mouth.

"What?" I said, savoring the creamy sweetness. "You can have some too."

Shaila shook her head. "I thought Parveen said you weren't supposed to eat sweets."

"Who died and made her queen? I'll eat as many sweets as I like," I said, defiantly sinking my teeth into a plump, slightly dripping gulab jamun.

Shaila just rolled her eyes in response.

"Anyway, how are you planning to call Sohail? Do you even have his number?"

"No, I don't. Mom has it on her phone, but I can't get it without her noticing."

"I think my dad might have it in his contacts list in his study," Shaila said. "I can try to get it when they're out."

We waited until evening, when my parents and Shaila's parents went to a function. We were supposed to go as well, but I feigned a bad headache and Shaila volunteered to stay behind with me. As soon as their car was out of the driveway, Shaila and I went into her dad's study. She looked up Sohail's contact on the computer and I quickly typed the number into my phone.

"Sohail, it's Rukhsana," I said when he answered after the third ring.

"Well, this is a surprise." The sound of his voice was inexplicably soothing to my raw nerves and I almost started crying again. "My mother tried calling several times after our dinner together, but it seems your parents weren't available. I was kind of disappointed, to be honest. I thought we hit it off pretty well."

"That's what I'm calling about," I said. "I need to talk to you."

"Oh? What about? Is everything okay?"

"Well, I'd rather not say over the phone. Could we meet?" I held my breath.

"Actually, I was hoping to talk to you about something as well," he said.

What could he want to talk to me about? I guess there's only one way to find out.

"Great," I said. "How about Terra Bistro, tomorrow morning at ten?"

"I'll see you there."

● ● ●

"Rukhsana, good, you're dressed and ready," Mom said when I entered the living room the next morning. She poured me a cup of chai. "Shaila wants to take you to look at mehndi patterns."

"Mehnaz is really talented and I promised her I'd bring you by," Shaila said.

I picked up my cup, breathing in the spices. "Sounds good to me."

"That was pretty convincing," I said to Shaila, who grinned back at me as we weaved through the morning traffic.

"Did you tell Sohail to meet you at the café?" she asked in a low tone, so the driver wouldn't overhear.

"Yes, he said he'd be there. Can you pick me up in about an hour, please?"

Shaila nodded. "Take all the time you want. I'll go to the mall and pick up some actual mehndi patterns to show Zuby Phupi when we get back."

"Good thinking," I said, jumping out when the driver stopped in front of the café entrance.

When I opened the door, a wave of cool air pushed past me and out into the sultry morning. My eyes took a moment to adjust to the dim lighting. Dark blinds valiantly attempted to keep out the sunlight, and the air-conditioning provided a welcome relief from the sweltering heat.

I spotted Sohail by the glass display case, checking out the pastries. I watched him for a moment, bathed in the warm glow of the sparsely arranged lamps. With his high cheekbones, chiseled jawline, and perfectly styled Bollywood hair, I could see how he'd be considered quite the catch. For someone else.

He turned just as I walked up to him, and smiled.

"It's nice to see you again," he said, gesturing to a small table by the window.

"You too. Thanks for agreeing to meet."

"Of course. Shall we order first?" he asked as the waitress approached.

"Sure. I'll have a latte, please," I said.

Sohail ordered a black coffee for himself, as well as some pastries.

"So, what did you want to talk to me about?" I asked, deciding that I'd rather hear what he had to say before I compromised myself.

"I just thought we should discuss some things before making any decisions," he said.

I fiddled with the ends of my orna. "What kind of things?"

"Well, I know you weren't keen on this whole arranged marriage thing when we met last time."

The waitress came back with our coffees and pastries, and I used the time to think up a suitable response.

"I just think that people should be allowed to marry whoever they want," I said, watching him carefully.

"I agree completely," he said. "I mean it's my life. I'll be spending it with that person, so I should get to choose who that will be."

I took a careful sip of my latte.

"So why haven't you said anything to your parents?" I asked.

"Because I don't think they will ever accept the person I want to marry."

My ears perked up. So he had a person. Hmm, this was getting interesting. I took a bite of mango pastry. "How can you be so sure?"

"Well, let's just say he's not exactly someone they would want me to marry."

A piece of pastry went down the wrong way, causing me to cough up my left lung. I struggled to process the information he had just casually dumped on me.

He is gay. HE IS GAY.

I could actually feel light bulb flashes going off in my head. This changed everything. Sohail's eyes were wide with alarm and I was pretty sure he would come around the table and start thumping me on the back if I didn't regain my composure and say something.

"Okay . . ." This was the best I could muster. My mind was trying to string together coherent thoughts from the supernova of feelings that were exploding inside me.

"Okay?" he echoed rather loudly. Then, realizing, he lowered his voice to a whisper once again. "Is that all you can say?"

"I'm sorry. I just wasn't expecting this."

"Clearly. Do you have a problem with it?" He looked suddenly vulnerable and I was confused. Then it hit me. The notion that I would have a problem with him being gay was so absurd, I laughed out loud. His eyes widened and I groaned inwardly.

"No, of course not," I said, and he relaxed his shoulders. "I thought you were going to tell me something else, that's all."

"Like what?" He smiled, and a small dimple appeared on his right cheek. *How have I not noticed that before?*

"Honestly, I just thought you had a girlfriend," I said. His dimple deepened as he shook his head.

"I did . . . several . . ." he said ruefully. "But I realized I was just lying to myself."

"So, when did you know?" I asked.

"When I met Mushtaq." He blushed a little and it was the cutest thing.

"Mushtaq. So where did you meet?"

"At Columbia. I had just started my master's and he was finishing up his undergraduate program. We met at a talk by a visiting lecturer and later we started talking and then before we knew it, hours had passed."

"And how did you know that it was serious?"

"Well, we found excuses to bump into each other," he said. "Until Mushtaq told me that maybe we should just try going out on a real date." He smiled in that disarming way he had and I realized that I was beginning to really like him.

"And you've been together for three years?"

"Yes, I can't believe it's been that long already."

He got this look in his eyes that I recognized well.

"So where is he now?" I asked, finishing the last of my coffee.

"He's in Chicago getting his MBA. I'm planning to join him there as soon as I can." He smiled wistfully and in my heart I wished him and Mushtaq all the happiness in the world.

"What about your parents?" I asked, even though I knew the answer.

"Well, I've thought about telling them so many times, I've lost count. But I know what they'll say, and there's just no point. They'll never accept me for who I am."

I nodded. I was painfully familiar with that notion of futility, that empty feeling when you realize that your own family would never understand the real you.

"I'm so sorry, Rukhsana," he said suddenly. "Here I am, going on and on about myself. Didn't you have something you wanted to talk to me about?"

I nodded.

"I do. But same deal," I warned. "This has to stay just between us."

He smiled again. "I trusted you with my secret, didn't I? Now you have to trust me with yours. I promise, I will not tell a soul."

This time I leaned over the table conspiratorially and whispered.

"There's someone special in my life too."

"Are you going to tell me more?" he whispered back with a smile.

"Her name's Ariana."

His eyes narrowed as he looked at me wordlessly.

"Is this some kind of joke?" he said finally.

"No, of course not. Why would I joke about something like this?"

I wasn't sure what reaction I expected him to have, but it certainly wasn't a booming laugh that made the four other people in the coffee shop turn around and stare at us.

I sat and watched while he caught his breath and looked at me, his mouth still twitching. I was not amused.

"I'm sorry," he said, still snorting a little. "But can you imagine if our parents could hear us now?"

That notion was a little funny. Actually, now that I remembered my mom's excitement when she'd first met Sohail, it did seem hilarious. Would she find a way to blame me for this too? Maybe sending us out into the garden at night hadn't been the best idea. I could have infected him. It was still too soon for me to laugh about it though. Plus, I didn't want the jinn to jump back into me on account of laughing too loudly.

"You're lucky your parents don't know," I said. "Mine found out in Seattle. That's why they brought me here."

And then I told him everything. I left nothing out. And after all this time, it felt so good to tell someone. Somebody who really got it.

"Wow," he said after I was done. "I'm so sorry, Rukhsana. I can't even begin to imagine what you've been going through."

"I find it hard to believe myself," I said. "A month ago, I had a pretty normal life. I was about to graduate and go to Caltech with Ariana. Now I feel like a character in someone else's life."

"That's why I never told my parents," Sohail said. "I knew they'd freak out completely and then who knows what kind of guilt trip they'd lay on me. I mean, I love them, but I'm not going to lose Mushtaq over them."

I felt closer to him at that moment than I did to anyone. Even Ariana. Because he understood all of it. No explanations were needed. I was so tired of having to justify everything to everyone. I just wanted someone who would accept me exactly the way I was. No conditions, no caveats.

And as if he read my mind, Sohail leaned over.

"Can I say something really cheesy?"

"Sure."

"I know we just met, but doesn't it feel like we've known each other for much longer? Like we were meant to meet and be in each other's lives. Is that weird?"

"Not even a little bit," I said. "I'm just so done with defending myself. I mean, is it bad that I care about my parents and don't want to ruin their lives? Even though they're going out of their way to ruin mine? Ariana and my friends always act as if it should be so easy for me to walk out and just live my life."

He nodded. "It's hard to explain to someone who hasn't grown up in the kind of environment we did."

"Right? And I do realize that I am in fact running away and ruining my parents' reputation, but I had to at least try and see if they would come to their senses. And I really tried. But after what they've put me through, I don't think I can ever forgive them."

"I didn't have to deal with that part because Mushtaq's family is just as conservative as mine. But it does tear me up that I'm lying to my parents every day."

"Do your friends know?"

He sipped his coffee before replying.

"Only my closest ones. Obviously, I'm not the only one; there are other gay people in Bangladesh. But they have to stay in hiding mostly, because it's too dangerous for them to be out here."

I knew all about the dangers. The arrests and disappearances. My parents had made it a point to make sure I was fully aware of the position I was putting all of us in. But just because something was illegal didn't make it wrong. I wouldn't allow them to reduce my existence to something that could be controlled by others. I was who I was, and I would not be erased.

Sohail eyed me intently as he finished the last of his coffee.

"You look like you could kill someone."

I laughed nervously. "I was just thinking how much worse it is here. You know . . . to be in your situation." I glanced around, suddenly very conscious of everyone around us.

"It is definitely risky, and you have to know whom to trust. But can you honestly say that it's that much better in the States? I mean, from what Mushtaq tells me, you have your own share of homophobia and hate crimes to deal with."

My phone buzzed.

Panicked, I checked the time. How was it so late already?

I said a quick goodbye to Sohail, and a few minutes later the driver pulled up in front of the café.

"I'm so sorry," I said to Shaila again as I climbed into the back seat. "You will never guess what Sohail wanted to tell me," I whispered. I could barely contain my excitement, but Shaila glanced surreptitiously at the driver.

"Later," she mouthed, and we both settled in for the long ride home.

• • •

"He's gay." The words burst out of my mouth as soon as I shut the door to my room.

Shaila collapsed on the edge of my bed with her mouth hanging open.

"No way. Are you serious?" she asked incredulously.

I nodded, unable to suppress my smile. "I swear, Shaila, this is better than I'd hoped. Do you know what this means?"

Shaila shook her head.

"It means I'm finally getting out of here."

• • •

Ariana was calling. It was five in the morning and I thought I might be dreaming, but then I heard her sweet voice and I was wide awake.

"Rukhsana, it's me. Are you okay now?"

"Yes, I am, but where were you?" I said. "I was so worried."

"I know, I'm sorry. My parents took me to our cabin and they made me leave my phone at home."

"Jen told me that you . . . I'm so sorry that I couldn't call you. My parents—"

"I know," she said softly. "Jen told me what happened. Are you really okay?"

"Not really. But I have a plan. This time it's going to work."

I wasn't sure if I was trying to convince me or her.

"That's what you said last time," Ariana said, as if I needed to be reminded.

"It's different this time. There's someone who will help and wants to get out of here as much as I do."

"What do you mean?"

I told her all about Sohail.

"The guy your parents want you to marry is going to help you get out?"

"I know it sounds weird, but he's a really great guy."

"Are you sure you can trust him?"

"Yes, I can," I said. "I just told you. He's gay and has as much to lose as I do if this doesn't work."

"Okay, I hope it works this time. I didn't know what to think when you didn't show up at the airport last time."

"Ariana, I'm so sorry I put you through that."

"You were dealing with worse, Rukhsana. I feel so useless. I'm sorry I can't do anything to help."

"Please don't say that. I was so scared when—"

"Rukhsana." Mom's voice came from just outside the door. Shit.

"It's my mom. I have to go." I hung up, put my phone under my pillow, and closed my eyes. What was she doing up so early? She probably got up for her Fajr prayer, so she'd have more time to torture me during the day.

"Rukhsana," she said again softly. I held my breath. *How long has she been outside my door? Does she suspect anything?*

I heard the door close softly, but I was too scared to open my eyes. Eventually I drifted off to sleep, but not before I promised myself that no matter what, I would make it out of here and back home to Ariana.

chapter
twenty-eight

"I have great news," Mom announced later that day, practically bouncing into the living room, where another selection of saris surrounded me. My brain hurt from having to make such life-altering decisions as which sari would be appropriate for visiting extended relatives of my yet-to-be-found in-laws.

"What happened?" I asked, feigning disinterest.

"Sohail's mother called. It seems that he has made up his mind about you."

I could proudly say that I had now perfected my poker face.

"Rukhsana, you should be happy. Why aren't you more excited? Sohail is a catch. You are very lucky that he has decided he wants to marry you." She looked proud of me and I wondered what exactly she thought I had accomplished here. Extreme likeability?

"Did she say what finally made up his mind?" I asked cautiously, wishing desperately that I could have listened in on that call.

"Not really. Just that she convinced him that this was the best thing for him. He is a good boy, he listens to his parents."

As opposed to me, evil incarnate.

Later that evening, Sohail's family came over for dinner to celebrate. We sat around the table, surrounded by an elaborate feast. I didn't know how Rokeya threw this all together so fast. I imagined her in the kitchen like Molly Weasley in *Harry Potter*, using some sort of magic to make several dishes at the same time.

Sohail glanced surreptitiously at me and I looked away. If I started smiling, I might not be able to stop.

After dinner, our parents got down to the business of hammering out details like wedding dates and potential venues until the early hours of the morning.

• • •

The next afternoon Mom came to my room.

"Rukhsana, come downstairs with me. All the relatives are here, waiting to see you."

She fanned herself with the aanchal of her sari.

"Sohail's mother said the wedding has to take place in two weeks because he has to get back to work. I have so many things to do. I'm sending the wedding invitations for Aunty Meena and Uncle Maruf. Aamir will come with them."

Joy surged through me at the thought of seeing my brother again. I'd feel so much better once he was here with me.

"When are they getting here?" I asked.

"They won't be here until the day before the wedding, because Aamir has to finish up his exams. Aunty Meena was so disappointed that she won't be here for the preparations. But at least they can come. I don't know how I will do all this without her."

At the mention of Aamir's exams, I felt anger rising in me again. She didn't care a bit about what this whole thing was doing to me. I should have been preparing for my finals, not picking out fabrics and getting beauty treatments. I'd worked hard to get good grades all my life, and now it was all ruined.

Some of my many cousins and aunts and uncles sat in the living room surrounded by boxes of sweets. I sat on the couch next to my grandmother and one by one they all congratulated me as they put pieces of sweets in my mouth. They wished me a happy married life, and as I smiled and hugged them, I couldn't help wondering how they were able to shut out reality so completely. They had to know that something was going on, because there was no way Nusrat Mami would have kept her mouth shut. But they all acted as though this was a happy, normal occasion.

Mom was practically bouncing as she called even more family members. I had never seen her like this.

When I finally got a moment to myself, Nani took my hand and held it, silent at first. Then she turned to me and looked me deep in the eyes.

"My little spring bird, are you sure this is what you want?"

"Nani, you know I don't have any other choice." I gave her hands a tight squeeze. "Please don't worry about me. I'll be fine."

I didn't want to talk about it here with everyone around, but she looked so worried that I couldn't bear it.

"I have a plan. But I can't tell you here," I whispered in her ear.

She shook her head as she looked at the rest of the family sitting around the table, laughing and talking. "Not one of them cares about what you want," she said bitterly. "How did I let them become like this?"

"It's not your fault, Nani." I tried to reassure her, but I knew she didn't hear me. She was lost in her own guilt and powerlessness over what was happening to me.

Much later, after most of the guests had left, I took Nani up to her room to help her get settled in bed. Then I told her about Sohail and our plan.

"He sounds like a very good boy. I am happy that you have found someone who is kind and who will help you." Her eyelids were getting heavy and I remembered how late it was.

"You should go to sleep," I said softly, before sliding off her bed.

"Just like my Raju," she murmured as I quietly slipped out the door.

• • •

"Have you talked to Ariana again?" Shaila asked me the next day, while we drank chai in my room. I was supposed to go down when the tailors came, but in the meantime, I was enjoying the break from Mom in her intense wedding prep mode.

"I did last night."

"How is she doing with all this?" Shaila stood to put a stack of saris in the cupboard.

"To be honest, I'm not sure. I finally told her about the whole jinn-catcher thing," I said. "And my friend Jen told me that Ariana had to go away for a few days after I didn't show up at the airport."

"How did she react? What do you mean go away?"

"Apparently, her parents took her to their cabin. She seemed reluctant to talk about it when I asked her."

Shaila sat back down and finished her tea.

"She probably feels weird talking about it after what you've gone through, you know?"

"But why would she?" I said. "I asked her about it because I wanted to know."

"Maybe she feels like her problems seem trivial compared to yours."

That was pretty much what Ariana had said.

"Probably," I said. "Telling her about the jinn-catcher definitely didn't help. I need to make sure she knows her feelings always matter."

Shaila pressed her lips together like she was going to say something.

"What?" I asked when she looked like she was going to burst.

"It's just that . . ."

"What?" I said, a little too loudly.

"Nothing, I just don't think it's that simple."

"What do you mean?"

"I mean, what's your plan exactly?" Shaila stood and began to pace. "Let's say it all works this time. Where are you going to go? Even if you both end up going to Caltech, what happens to you and Ariana then? Your family will never accept her, and it won't be long before she resents you for that."

I did not like the turn this conversation was taking. But like it or not, there was some truth to what Shaila was saying. I just wasn't ready to face it. I hadn't really thought about what would happen after I got back to Seattle. I'd been a little preoccupied with just getting there. I figured I could stay with someone, maybe Jen or Rachel, until the end of the school year. But I couldn't avoid my family forever.

"Look, Rukhsana." Shaila came and sat beside me on the bed again. "All I'm saying is that you're not the only one who'll be dealing with this. Ariana is going to be as much of a target as you are. So, you have to decide if you're willing to put her through all of it."

I felt a little betrayed by Shaila in that moment, so I stared back at her in stony silence.

● ● ●

The cloying sweetness of incense filled the air. I watched helplessly as the jinn-catcher came closer, his piercing eyes looking deeper into mine, until it felt like he could see into my soul. Suddenly I was gazing down at myself. But then everything rearranged itself and it was Ariana lying there. She was terrified, her eyes wide and fearful as she looked beyond me at something I couldn't see. I heard a resounding crack and my mom was bent over Ariana, who was crying for help. I tried to reach out to her, but I couldn't move. I couldn't do anything to help her and I began to scream.

I woke up with a start, my lungs starved for air. My sheets were damp with sweat and it took me a moment to figure out whether I was awake or still having a nightmare.

I lay back down and stared at the ceiling, waiting for my heart to stop pounding. I wanted to talk to Ariana again, but Shaila's comments rang in my ears. I hated what she said, but I couldn't deny the truth in her words.

The question was, could I guarantee that I wouldn't put her in such a situation again? I had no way of knowing what was going to happen in the coming months. And I had to wonder, did Ariana have any idea what she was signing on for?

Was I willing to drag her into this mess my life had become? It would never end; I knew that. Even if I was able to get back to Seattle, it wasn't as if I could pretend my family didn't exist. How could I let Ariana become a target of such overt homophobia? They would never leave us alone. She deserved better than that. In my heart, I knew what I had to do, no matter how difficult it would be.

But then again, I couldn't not have Ariana in my life.

After a while, I realized I was just going around in circles. Clearly any decision I made tonight would be a bad one.

I woke up the next day determined not to think about Ariana because I needed time to clear my head. I also didn't want to be around Shaila because I was still angry at her. I knew it was childish, but I just wanted her to be on my side.

A couple of days flew by as Mom went all out to satisfy Parveen's demands. Deep inside, I was glad for the distraction and was able to push away all thoughts of the decision I knew I had to make, until I checked my phone and found several missed calls from Ariana. She must have called while I was in the shower.

I sat on my bed for the longest time, staring at the phone and going over everything in my head. I had no idea what I would say to her or exactly how I would break her heart. Maybe she would be relieved. But I knew I couldn't put it off any longer.

She answered on the second ring.

"Rukhsana . . . are you okay?" she said, a little breathlessly. It was early morning in Seattle and I pictured her in bed, her brown hair tousled from sleep.

"Yes, I'm fine." My voice was steady, concealing my lie. "I'm sorry I haven't called; things have been so hectic."

The truth was that I'd been avoiding her. Because since my conversation with Shaila, all I could think about was this. If I really loved her, I wouldn't want her to be with someone like me. Someone with so much baggage that every little step felt like an uphill battle.

And, if I was being completely honest with myself, I had to accept the fact that Ariana would never be able to truly understand the reality of my situation, the pressure and the guilt. It would follow us, no matter how far away we got. And I knew I'd rather break up and preserve the good memories than put her through all of that.

"Ariana, there's something I have to tell you." I swallowed the lump in my throat. "I can't do this anymore."

I could almost see her processing what I was saying across the silence that hung like a weight between us. "What do you mean?" Her voice shook, but I had to push through.

"I mean that staying together is too hard. And trust me, if I've learned anything in the past few weeks, it's that it won't get any easier for us."

"So, what, now you just want to throw it all away? After everything we've been through?" I could feel the hurt in her voice and my heart broke piece by piece. It wasn't too late; I could take back what I'd said. But something inside me wouldn't let me take the easy way out.

"I love you, Ariana, you know that. Nothing can change that. You don't know what it's like. And I'm sort of glad that you don't. But I don't get a choice in this matter. My family, my community, they're never going to accept us. And I can't put you through that. I love you too much."

There was silence at the other end. I couldn't tell if she was crying. I wanted to reach out to her, to hold her and tell her we would figure it all out. But I would be lying. I couldn't see a way through this.

"Do I get to have a say in all this?" Ariana's teary voice came over the phone. "Or is it entirely up to you? I can decide for myself whether I want to be in this relationship or not. And I've decided that I do. I don't care how hard it is."

My heart dropped in my chest. In that moment, I loved her more than ever. And that made it even harder for me to say what I knew I had to.

"Ariana, try to understand. This won't work." I tried to make my voice as firm as I could; I didn't want her to know that I was falling apart on the inside.

"I don't believe you." Ariana's tone was sharp. "You've just been through a lot, and maybe you can't see it right now. But I believe in us. I'll never stop believing in us." The last few words came out shaky and I knew she'd started to cry. I choked back my own tears as my breath shook.

"Ariana, I think it's best for you to move on." There. I'd said it. The final nail in the coffin. It was better this way. She would find happiness with someone else. And somehow, I would live my life without Ariana by my side. At this moment, it felt like an impossible task. But knowing that Ariana might at least have a shot at a normal relationship made it worth the pain that was flooding my heart.

"Don't do this, Rukhsana." Her voice came through, defeated and small. I forced back a sob. I couldn't let her know how much this hurt me.

"I love you, Ariana. I'm so sorry."

And then I hung up, severing the final thread that bound us together.

chapter
twenty-nine

I woke disoriented, my pillow wet. The memory crashed into me like a wave. Ariana. My heart ached for the sound of her voice, the touch of her skin against mine. I didn't want to move, to feel. I just wanted to hold on to that space where I'd spoken to Ariana, that moment where I was still connected to her.

I heard a gentle knock and Shaila walked in. Worry lined her face as she sat on my bed.

"Rukhsana, I'm sorry for what I said to you the other day. You know I've always been too scared to go against my parents. But I look at you, and you're fighting for something you believe in."

She couldn't have picked a worse time to tell me this. But it wasn't her fault. The decision had been mine. She'd just told me something I already knew deep down inside.

"No, you were right. It would never work and it's not fair to her." My voice caught in my throat. The wound was still so fresh and I would have to build a shield around my heart, bit by bit, just to hold it together.

"What are you saying?"

"I broke up with her last night." I began to sob and Shaila moved to wrap her arms around me. I felt empty inside, and the worst part of it was that I had done this to myself. Even though I knew it was the right thing to do, Ariana's voice kept echoing through my head.

Do I get to have a say in all this?

I had decided for the both of us, and if I had made the wrong choice, then she would pay for my mistake.

After I calmed down a little, I washed my face to get rid of any telltale signs. The last thing I wanted to do was make my parents suspicious.

"I know that you're upset right now," Shaila said. "But please don't lose hope."

• • •

"Do you think I could see a picture of him?"

Sohail and I were back at Arirang House, the Korean place where we had our first date. We had ordered a tabletop sizzler of assorted seafood. I stirred the pieces around on the grill, my mouth watering from the tantalizing aroma of the spices.

He handed me his cell phone. Mushtaq's smiling face looked back at me. Some stubble, dark eyes crinkled with laughter, and the same hairstyle as Sohail. I smiled as I gave him his phone back.

"Oh, he's cute!" I said. "I hope I can meet him some day."

He nodded. "Your turn," he said, holding out his hand for my phone.

I hesitated, then looked down at my phone. My wallpaper was a picture of Ariana and me, taken last Christmas at her house. We were both smiling into the camera, my arms around her from behind. We'd just started seeing each other, the glow of newfound love still fresh in our eyes.

I handed him the phone, wondering what he would say if he knew I'd broken up with her. But I couldn't tell him yet. Saying it out loud to him would make it real again.

So I said nothing, watching him silently as he looked up from the phone.

"She's beautiful," he said softly. Then he raised his glass of water. "Here's to all of us getting together one day soon."

I could toast to that.

For the first time in weeks, I was actually kind of happy.

But something felt off. I didn't notice the men at the table in the corner at first. Being stared at wasn't unusual here, and I had to get used to it again whenever I came to Bangladesh. But there was something in the way they were staring that felt malicious somehow. Not the usual undressing with the eyes deal.

"Sohail." I nudged him gently under the table. "Don't turn around, but I think those guys are staring at us."

He nodded and then discreetly turned, pretending to look for the waiter. Then he signaled for the waiter to come to our table. When he looked at me again his face was ashen.

"Rukhsana, we should leave."

"Do you know those guys? Who are they?"

The waiter came over and Sohail asked him to pack up our food to go.

"Let's get out of here. We can go to my office and eat there. It's pretty close by." He paid the bill when our packed-up food arrived, and we left. The entire time I could feel eyes on me, watching our every move.

"Who were they?" I asked as he pulled up in front of a tall office building.

"Just some guys who like to make trouble wherever they go." Sohail's office was on the fourth floor, a set of glass doors leading into a large, open area with desks arranged along one wall. He led me to a private office in the back and I set the food down on a small table in the corner.

"Are they dangerous?"

"Yes, they belong to a group that dabbles in extremist beliefs. They've threatened some friends of mine before."

"Did they hurt them?"

"No, but the threats were pretty bad. My friends had to go into hiding for a while. You can't be too careful."

My stomach reminded me that we hadn't eaten yet. I began to unpack the food and Sohail disappeared down the hall. He returned a few minutes later with plates and silverware.

"Rukhsana, there's something else you need to know about me," he said, helping himself to some food.

I was already eating, so I just waited for him to continue.

"I have a website where I write about some very polarizing topics."

"Like what?"

"Mainly LGBTQ issues, but also religion and politics. You know, all the fun stuff."

"I see. That must upset a lot of people."

He bit his lip before replying.

"Well, there are a lot of freethinking individuals in Bangladesh. But there are also those who would like to take us back to the Stone Age."

I nodded. Thanks to my parents' regular social functions, I was usually on top of Bangladeshi current affairs.

"Do you think those guys at the restaurant recognized you?"

"I'm fairly sure they did," Sohail said. "I mean, to be honest, I think they're just trying to intimidate me. But I didn't want to take any chances, so I thought it would be better if we left."

"Are there a lot of people who follow your website?" I was curious, because judging by the way my parents and their friends talked about gay people, I wouldn't expect a lot of people in a Muslim-majority country to be sympathetic to Sohail's views.

"I think I have about twenty thousand weekly readers," he said. "There are many intellectuals here who believe in a secular Bangladesh and don't approve of extremist views."

"That's really surprising," I said. "Whenever I hear Bangladeshis talk about this stuff, it's always so homophobic."

"There's a lot of that here too, obviously," he said. "But not everyone thinks the same way, especially among the younger generation. Fortunately, enough people want to see things change and want to make it a better place for everyone. But that's going to take a very long time."

We finished our food quietly after that and then he drove me home. Mom and Dad were watching a Bollywood movie when I walked in.

"Did you and Sohail have a nice dinner, ammu?" Mom said. "Where did you go?"

"Arirang," I said, marveling at the change in her demeanor. She was like a different person. All because she thought I was marrying the right guy.

"You should ask him to come for dinner tomorrow. There is so little time left before the wedding, we want to get to know him better while we can." I nodded and went up to my room. It had been a long day and I needed sleep.

• • •

Because Sohail's family wanted the wedding to take place so soon, everything had to move fast. There would be several different ceremonies leading up to the wedding. I would have to get through them all before I could make my escape. At least I'd be able to spend more time with Sohail until then. I genuinely liked him and felt like we were growing closer.

When I walked into the living room, Mom was on the phone talking to Parveen about the exchange of gifts that would take place during the engagement ceremony and the wedding. She was relieved that Sohail's family didn't believe in dowries, so instead both Sohail and I would receive one or two expensive gifts from each other's parents. I overheard something about a gold watch, so I assumed I would be getting heavy gold jewelry as well.

On the dining table, an array of velveteen boxes lay open, displaying their glittering contents. I hadn't noticed the man in a chair in the corner until now. Mom waved me over and covered the mouthpiece of the receiver with her hand.

"Rukhsana, the jewelry store has sent over these for you to pick from. Parveen says they have the best selection. You can pick three or four that you like, okay?"

She went back to her conversation while I looked at the accessories on the table, stunned by the excessiveness of the situation. There were gorgeous earring and necklace sets with matching bracelets, all made of 22-carat gold. A bride would typically wear at least four or five of these sets on the wedding day. The front of her torso would be dripping with gold, placed carefully to display the families' wealth to their guests. I'd been to one wedding where the bride had run out of earlobes and decided to wear the rest of her earrings dangling in her hair.

I watched with a detached fascination as my mom bargained with the jewelry store employee, attempting to negotiate the cheapest possible price for the three pieces I'd picked out. Finally, after copious amounts of chai and singharas, money exchanged hands and the man left with the remaining jewelry.

Next my mother began calling all her extended relatives with the wedding announcement and an invitation to come by and visit as soon as they were able. This was a long-standing tradition by which the bride's family was able to show off their wealth. And it was all accomplished without openly bragging about the gold they were sending with their daughters.

As expected, hordes of visitors descended upon the house throughout the day to congratulate me, but more to see how well the foreign returned family was doing.

While Mom was flitting around being social, Sohail called and asked if I was free for dinner to meet some of his friends. Of course I was, and I had no doubt that Mom would happily let me go.

Half an hour later I was in Sohail's car as we drove to his friend's house.

"I thought you might like to meet some of my friends who help me run the website."

"I'd love to meet them. But do they know about . . ."

"Yes, they do. I told them everything." He threw a quick glance in my direction before returning his attention to the road again. "Well, not everything, of course. Just enough so they know."

"Do they think it's weird what we're doing?" Not that it mattered, but I was curious how supportive his friends were about his fake marriage plans.

"Not even a little bit. They totally get it. A lot of them are in the same situation. We all have to be really careful so no one finds out what we're involved in."

We were stopped at a red light and I looked at his face in profile.

"Does it ever scare you? You know, doing something that incites so much anger and violence in people?"

"Every minute of every day." He smiled and reached out to touch my hand. "Are you worried about me? That's so sweet. And here I thought you only wanted me for my body. *Literally*. I thought you only wanted a body for the wedding." He laughed at his own joke and I couldn't help but smile. He was also incredibly sweet, and I was so happy that fate had brought him into my life. Even if it was in the shittiest of moments.

"I'm glad you think you're so hilarious, but I'm serious. What if something happened to you? What about Mushtaq? Doesn't he worry?"

I'd be terrified if Ariana were involved in something that could potentially get her killed.

"He does, of course. But he knows how important this is. He was there when we started all this. But he's definitely glad I'm getting out."

"Are you going to continue writing after you're in the US?"

He pulled into a wide driveway and turned off the engine.

"Yes, I am. The good thing is that I can do so much more if I'm not constantly having to look over my shoulder."

"And your parents have absolutely no idea that you're involved in all this?"

Sohail shook his head as we stepped out of the car. He leaned against the hood, staring up into the night sky, a dark blanket dotted with thousands of tiny, sparkling lights. I followed his gaze and wondered if Ariana and I would ever stand like this together again and look up at the stars. There were moments such as these when I wondered if I was fighting a battle I could never win. If it wouldn't be easier just to accept my circumstances and allow myself to flow along wherever the tide took me. But then I imagined myself a few years later, a hollowed-out version of myself, the very essence of me drained, until there was nothing left of what made me Rukhsana. And then I knew I could never allow that to happen. Even if Ariana never forgave me.

"Ready to go in?" Sohail smiled disarmingly and pulled me close into an unexpected hug. I stiffened at first, but it felt so good to be in the arms of someone who actually cared and accepted me for who I was.

He pulled back a little and looked me deep in the eyes.

"We're going to get through this together, okay?"

"It doesn't feel like it right now." I breathed in deeply, inhaling the sweet and heady scent of the jasmine that filled the night air.

"Trust me, Rukhsana, I will make sure that you get out of here. No matter what." He sounded so sure. Some of his confidence seeped into me, allowing my body to relax a little.

"So, are we going inside or what?" I stepped back and touched his cheek. "Thanks for, you know, everything," I said softly. "I don't think I could get through this without you."

He dazzled me with another smile then and took me by the hand as we walked to the front door.

We entered the air-conditioned interior of his friend's house and I was immediately enveloped by the fragrance of meat baking in a tandoor oven. The smell of garlic, onion, and cumin made my mouth water.

A short man about Sohail's age approached us.

"Sohail Bhai, you made it," he said, his voice friendly and booming. He turned to me. "And you must be Rukhsana. I'm Omar. I'm so happy you could come tonight. We've all been eager to meet you."

I blushed a little at the thought that Sohail had been discussing me with his friends.

"Thanks for having me. It's so nice to meet you," I said, taking in the elaborate décor of Omar's house. There were intricately embroidered nakshi kanthas hanging on the walls and earthen pots standing in various corners in the foyer.

"Something smells amazing," Sohail said as Omar led us inside.

"Everything is prepared. We were just waiting for you both to arrive before we sat down to eat." He called out in Bengali to a young man to set out the food.

Two other men were in the living room, one playing a tabla set while the other coaxed beautiful sounds from a sitar. After they introduced themselves we were ready to eat. I was elated to see a variety of kebabs on platters, with hot, buttery naan, sliced red onions, and raita spread out on the dining room table. My stomach groaned from hunger and I realized I hadn't eaten anything all day aside from some sweets this morning.

"So, you all started this website together?" I asked between bites of seekh kebab and naan.

Omar nodded. "Actually, Hassan over here came back to Dhaka after finishing his undergraduate degree in Texas a few years ago, and this was all his brainchild."

Hassan smiled bashfully as he helped himself to another piece of naan.

"Omar Bhai, you're being too nice. If it wasn't for you and Zahir, I don't think I would've been able to get the website or magazine going."

Zahir looked like he was a few years older than the rest of the group. I gathered from the affectionate glance he threw Hassan that they were together.

"I didn't know you also had a magazine," I said. "That's so cool."

"Yes, we started it after we got a lot of requests from the community for articles and resources on issues that concern us," Hassan said. "We couldn't really find those anywhere else before."

"And how did you all meet?" I said.

"Zahir and I actually knew each other from Texas A&M," Hassan said. "But he returned to Dhaka before I did. And then we reconnected when I came back last year."

"And I just get to watch these two making eyes at each other," Omar said, grinning at his friends.

"I think it's so great that you all are doing this together," I said. "In spite of all the risks."

Omar nodded. "It is very risky. But we really don't have a choice. We need a voice, and sometimes you just have to gamble with everything you've got."

"The LGBT community in Dhaka is very tight-knit," Zahir said. "As you can imagine, safety is an issue, so we have to be able to trust one another completely."

I couldn't help but be in awe of all these guys. Their circumstances were terrifying, yet here they were, facing everything head-on.

"So, Rukhsana," Omar said, "Sohail tells us that you have someone special back in Seattle?"

"I do," I lied. "But my parents caught us together and now they're forcing me to marry Sohail."

"Yes, that has to be the worst," Hassan said with a grin. "I don't know how Mushtaq puts up with him."

"Well, luckily for Rukhsana, I came up with the perfect plan."

"Um, excuse me, you mean you listened while I told you about the perfect plan I came up with," I said haughtily.

"Do we get to find out what the plan is, or do we just have to listen to you two brag about how perfect it is?" Zahir asked.

I was loving this whole exchange. These guys were great.

"Okay, so we do the engagement," Sohail said. "But then three days later, on the wedding day, we're just not going to show up."

"Why not just leave now?" Omar asked.

"It's too soon. I need a couple of days to get my affairs in order. I don't know when I'll be able to come back."

Zahir raised his glass. "To the happy couple."

We all joined him.

"To runaway brides and grooms," Omar said.

"May you both be happy without each other," Hassan added.

• • •

"Rukhsana, the tailors are here," Mom called out to me while I was on my way to the study. When I found her in the downstairs guest room, a makeshift worktable had been set up and two men sat on stools in front of sewing machines.

"They need to take your measurements," she said.

"Why can't we just buy what we need at the mall?" Even though I'd promised I wouldn't argue with my mother about anything, I didn't want these men anywhere near my body. It was a well-known fact among Bengali women that most tailors would cop a feel while checking your breast size and the length of your inseam. I was disgusted when Shaila told me this a few visits ago, but she said it was so commonplace that nobody said anything.

"There is no time to go shopping and get alterations done," said my mother. "This will be faster and you can pick any color and style you like."

I looked around at the bales of silk, chiffon, and organza in bright and subtle hues stacked against the wall. There were fashion magazines lying open-faced on the long table.

Normally, I'd be ecstatic at the prospect of having my own design team prepare my trousseau, but instead I felt like a cow being led to slaughter. None of this fuss was actually about me. It was about my parents and their reputation in the community. It was always about that and it would always be about that. It was a great relief to accept that. I'd felt guilty for so long for who I was and for being the cause of their pain. But now I knew that if I didn't take back control of my life, I would end up like my grandmother. Alone and unhappy.

I set about choosing materials, colors, and styles. At least it made the day go by faster. And I didn't flinch when the tailor brushed his arm against my breast. Every part of me wanted to punch him, but I forced myself to think about how surprised Ariana would be when I showed up at her place next week. That was what kept me going. Seeing her smile, the way her eyes lit up when I made her laugh. It kept me moving forward even through moments of despair. But I couldn't let her down, not again, not after the way I'd ended things with her. She thought it was over between us, but I knew deep down inside she wouldn't give up so easily. She knew me well enough to know that I would keep fighting to find my way back to her, no matter the cost. I had to believe that.

I decided on the mauve silk and the floral-patterned organza and left the tailors to their own devices. According to Parveen, who had popped in earlier to see how things were going, these two were the best in the city and in very high demand. But because of her connections she had been able to secure their services at short notice. I would have expressed my undying gratitude to her if I'd cared enough. But I didn't. Plus, she was making a hefty commission off this wedding, so she was one person I did not have to make nice with.

Dad had gone to confer with the caterers and I found Mom and Nusrat Mami talking with some women in the living room, who turned out to be the florists. The wedding hall had to be decorated, and we needed flowers for the engagement party as well as for the house. We ordered special garlands for the groom and for both mehndi events.

As I sat back and observed it all, I couldn't help but fantasize about the wedding Ariana and I would have. We had never actually talked about it, since neither of us had any intention of getting married so young. But with all that was happening, it made me wonder if I wanted to waste any more time. We would both be eighteen soon, and once we were legally married no one could do anything to keep us apart. We could live our lives in peace, and if my parents wanted to be part of it they could. Otherwise I accepted that they might completely cut me out of theirs.

chapter
thirty

The engagement party took place the following day. I had to start getting ready by midmorning even though the actual event was in the evening.

For the next few hours, I had bleaching cream lathered on my arms, legs, and face. I was plucked and waxed while aestheticians worked on my nails. Then makeup and an elaborate hairdo. Finally, after about five hours, I was deemed pretty enough for my husband-to-be.

Sohail's parents had sent an exquisitely hand-embroidered Benarasi silk sari in hues of pink and purple. I looked in the mirror after Shaila had draped me in it and secured the aanchal and the pleats with giant safety pins tucked under the folds. I had to admit, I looked radiant. My skin glowed, and the rosy color set off my brown skin beautifully. I didn't feel like I was looking at my own reflection. I saw a stranger looking back at me, poised and untouchable.

"You look stunning, Rukhsana," Shaila said, hugging me carefully from behind. The last thing either of us wanted was for the painstaking hours at the salon to go to waste.

When the time came, we drove to the hotel where the ceremony was going to take place. I felt anxious, my palms sweaty. I wasn't sure if this was because of the hundred-degree temperature or my nerves.

The room was buzzing when we walked in. A stage had been set up, with separate chairs for Sohail and me. To call them chairs was an injustice; they were closer to thrones. The florists had decorated the stage with garland upon garland of roses and jasmine. A cloud of their scent surrounded us as we sat down. There were also a few chairs for the parents, and Mom was almost giddy with excitement as she sat down beside me.

"Isn't it gorgeous?" she gushed. There had to be almost two hundred people, which wasn't unusual for an engagement party. You had to pace yourself when making up the guest lists. The engagement was for family and close friends. The holud ceremonies were for the respective family members, a slightly less formal affair and an excuse for the younger guests to enjoy themselves. But the wedding, hosted by the bride's parents, was where anyone with the remotest connection to the bride's family was invited. It wasn't uncommon to invite all of one's colleagues and their families to your daughter's wedding. Then a couple of days later was the reception, this time hosted by the groom's family, an event to present the married couple.

Whenever I went to one of these elaborate affairs I always marveled at the amount of money spent and thought that one could feed a small village in Bangladesh instead. But clearly my parents had different priorities.

I watched Sohail as he bent his head to listen to his mother. He looked incredible in a dark grey suit and deep purple tie, obviously chosen to match my sari. I scanned the hall, looking at Sohail's side of the family. They seemed nice enough, all of them dressed to impress.

He turned and our eyes met. As we smiled at each other, I felt the tight knot in my stomach unfurl a little.

The ceremony was just an exchanging of rings, but somehow, they had managed to turn it into an extravagant celebration. Yet no matter how hard I tried to brush it off as a farce, when the time came for him to put a ring on my finger, an icy shiver rippled down my spine. I felt like I was cheating on Ariana, even though it meant nothing to me. But as I slipped the ring on his finger, I knew I was doing the right thing. For all four of us. Ariana and me. Sohail and Mushtaq.

There was a long line of elderly relatives whose feet we had to touch and who gave us their blessings. Once the rest of the guests had finished congratulating us, it was finally time to eat.

After dinner, a local artist performed classical music. I sat back on my throne-chair wondering how I would make it all the way to the wedding.

We didn't get back home until well after two in the morning. My feet were killing me and I was relieved to take off the strappy silver four-inch heels. As I undressed and washed the evening away, I thought about Ariana and what she was doing now.

When I came out of the bathroom, Mom was standing by the bed. I froze, my mind going immediately to the passport Shaila had stashed away safely in her room. Had they found it? This could not be happening again. I couldn't tell from her face if something was wrong, but she said nothing and handed me an envelope.

"What's this?" I asked, taking it and peeking inside. It was filled with money.

"It's the gift money from your engagement," she said. "That was a lovely party, wasn't it?"

I nodded, hoping she wouldn't ask me if I was happy. I didn't think I was that good of an actor.

• • •

It was almost four in the morning when I finally fell asleep. I had a day off between events, and then my holud ceremony was the following day. And then the day after, the wedding. That meant I had less than three days to perfect my plan.

The sun was high in the sky when I awoke. A quick look at the clock showed me it was noon. A tray with toast, jam, and chai was on the desk. Whoever had come by, probably Rokeya, must have thought it better to let me sleep.

Sohail and I were meeting in a couple of hours for one last time before the wedding. He had booked us both on the same flight out to Los Angeles. From there we would each go our separate ways. He would be flying to Chicago to be with Mushtaq, and I would go back to Seattle. Irfan had already promised to pick me up from the airport, and Sara had invited me to stay with her for a few days. I would have a lot of straightening out to do with my school counselors. Since I had missed finals, I would have to sign up for summer school. And I was fairly certain I had lost my scholarship. My only hope was to explain my situation to the admissions committee at Caltech and pray that they would make an exception.

I had Malik drive me to the mall, where I met Sohail in the food court. We got some kebab and naan and found a table in the midst of the bustling crowds.

"Here are your flight details," he said, handing me a printout. I looked at it briefly before folding it carefully and putting it in my pocket. I would give it to Shaila later at home to stash away with my passport just in case Mom decided to go through my stuff again.

"Thanks so much for taking care of everything," I said. "I can't believe we're really doing this."

"I know. I can't help feeling guilty about all the money my parents are spending on this wedding. But I can't see any way out of this either."

"Have you tried to tell your parents recently? About you and Mushtaq?" I knew the answer already, but I couldn't help wondering.

"I've thought about it so many times, but in the end, I just couldn't do it," he said wistfully. "I guess this way I'll never have to find out how they would look at me if they knew."

I knew exactly what he meant. The way Mom had looked at me when she caught me with Ariana made me wish I could erase that memory.

"Every time I start feeling guilty, I just tell myself I deserve to be happy. And if they can't see that and they don't care about that, then I'll just have to forget about them."

He nodded slowly.

"I'll have to do the same. But I can't keep lying to myself. And I just don't want to anymore."

We ate in silence for a little while, looking around at all the people milling about.

"Do you think we'll ever see each other again after we get there?" I had been wondering a lot about that recently. I really liked Sohail and I knew I'd miss him after this was over.

"I hope so," he said, sounding a little offended. "I mean, only if you want to, of course."

I couldn't help laughing at the hurt expression on his face.

"Of course I want to. I'm just saying, I don't even know what's going to happen to me once I'm back. With school and everything."

"It'll be fine. You'll figure it out, and when you do, Mushtaq and I will come visit you in California." He smiled at me then and my apprehension faded away.

"I think I should head back now," I said, checking my watch. "I'll see you at the airport the day after tomorrow. Don't be late."

chapter
thirty-one

The next morning I went to take a bath, and when I came out, a cream silk sari with a vermillion border lay on my bed. I went down to look for Shaila and found several of my cousins who had come over to help set up for the holud ceremony.

"Rukhsana Apa, have you talked to Sohail Bhai yet?" asked Seema, one of my thirteen-year-old cousins.

"No, but do you want me to call so you can talk to him?" I asked innocently.

She dissolved in a fit of giggles and suddenly they were all laughing themselves silly. I shook my head at them as we finished breakfast.

"So, who wants to get mehndi done tonight?" Shaila asked after we were all done eating. A second later, they all surrounded her. Her henna skills were legendary.

"Rukhsana, remember not to wear any makeup today, okay?" Mom yelled at me from somewhere in the house. "Otherwise the turmeric paste will not go on properly."

"Okay, Mom," I yelled back as I joined my cousins to choose which henna patterns Shaila would do for each of us.

I hugged her before I went to watch the preparations.

Trays of rose petals lined the doorway at the front of the house, to be used later for greeting the groom's side of the family. Traditionally only women were invited to the bride's holud cere-mony, but sometimes some of the more daring younger friends of the groom snuck in to catch a glimpse of all the pretty young girls. I wandered outside the front entrance, where my cousins were hard at work creating an elaborate design on the ground.

"Rukhsana Apa, do you like our alpona?" said Shamma, another one of my cousins. She held a container of red rice powder and was using it to make a circle on the ground. Other girls had similar containers with different colors and filled in the large cir-cle with vines and flower shapes.

"It's beautiful," I said, smiling at her. "I love it. You've gotten really good at this." I left them to continue their artistry.

In the living room, a raised platform had been set up. I assumed I was going to be sitting there later when each of my relatives would smear a small amount of turmeric paste on my face, arms, and legs. Above the platform hung a breathtaking canopy of strung flowers, bright marigolds providing a burst of orange against the stark white of the platform.

"Rukhsana, you should get ready now." Mom's head popped out around the corner. "Shaila, can you help her?"

"Yes, Mom."

"Yes, Zuby Phupi."

We grinned at each other and ran up the stairs to my room. As Shaila helped me do my hair, we talked over the final details of my escape plan.

"It's a good thing they're not doing the nikaah earlier, isn't it?" Shaila said as she braided my hair.

"I know, right?" I said. "Otherwise I'd be so screwed."

The nikaah was the religious ceremony that took place just before the big celebration. It was officiated by an imam of the mosque and was considered binding in the eyes of God. Although I was willing to leave my parents to deal with this mess, I was not willing to enter into a religious or legally binding agreement of marriage. The last thing I needed was that following me for the rest of my life.

"Mom and Dad said they'd be going to the wedding hall earlier to make sure everything is set up properly. They said Malik can drive us there when we're ready."

"Good, because my parents are taking Nani, so it'll just be us in the car," Shaila said.

"What about Malik?" If he called my parents and told them, I'd be in big trouble.

"I'll figure something out, don't worry," Shaila said reassuringly as she pinned strings of marigold in my hair and wrapped some around my wrists.

A loud knock startled us and Shaila almost dropped the bowl of flowers.

The door opened slowly with a creak and I froze. The next moment, Aamir's face appeared. He was grinning that stupid grin of his and at first my brain didn't register who I was looking at. But then I flew to him, my sari almost tripping me and the carefully strung strands of marigolds falling to the ground, but I didn't care. I was like a person drowning who'd been offered a few last gulps of air. I clung to my brother as waves of immense relief washed over me. He pulled away for a moment but saw the tears running down my face and stroked my hair until I had composed myself.

I was a mess. The beautiful flowers Shaila had painstakingly woven into my hair were ruined. I looked guiltily at her, but couldn't wipe the big smile of happiness from my face.

"Good luck fixing that, Shaila Apa," Aamir quipped as he plopped on my bed.

I sat down while Shaila tried to repair the damage. I'd never been happier to listen to my brother's insults.

"So, what's the plan? I hope you're not actually going through with this." Aamir propped himself up on his elbows to look at me.

I told Aamir about our plan and he agreed that the best time to get away would be just before the wedding. But he wanted to be the one to ride with me to the airport. I was relieved and touched to know that he was willing to risk my parents' wrath just to help me. But I was worried about him too.

"Aamir, they're going to be so mad at you. I don't want to be the reason you have a screwed-up relationship with Mom and Dad."

Strangely enough, even after everything they'd done, I felt guilty about ruining Aamir for them too. They would never look at him the same way again.

"That's their problem, Rukhsana. What they're doing is screwed up. They're not backward people from some village, forcing their daughter to get married. But they're sure acting like it."

"It'll kill them when they find out." I still wanted to give him an out. Just in case he needed it.

"Then that's what they deserve," Aamir said, and I'd never heard him sound so bitter. "You know it's all fun and games when they let me get away with stuff and you can't. But this is your life they're messing with. So I really don't care what happens when they find out."

He stood and put his hands on my shoulders. "I will make sure you get to the airport. The rest is up to you. I'll try to buy you as much time as I can."

I don't think I'd ever loved my brother this much. I was too choked up to say anything, so I just nodded and threw my arms around him again. Shaila, who'd been standing off to the side during our exchange, joined in the hug.

After a few seconds of this, Aamir extricated himself from the group hug.

"Okay, I'm getting out of here before you all start crying again. I'll see you downstairs."

Shaila finished fixing my hair and by the time we went back down, our guests had started arriving. My little cousins greeted them at the door with rose petals, and then they came through to where I was sitting. One by one, they all came up, put a dab of turmeric paste on me, and showered me with their blessings and good wishes. Some chose to feed me tiny bites of sweets. After about two hours it was finally over.

"Time for mehndi," Shaila called out, stepping onto the platform. She placed both my feet on a short stool, and sitting across from me proceeded to paint the top of my feet and ankles in the most exquisite henna designs. It took several hours to complete my feet and then my arms up to my elbows. When I looked at the finished design, I couldn't believe my eyes. She had created an intricate pattern on each hand and foot and the end result was stunning.

"Shaila, your back must be killing you," I said as the photographer took pictures of my hands and feet.

"It is," she groaned as she stood up stiffly. "Let's go get you something to eat before you pass out."

I got up gingerly with Shaila holding up my sari so the bottom wouldn't ruin the mehndi on my feet. I was useless for the rest of the evening since I couldn't use my hands while the mehndi was still wet. Luckily, a slew of cousins fed me and made sure I stayed well hydrated.

As I looked around at all of them, excited for me and enjoying themselves, I couldn't help but feel a little bit sad. I was going to have to give up all of this . . . this feeling of belonging to something much bigger than just my family in Seattle.

I pulled Shaila aside when the little cousins went off to show their mehndi to the rest of the family.

"Hey," I said to her in a conspiratorial whisper when I was sure we were alone. "How is Alam doing?"

"He's alright," she said. "Rukhsana, I want to talk to you about something."

"Sure," I said. "What's up?"

"Remember how you asked me why Alam and I won't fight to be together?"

I nodded. I remembered very clearly.

"I do," I said. "It's just that . . . it's easy to see how much you love each other."

"We do," Shaila said. "But we also love our families, our lives with them. We don't want to jeopardize that either. Look at what you're going through. You and your parents both. I don't want to put them through that."

I wanted to say that if her parents really loved her they would want her to be happy, truly happy. But I didn't say that to her. Just because I was ready to go off on my own didn't mean it was the same for her.

"I understand. It's complicated, and as long as you're happy, then that's all I care about." I didn't want to tell her that we would probably never see each other again. Once I left on the day of my wedding, I was pretty sure the rest of the family would cut ties with me. They all had daughters to marry off, and rumors that there might be a lesbian cousin in the mix would most certainly ruin their chances.

By midnight, the mehndi was dry, but Shaila still had to help me get changed before bed. I could tell she was exhausted after hours of sitting hunched over doing all the cousins' mehndi. She just couldn't say no to the little ones. Before getting into bed, I went over all the details in my head one more time. I had to make sure to see Nani one last time before there were too many people in the house crowding her room.

I made a mental note to hide a change of clothes between the folds of my trousseau. Malik would be putting all my suitcases in the car beforehand since I was supposed to go home with Sohail to his family's house after the wedding.

I'd stashed the money from the engagement in my purse, and Shaila would give me my passport just before I left. Sohail planned to meet me at the airport, and we would check in together. Aamir would be taking a cab with me to the airport and then going on to the wedding venue. Our parents would be too busy making sure the guests were happy and well-fed to notice how late it had gotten and that I was still not there.

I could hardly sleep with all the thoughts swirling around in my head. If everything went according to plan, this would be my last night here. By this time tomorrow, I'd be halfway back home, back to Ariana and my own life.

chapter
thirty-two

I awoke the next morning to the wailing sounds of a shehnai outside my window. I was pretty sure it was supposed to be playing when the groom's party arrived, but somebody was probably having some fun with it.

I pulled out my suitcase from under the bed. I wasn't taking any luggage with me, other than the carry-on duffel bag that I had traveled with from Seattle. I wanted to be as unencumbered as possible when I was making my getaway.

I'd already put in some of the outfits from my trousseau, but now I added a couple of T-shirts, two pairs of jeans, and a light hoodie between the layers of silk and chiffon. Next, I collected my everyday makeup items, put them in a small plastic pouch, and put it in my purse. I looked around. Was I forgetting anything? Nani.

I walked quickly across the landing to her room. Luckily, she was awake, and there was no one else in her room yet. Bending down to hug her, I took her hand and sat on the edge of her bed. I brushed away the grey hair on her forehead and tried not to think about how much I would miss her.

"Is everything taken care of, Rukhsana? Is there anything you need?" she asked me, cupping my cheek.

"No, Nani." I shook my head. "Aamir is helping me. And when I'm back home I'll get in touch with you somehow, I promise."

I hoped I could keep that promise. Otherwise, I wouldn't be able to live with myself.

"Ammu, bring me my purse from over there," she said, pointing to a chair across the room. I jumped up and brought it to her. She fished out an envelope. "I was going to give this to you as a wedding present someday. Since I don't know when I'll see you again, why not today?" she said, handing it to me.

I opened it. Inside was a lot of cash.

"Nani, I can't take this," I said, in shock. "It's too much."

"Rukhsana, you are my granddaughter. The heart of my heart. Nothing is too much. What will I do with all this money? I will die soon. But you . . . you have your whole life to live. And you have chosen a difficult path. I know how hard that can be."

"Nani . . . I can't . . ."

"Are you going to refuse your nani this little bit of happiness? Rukhsana, knowing that I have helped you even a little bit makes me so happy. Don't you want me to be happy?" she said, her eyes twinkling.

Nani was always a master at persuading me.

I bent down to kiss her forehead. "You've helped more than you can ever imagine, Nani. You're standing by me and I'll never forget that." I lifted her hand to my lips and kissed it. "I have to go now, Nani. I love you." I could barely see through my tears, but her voice floated after me.

"Come back one day, my spring bird."

I carried her words in my heavy heart as I went back to my room for the final preparations.

I had convinced Mom that I wanted Shaila to do my makeup for tonight. She was too preoccupied with everything else to pay too much attention to me. At least I wouldn't have to change from full bridal mode to casual traveler somewhere between here and the airport.

Our flight to LA was at two o'clock in the morning, and Sohail and I would have to get to the airport by eleven o'clock tonight. We both lived fairly close to the airport, but with traffic it would take at least two hours to get there. That gave me until nine o'clock tonight to sneak out. Thankfully Bengali weddings traditionally started late and went on until well past midnight, so I wouldn't be expected to leave the house until later in the evening anyway. The last thing I wanted was to make my parents suspicious.

Dad and Tanveer Mama had gone to check on the caterers, and Mom and Nusrat Mami were sorting out gifts of jewelry that some relatives had chosen to deliver to the house rather than risk having it stolen at the busy wedding venue. I used this opportunity to pop into the study and send off an email to Irfan, who was meeting me at the airport. I made sure to leave no evidence of my correspondence on the computer. Once they realized I was missing that would be the first thing they would check. I also had to figure out a way to protect Shaila from any fallout. I would not let anything bad happen to her this time.

By four in the afternoon, I was ready and packed. I took a long bath and dried and straightened my hair. Mom came by around six.

"Rukhsana, Daddy and I are leaving for the hall to check on everything. Make sure you start getting ready on time, we don't want to keep everyone waiting."

She stepped closer and cupped my face in her hands.

"I am proud of you, for making the right choice. You have remembered your values, I'm very happy to see that. You have not let us down," she said with a satisfied smile.

If there was even an ounce of guilt left over what I was about to do, it completely dissipated. And any shred of respect I had left for my mother disappeared along with it. I was glad we'd talked, because she had just made my decision a hell of a lot easier.

"Don't worry, Mom, we'll get there on time. Although I might send Shaila ahead of me with my stuff. She can look after Nani. You all will be pretty busy, right?"

"That's a good idea. I'll send Malik back for you. The nikaah is not until nine o'clock, and knowing these people, they're not going to come on time. No use for you to wait and get all sweaty. Okay, ammu, I will see you there."

Suddenly it hit me. This was probably the last time I would see my mom. Or at least the last time she'd want to see me. I stood and gave her a long hug.

"See you there," I said softly as she turned around and left the room.

Okay, so Shaila was in the clear. Malik wouldn't get in trouble because I wouldn't be here when he came back for me. Once Shaila left, the house would be empty, so no one would notice Aamir and me getting into a cab. He would ride with me to the airport in a cab and make up some excuse about why he was late to the venue.

An hour later, Shaila showed up in my room with my passport and put it in my purse immediately. I flitted around the room picking up little things here and there that had accumulated in the last two months. It was hard to believe that it had been that long already. I stopped in the middle of closing my suitcase and looked over at Shaila, sitting on the edge of my bed.

"Shaila, I don't know when I'm going to see you again. I'm going to miss you so much." My eyes welled up with tears.

We put our arms around each other and stood like that for a long time.

"I know it won't be anytime soon, right?" Shaila stroked my hair. "You promise you'll be in touch with Aamir to let us know that you're alright?"

I nodded. We'd planned for Aamir to be the go-between for Shaila and me. Shaila would keep Nani updated so that she didn't worry about me.

"As soon as I can. And you have to promise that you'll do what makes you happy. And tell Nani I love her."

I hadn't told Shaila about the diary. I'd thought about it, but I felt as if I'd be betraying Nani's confidence. It would remain our little secret.

"You should get going," I told her now. "I don't want them getting suspicious."

Footsteps approached outside the door.

"I thought everyone was at the hall," I whispered.

"Quick, get in the bathroom." Shaila waited for the door to open as I disappeared.

There was a knock. I heaved a sigh of relief. Mom never knocked.

"Shaila Apa, Malik is here and ready to take you." It was Rokeya.

"Okay, tell him I'll be down in ten minutes."

After Rokeya left, I came out.

"Oh my God, I almost peed in my pants there." I laughed shakily. My whole body was trembling. For a second I'd thought that Mom had suspected me all along and was just tricking me so she could catch me in the act.

"You need to go now, Shaila. Aamir said the cab will be here soon. I think I'm just going to change now. I don't want to drag the suitcase down the stairs. Rokeya might hear me."

I gave her one last hug and then I stepped back as she left the room. I would see her again, I promised myself. I would not lose my cousin . . . my sister.

After I changed my clothes, I sat on my bed, waiting for Aamir to text me about the cab. He had asked the driver to park a short distance away from the house, so Rokeya wouldn't see anything.

A few minutes later, my phone pinged with a text from Aamir.

In the cab, outside. You ready to do this?

My pulse quickened as I took one last look around, grabbed my stuff, and went out. I was careful to tread softly down the stairs in case Rokeya was close by. After every few steps, I paused to make sure no one was coming. It looked like the coast was clear.

Taking a deep breath, I sprinted down the remaining steps and dashed out the front door to freedom. I didn't relax until I was finally in the cab with Aamir, heading toward the airport.

I squeezed Aamir's hand tightly as we sat in the back seat. Words weren't necessary. He was my brother and he would always have my back, just like I would always have his.

As expected, it took us almost two hours to reach the airport.

The cab dropped me off at the international departures terminal. After refusing to let Aamir come in with me and one last tight hug, I got out, only to find myself swarmed by the dozens of coolies who were hoping to make a little money by carrying people's luggage for them. When they saw I didn't have anything except my duffel bag and purse, they dispersed, looking for more lucrative opportunities.

I went in and checked the board for flight information. As I scanned the digital display, I groaned. My flight was delayed due to technical difficulties.

I debated checking in and waiting at the gate. But in the end, I decided to stay outside security and wait for Sohail. We would have plenty of time after he got here.

> Just got to the airport, Sohail. Are you close?

Ten minutes after I sent the text, there was still no reply. I looked at my watch. Eleven fifteen. Technically he was late, since he didn't know that our flight was delayed. Or maybe he found out and decided to come a little later. It would have been nice if he'd texted me back.

What if his parents caught him?

The thought came to me unbidden and I glanced around nervously. I felt as if there was someone watching me. I shook myself mentally. I was just being paranoid. My parents and the rest of the family were all at the wedding hall, receiving guests. By now they would have started trickling in, the ladies all decked out in their best finery, the young ones vying for attention, hoping to catch the eye of some young man from the groom's side. Or maybe a mother looking for a bride for her son would take a liking to one of them and send out inquiries in the next few days. No one would expect to see me until much later. It was the prerogative of the bride to take her time.

I checked my phone again. Eleven forty-five.

> Sohail, I'm freaking out a little. Where the hell are you?

The line at the check-in counter was getting longer, winding around the belted security stands. I decided it was time to get going and joined the line.

As I stood there waiting, I wondered if anyone had noticed that I was missing yet. Maybe Mom had called home to find out what was keeping me. Rokeya would have come to find me. She would see the suitcase with half my trousseau lying on the bed. She would check the bathroom, then look for me in all the other rooms before telling my mother that I was gone.

Would Shaila be able to lie convincingly? Would they get angry at her?

I texted Aamir.

> Sohail isn't here yet and I'm really worried.

My phone pinged immediately.

> I'll try to reach him and get back to you.

No missed calls from my parents yet. So, the alarm hadn't been sounded yet. If I could just get through the check-in line and airport security, I would be home free.

The line moved at a painstakingly slow pace and it was another thirty minutes before I was finally standing in front of an agent. I checked in and then made my way through all the security checkpoints. Finally, another half hour later, I was walking toward my gate.

Just then my phone buzzed.

Finally. It was about time that he called back.

But the number wasn't Sohail's. It was Tanveer Mama's.

So, they had finally discovered that I was gone. Or maybe they were still trying to figure out why I hadn't shown up yet.

I let the call go to voicemail and checked the departures board again. Thankfully, there were no more delays.

My stomach growled and I realized I hadn't eaten in over eleven hours. I walked over to the café to get some food before settling into a spot by the gate to await boarding, watching as the waiting area slowly filled up.

I looked at my phone again. Still nothing from Sohail. But about a dozen missed calls from Tanveer Mama's number. Obviously, they had figured it out by now. And even though I was confident they couldn't just waltz through security and drag me away from here, I couldn't stop the sliver of panic that crept through me.

The flight status had been updated. Boarding would begin in thirty minutes. I took out Nani's diary, flipped to the page where I had stopped last time, and began to read.

It has been many months since I have written here. By the mercy of Allah, I had a baby boy. Arif and mother-in-law were very pleased and have been treating me well. They named him Tanveer and had a big celebration for his naming ceremony. Many people were invited and even my parents came. Two goats and a cow were slaughtered for the korma and biryani that were served. Mother-in-law made the sweet rice herself. She said she will teach me how to make it one day. She does not put Tanveer down at all. He is always in her arms, while she sings and talks to him all day. Arif is always in a good mood when he comes home nowadays. He will pick up the baby and make silly sounds for a long time. Zubaida watches him, but she does not go to him that much anymore. She has become very quiet. She's not my naughty girl anymore. When Arif comes to me at night, he is gentle. He doesn't want to wake Tanveer.

I am still doing all the housework while mother-in-law plays with Tanveer. She calls me when it is time to feed him and change him. Then she takes him back and tells me to finish my work.

I looked up as a mother and son took the two seats beside me.

As they settled in, I thought about Tanveer Mama. His birth had changed my grandmother's life. It sounded like things had gotten better for her. But I felt sad for my mother. It must have been hard growing up knowing that your father didn't love you. And to see him showing so much love to his son must have hurt. I knew a little bit about that, and I wished I could have talked to Mom about why she always favored Aamir over me as I was growing up.

I flipped to a later section of the diary. I was impatient to see if she had written anything about my mom when she was older. I found a page that looked promising and began to read again.

Today Tanveer turned six. Every year on his birthday, Arif buys a goat to sacrifice in Tanveer's name. Then he asks me to cook the curry. In the evening, his relatives will come and mother-in-law will brag about Tanveer's cleverness to them. Zuby turned ten years old this summer. She is blossoming into a young woman. I was only two years older than she is now when I came into this house. Where have the years gone? I no longer recognize myself when I look in the mirror. Yesterday I saw Raju at the fish market. I don't know if he saw me or if he would even recognize me. He looks

stronger now, tall and well-muscled. He was
wearing a lungi and a white shirt. when I am
very sad sometimes, I think about him. He used
to tell me he would marry me when we grew
up. He would build a small house just for the
two of us and our children. we would have a
boy and a girl. The boy would be older so that
he could protect his sister. He promised he would
buy me a string of jasmine flowers every day to
put in my hair. He knew I loved jasmine flowers.

So this was the mysterious Raju. I closed my eyes and tried to picture Nani with him, both just children when they were torn away from each other. Sadness engulfed me as I thought about how Nani must have longed for her Raju all those years when she was suffering. I wondered if they ever had a chance to meet again, and I was about to turn to the next diary entry when I heard the garbled sounds of an announcement for my flight. I couldn't really make out most of what was being said, but from the sudden rustling of jackets and shuffling of bags, I gathered that our flight was ready to board.

Where the hell was Sohail?

> Sohail, I don't know what happened to you. I'm sorry, but I have to get on the flight. Please text me back as soon as you get this. I'm really worried.

I was grateful to have a window seat, especially on such a long flight. I looked out the window when the plane started to move. The lights of Dhaka became smaller and fainter until they disappeared entirely into the darkness.

chapter
thirty-three

I stood in the arrivals lounge at the Seattle airport looking for Irfan. The connection at LAX had been tight, but I'd still had enough time to grab some food before the final leg of my journey. Sleep deprived and with a pounding headache, I found a seat near baggage claim and slumped into it.

A few minutes later, Irfan and Sara found me. Sara had her arms open before she even got to me, which was a good thing because I fell into them. Irfan patted me awkwardly on the back while I tried valiantly to hold back tears of relief. I was finally home and safe.

"Did Sohail make it off to Chicago okay?" Irfan said.

I shook my head. "He never showed. I have no idea what happened."

"Do you think they found out before he could leave?" Sara asked.

I shook my head. "I don't know. I haven't had any missed calls or texts from him. There were so many voicemails from my parents, but I haven't listened to any of them yet."

"Okay, well, let's get you home first," Irfan said. He picked up my duffel bag and we walked outside. It was refreshing to inhale clean air after months of the smog-laden, humid kind. The traffic outside seemed so tame after the insanity of the roads in Bangladesh. But strangely enough, I missed the hustle and bustle of all the people on the streets, the colorful array of saris and the singsong of the vendors.

When we got to her place, Sara went into the kitchen and emerged a short while later with a bowl of grapes, some slices of watermelon, and a platter of cheese and crackers.

"I have to get back to work," Irfan said after we'd eaten. "I'll come by again this evening."

"And I have to meet with my study group in a bit," Sara said. "Rukhsana, will you be okay by yourself for a few hours? My parents are away for the week, but they left tons of food in the fridge, so please help yourself to whatever you want."

"Thanks so much, you guys. I really appreciate you going to all this trouble for me," I said.

"It's no trouble at all," Sara said. "Just get some rest and we'll talk more when we get back."

After they left, I sat down to check my voicemail.

There were dozens from Tanveer Mama's number.

"Rukhsana, ammu, you're taking a long time. People are starting to ask where you are." That was the first one, close to eleven. Then a few more identical ones, urging me to hurry up.

"Rukhsana, where are you?" Mom's stern voice had underlying tones of nervousness.

As I continued listening, I could hear Mom's voice becoming more and more agitated.

One message was from Dad.

"Rukhsana, this is your father speaking. Please call us back immediately. I don't know what you think you are doing, but you must come here right away." This one was left just after midnight.

By then they would have had no more doubts in their minds. They would have known I had run away.

Goose bumps erupted on my forearms and my stomach clenched. Even though they couldn't do anything to me now, I still felt uneasy.

The next voicemail was from Shaila.

"Rukhsana, something terrible has happened. You have to call me immediately." She sounded terrified and my hands went numb.

My fingers fumbled as I tried to call her back, and I had to try three times before I got it right.

"Rukhsana . . . oh my God . . . are you alright?" The panic in Shaila's voice was clear and my stomach heaved.

"I'm okay, I just landed a little while ago. What happened?" A part of me didn't want to know. Another part of me knew it was about Sohail.

"Rukhsana . . . I don't know how to tell you. I'm so sorry. It was horrible. We thought you——"

"What are you trying to say?" I asked as calmly as I could.

"Sohail was attacked before the wedding. He's dead." She sobbed.

My blood turned cold.

Sohail's charming and devilish smile flashed before my eyes. He couldn't be dead.

"Are you sure?" My voice sounded small and thin. Maybe this was all a horrible mistake. Maybe my parents had put her up to it to punish me for running away.

"Yes." More sobs. "I thought they had killed you too." She could barely get the words out between her crying. "But then Aamir told me Sohail never made it to the airport."

My eyes were completely dry. I felt no tears. In fact, I felt nothing at all. I was numb from head to toe. None of this was real.

Sohail must have caught a later flight. Any minute now he would call me and apologize for worrying me. I would hear the happiness in his voice and he would tell me how great it was to finally be back with Mushtaq. But none of that happened. Instead, the only sound I could hear was Shaila crying.

"How did it happen?" I could barely recognize my own voice, cold and detached.

"I don't think—"

"Please, Shaila, I need to know exactly what happened."

"He was attacked by some guys near his office." Shaila's voice quavered.

"What did they do to him?"

"He was found covered in large gashes all over his body. The police think he was killed with a machete. So barbaric."

Bile rose in my throat and I ran to the trash can before I vomited. I didn't need to hear any more.

From the far recesses of my mind, I remembered. Sohail and I at a restaurant. A group of men staring at us. It had to have been them. What if we'd gone to the police that night instead of his office? Would he still be alive today?

I realized I had dropped the phone on the couch. I picked it back up, but the call had disconnected.

I felt empty inside, hollowed out. Then a terrible thought struck me. Mushtaq. He had to be going out of his mind with worry. No one would have even known to call him. I quickly scrolled through the contact list on my phone. Sohail had added Mushtaq's number, just in case.

My palms were sweaty and there was a hard lump in my throat.

I put the phone down. I couldn't do this. How could I tell him such awful news? I'd never even met him and now I was going to tell him the worst news of his life. But then I saw Sohail's face in my mind again. That tender look whenever he spoke about Mushtaq. The way he looked off into the distance when he told me about their plans for the future. I had to do this for him. I had to do this last thing for Sohail, my friend, my confidant.

I took a deep breath and made the call with shaky fingers.

He answered on the second ring.

"Hello?"

"Mushtaq? This is Rukhsana, Sohail's friend from Dhaka," I said hesitantly.

A moment of silence.

"Rukhsana, it's so nice to finally speak to you. Sohail's told me so much about you. Actually, I'm so glad you called. I'm starting to worry. He should have been here by now."

I held back a sob.

"Mushtaq." I tried to keep my voice steady. "I'm afraid I have some bad news."

The silence was deafening. I knew exactly what he was feeling, because I had felt it myself moments ago.

My heart twisted inside my chest. Time to rip off the Band-Aid.

"Mushtaq, there were some guys. They attacked him outside his office."

"Oh my God. Where is he? I can catch the next available flight—"

"He's dead, Mushtaq. They killed him."

Silence.

"Mushtaq?"

"Is this some sort of cruel joke?"

"No, I'm sorry."

"Stop it. You're lying." His voice was cold and hard.

"Mushtaq, I'm so, so sorry."

"Just stop talking. Look, I don't even know you. You think this is funny?" His voice was starting to break and I knew realization was setting in.

"Mushtaq—"

"No, please don't—"

He was sobbing now and my soul was dying. I wanted to reach out and hold him. To cry with him and try to make sense of this insanity. But all I could do was say his name over and over again while his heart broke thousands of miles away.

"I didn't even get to say goodbye." His voice quivered with tears and mine finally came. I could do nothing to stop them. I didn't want to.

I tried to remember the last thing I said to Sohail, but I couldn't remember a single word. What if we had decided to drive to the airport together? Or if he had left just a little bit earlier? I wondered why he had stopped at his office at all. Those guys must have followed us from the restaurant that night. That's how they knew where he worked.

"I have to go now," Mushtaq said. "Goodbye, Rukhsana." Then he hung up.

My only connection to Sohail was gone.

chapter
thirty-four

"Rukhsana, wake up." An insistent voice pierced through the thick haze of sleep. I ignored it, but it would not go away. Someone shook my shoulder and I jerked awake.

"Your mom is on the phone," Sara said.

I was disoriented and groggy, and for a minute, I couldn't remember where I was. But the awful memories came rushing back and I looked at Sara and shook my head.

"I don't want to talk to her." My voice was hoarse from crying.

Sara nodded and walked away. I could hear her say something to my mother, but I didn't really care. The last thing I wanted to do right now was deal with my parents.

I sat up in bed but couldn't muster the energy to actually stand up. My head was heavy and my eyes burned. Sara came back into the room.

"Rukhsana, can I get you anything? How about some breakfast? I could whip up an omelet."

The mention of food made me gag.

"No, thanks. I don't think I can eat anything."

Sara sat on the edge of the bed and gently put her hand on my shoulder.

"I can't even begin to imagine what you're going through," she said softly. "But I just want you to know you're not alone. Irfan and I are here for you. Whatever you need, all you have to do is ask."

I squeezed her hand.

"I know, Sara. But I don't have the strength to feel it right now. I just can't handle anything."

"It's okay, Rukhsana. Let us take care of things for you. If you don't want to talk to your parents or anyone else, I'll make up an excuse." She put her arms around me and hugged me. "You take all the time you need."

Her kindness made my eyes well up again. As soon as she left the room, I fell back into bed.

There was an empty darkness growing inside me. Then an awful thought hit me like a sledgehammer. If I had been with Sohail, they would have killed me too. There were a million different scenarios in which I could have been there that night. The thought paralyzed me.

A faint voice found me through the dismal abyss, growing louder, and eventually I was out of bed and dressed. Sohail would have never wanted me to give up this way.

I had to talk to my counselor at school to find out if there was any way I could make up the credits I missed and still go to Caltech in the fall. I was pretty sure I'd lost my scholarship, and for that alone I would never forgive my parents.

Sara and Irfan had left a note saying they would be back soon with some food. My stomach rumbled and I put a slice of bread in the toaster.

While I waited, I called Jen.

"Rukhsana, you're back? Are you okay?" Her voice was shrill with excitement.

I realized that Jen had no idea who Sohail was, and I honestly didn't know how to tell her. Or if I even wanted to. It was strange, but I didn't want to share him. I didn't want to have to explain him to anyone. Not even Ariana, if she was ever going to speak to me again. It struck me that I hadn't thought about her at all since I got the call about Sohail. But now memories of her came flooding back. I wanted to hold her and I wanted to bury my head in her lap and cry. But I needed to keep it together and just get through today.

"I've been better," I said. "I got back last night, but I was too tired to call."

"I can't believe you're back. Hey, are you at home? I could come over right now. I'm dying to see you."

I looked at my phone. It was one thirty on a Friday afternoon.

"How come you're not at school?"

"I had a free period in last block, so I just came home to study for my chem final on Monday."

A wave of sadness washed over me. Jen and I had been in chemistry together all semester. We should have been studying together, cramming during late-night sessions. Now I wasn't even sure if I could graduate. I'd missed so many weeks, the only option left was summer school. Once again, rage shot through me. My parents had done this.

"I'm actually at Sara's place."

"Who's Sara? Is that the girl who's dating that Irfan guy?"

"That's the one. Hey, Jen, would you mind giving me a ride to school?"

"Of course. I'll be right over. And then maybe we could go for lunch?"

My spirits lifted. Maybe it was the enthusiasm in Jen's voice or the fact that I was doing something as normal as going to school with my friend. Either way I felt better.

"I cannot believe you're back," Jen squealed a short while later as she got out of her car to give me a tight hug.

"You have no idea," I said as I returned the hug with fervor.

"Okay, so once we're there, you go do whatever it is you have to do at school and I'll hang out and wait for you. But then you have to tell me everything." Her brown eyes shone with excitement and I felt much better just being around her.

"That sounds great. I just have to talk to Mr. Jacobs about my classes. Hopefully it won't take long."

"I'll text Rachel and see if she'll be done with her exam by then."

Spending the afternoon with my two oldest friends was exactly what I needed. But there was something I had to ask first.

"Have you talked to Ariana recently?" I had no idea how much Jen knew, but I assumed she was aware that we'd broken up.

"I did, just a couple of days ago," Jen said, keeping her eyes on the road. "You know, she was in really bad shape. She told me what you said."

We stopped at a red light and Jen looked at me. Was that disapproval in her eyes?

"Jen, things were really bad over there for me too. You have no idea what it was like."

The light turned green and Jen turned her eyes back to the road again.

"Ariana told us. But what I don't understand is why you would do something like that."

"Look, Jen, I know it all sounds strange to you, but it's not that easy for me. You've always known what my parents are like. And when they caught Ariana and me, everything just went batshit."

"I'm not saying it's your fault. It's just that maybe you could have handled it a bit differently."

I didn't know what to say to that. In hindsight, I wished I'd handled it differently too. But I wasn't sure if there was a nice way to break somebody's heart.

"I know. You're right. Do you think she'll want to talk to me?" I needed to help her understand why I did what I did. Maybe then, there would still be a chance for us to be together.

"She was a wreck after you broke up with her. But I can talk to her and see how she feels."

My heart plummeted.

"I've ruined everything, haven't I?"

Jen pulled into the parking lot at school, turned off the car, and faced me.

"I know things are awful right now. But it'll be okay, I promise. I'll talk to Ariana tonight. You know she still loves you. But you broke her heart, so give her some time."

I nodded. "Thanks. I guess I'll just have to be patient."

I got out of the car and went in to find my counselor.

Mr. Jacobs was surprised to see me but took me into his office right away.

I told him a tamed-down version of what had happened. I'd emailed him before we left, but now as he listened to me, he was visibly surprised.

"Rukhsana, I can't imagine how difficult this all must have been for you," he said, his voice filled with concern. "Look, I can contact the authorities if you would like me to. They can help."

I shook my head. "No, Mr. Jacobs, that won't be necessary. I'm dealing with it in my own way. What I'm more concerned with right now is what's going to happen with my graduation. I mean, I missed so much, and now I won't be able to go to Caltech in the fall. And I lost my scholarship."

To my horror, tears rolled down my cheeks and fell onto my hand. Embarrassed, I wiped them away, but not before Mr. Jacobs noticed.

"We'll figure this out together," he said. "First, I want you to listen to me carefully." He grabbed a box of tissues from his desk and handed them to me.

"I'm sorry," I blubbered, blowing my nose and taking some more tissues.

"I've known you for almost four years now. Trust me when I say that I will not let you lose this opportunity. You will go to Caltech in the fall."

I nodded, unable to say anything coherent. Somehow, his take-charge attitude was making me feel weepy and grateful at the same time.

"You will make up what you missed in summer school. I will contact Caltech and alert them to your situation. Then we'll evaluate your options again."

"What if they rescind their offer anyway?" I couldn't bear the thought of missing out on Caltech.

"If they are not willing to consider your circumstances, then you'll attend your backup school and transfer to Caltech next year."

It made sense. I couldn't change what had happened, but I wasn't going to allow it to ruin my future.

"Thank you," I said, trying to smile. "I really appreciate your help."

"Rukhsana, you've always worked so hard. I know it will all work out, and I'm happy to help in any way I can. Now go and get registered for summer school before all the spots are filled."

Afterward, Jen drove us to our favorite sushi restaurant for lunch, where Rachel waited for us. After a tearful reunion, we ate and caught up on everything that had happened while I was gone.

By the time Jen dropped me back off at Sara's house, Sara and Irfan were already there. Irfan made chai for us and I told them about my day.

"I'm glad you got that taken care of," Sara said. "I'm sure Caltech will understand. I mean, if these aren't exigent circumstances, I don't know what is."

"So, Rukhsana," Irfan said, settling himself in an armchair. "Have you thought about how you're going to deal with your parents? Aunty Meena says they've been calling nonstop."

"I can't think about them right now. What do they want anyway?"

"I'm not sure, but it might not be as bad as you think," Irfan said. "I think that with what happened to Sohail, they're reevaluating everything."

"Well, that's great for them. But I'm not interested. I mean, Sohail had to *die* for my parents to realize how wrong they were?" I felt that now-familiar anger surging through me again. "I just want to get on with my life."

Irfan began to speak, but Sara put her hand on his arm.

"Rukhsana, you take all the time you need. You've been through a lot, and your parents will just have to wait until you're ready."

Irfan nodded. "Sara's right. I'll ask Aunty Meena to tell them you need more time."

"And you can stay here with me for as long as you like. My parents aren't coming back until next week anyway," Sara added. "But maybe we can drive you to your place to pick up a few things?"

"That would be great. I know I've said it before, but I really appreciate everything you're doing for me."

"There's no need for that, Rukhsana," Sara said.

"If this was happening to my little sister, I would do anything to help her," Irfan said. He stood up and ruffled my hair affectionately. "Now, let's go and get you some clothes. You can't wear that sweatshirt forever."

• • •

That night I dreamed about Sohail.

We were out somewhere with Ariana, laughing at something he had said. Then out of the shadows, five men appeared, their faces distorted by the darkness. They began to beat Sohail, kicking and punching him, while Ariana and I begged for them to stop. They were deaf to our pleas, continuing their assault while I tried to reach out and pull Sohail to safety. But my efforts were futile, and I watched helplessly as he fell to the ground. Ariana and I screamed as Sohail lay there motionless, and the screams became louder and louder until I woke up and realized I was still screaming.

chapter thirty-five

It was strange being back in this house all by myself. That morning I had told Sara and Irfan that I wanted to move back home. As expected, they tried to dissuade me, but I had already made up my mind.

I went into the kitchen and opened the fridge. I held my breath, expecting a foul odor to hit me, but there was none. I checked the freezer. Mom had frozen all the leftovers so nothing would spoil. It looked like she had thought of everything, which made sense since she had planned this whole trip all along, knowing that it might be a while before they came back.

The light on the answering machine blinked accusingly at me. They must have called here after trying my cell phone. I didn't want to listen to anything they had to say. As far as I was concerned, I meant nothing to them. My happiness held no value in their eyes. And I was fine with that. But they would never manipulate me again. I would never relinquish control of my life to anyone. Only I had my best interests at heart.

I knew I was going to regret it, but I couldn't ignore the answering machine any longer. I pressed the button to listen to the messages.

"Rukhsana, this is your mother speaking. If you can hear me, please pick up. Hello? Hello? Ibrahim, she is not picking up. You should try, she will pick up if she hears your voice. Hello? Hello, Rukhsana?"

The next five messages were more of the same confusing prattle, until my dad decided he'd had enough. The next one was from him.

"Rukhsana, ammu, this is your father speaking." His voice echoed loudly in the empty house. He probably thought if he shouted the message I might answer. "If you are there, please pick up. It is very urgent. Please pick up or call us back when you get the message."

I shook my head and erased all the remaining messages.

chapter
thirty-six

I sat up with a start, disoriented from the darkness of my room. I heard shuffling somewhere inside the house and got up quickly. Relieved that I had thought to bring Aamir's cricket bat into my room last night, I grabbed it now from under the bed.

I crept downstairs, bat in hand, ready to strike. When I reached the bottom step, the lights in the entryway turned on.

I screamed and someone screamed back. I blinked against the harsh brightness of the lights and saw my parents and brother standing in the doorway.

"What the hell are you doing?" I yelled. "You scared me half to death."

"Rukhsana, we left you so many messages. We told you we were coming home tonight," Mom said, panting from the fright of being accosted in her own home.

The messages. That explained it. Maybe I shouldn't have erased them.

"If I'd known you were coming back, I would have stayed with a friend tonight."

"Why would you stay with a friend? What's wrong with your room?" Mom clearly didn't understand how hate worked.

I didn't have the energy to deal with them right now.

"I'm going back to bed. I have school in the morning."

Back in my room, my phone pinged just as I lay back down.

Jen said you wanted to talk.

It was Ariana. Jen must have gotten through to her.

I do. Can you come to our spot tomorrow after school?

The minutes passed, interminably long, as I waited for her reply.

But then—

I'll be there.

My heart skipped a beat. I couldn't help it. Maybe there was a chance that things would work out after all.

When I went downstairs the following morning, Mom and Dad were both there. They stopped talking as soon as I entered the kitchen.

"Don't stop plotting on my account. What is it today? You're planning to sell me to the highest bidder?"

I hadn't planned to say this. I hadn't even been thinking it. But I couldn't stop myself from spewing the venom that had been festering inside me for weeks now.

It was immensely satisfying to see the shocked expressions on their faces. For once Mom didn't have any retort.

"Rukhsana, this has to stop," Dad said. "We need to talk. We're a family, and we have to get through this as a family."

That did it. The floodgates opened, and it wasn't within my power to control what came rushing out.

"Family?" I said, my voice hard with rage. "You want to act like we're a family? Where was this family when you locked me up? When you drugged me?"

Mom was looking at me wide-eyed, and I'd be lying if I said this didn't make me feel good.

"Rukhsana. Please try to understand."

"Yes, please make me understand. I want to understand how my own parents would want me to lose everything just because I don't fit into your narrow little box." My blood was boiling. I could literally feel the heat coursing through my body. "My God, Sohail had to die before you could even try to understand me. Do you not see how screwed up that is? That a decent human being has to die because people like you can't understand and accept him for who he is?"

"But, ammu, we are trying——" Mom began, but I'd had enough.

"You know what? I don't need this. I don't want to talk to you, or be a family." I picked my bag off the floor and stormed out the door.

By the time I'd walked the two blocks to school I was a tiny bit calmer.

"Rukhsana." I turned at the sound of my name. Aamir stood behind me, backpack slung over one shoulder.

"You know Mom and Dad *are* trying, right?"

"Aamir, you don't know what you're talking about. You weren't there. You have no idea how senseless they were." Angry tears stung my eyes.

"Rukhsana, I'm sorry," Aamir said hastily.

He threw worried glances over his shoulder at the students walking past, but I didn't care who was listening. I didn't care about anything right now.

"I can't even begin to imagine how angry you must be right now. And I'm sorry I wasn't there for you when you needed me in Dhaka."

I was calmer now. "Aamir, it wasn't your fault at all. You helped me so much." I squeezed his hand. "But you're not getting it. I have absolutely no desire to talk to them. And I don't know if I ever will."

Aamir put his hands on my shoulders and looked me straight in the eyes.

"Rukhsana, I was there when they found out about Sohail. Just hear them out. That's all I'm saying." And with that he turned away and went into school.

chapter
thirty-seven

I waited for Ariana at our special spot, a little grassy area behind the library where we shared our first kiss. I was hoping that we could talk. Really talk, like we used to.

When she walked around the corner my heart did a little skip. She was wearing jeans and a white eyelet blouse. Her hair was shorter than the last time I'd seen her, and it looked really cute.

We both stood awkwardly looking at each other in silence for a moment.

"How've you been?" I asked, when the silence became unbearable.

"Okay, I guess."

"I like your hair like this."

She tugged at the ends of it, then smoothed the top and shrugged.

"I needed a change."

I nodded but didn't say anything.

"So . . . Jen said you wanted to talk." She played with the hem of her blouse. I wondered if she hated me so much that she couldn't even look at me.

"I just wanted a chance to explain," I began. "And to see you again," I finished weakly.

"I think you explained yourself pretty well the last time we talked," Ariana said, her voice cold and brittle. "I've moved on. I'm good."

She couldn't be telling the truth. This was just lashing out at me.

"Ariana, please just—"

Her eyes flashed at me, the anger and pain slamming into me like a solid object.

"Please just what, Rukhsana?" She spit out the words. "What did you think was going to happen today? You thought I was just going to be okay with everything because you've decided it's time to talk?"

"No, Ariana, I—"

"I don't care what you think you can explain to me. I don't want to see you. So, stop calling and texting me. JUST STOP."

And with that she turned and stormed off, leaving me standing there in the middle of the grassy patch that used to be our special place.

• • •

There was a soft knock on my door.

I ignored it.

"Rukhsana? It's me." Aamir's voice came from the hallway. I opened the door and let him in, hoping he wouldn't notice my puffy eyes and make a big deal out of it.

"Rukhsana, what happened?" he said as soon as he took one look at me. "Did Mom and Dad say something?" He scowled. "I swear, if—"

"No, no, it wasn't them," I said quickly, before he got too worked up.

He looked at me closely, and I avoided eye contact.

"I went to see Ariana," I said finally, when I realized he would just keep staring at me until I told him.

"Is she still angry at you?" I'd caught him up on our breakup when we were still in Dhaka.

"Angry would be an understatement. She hates me." My eyes filled up again and fat tears rolled down my face. Lately, it felt like all my conversations with Aamir ended up with me crying. A lot.

"Just give her some time. It can't have been easy for her either."

"You know what, Aamir? I'm getting really tired of hearing how hard this all has been for everyone else. Poor Mom and Dad, poor Ariana." I knew I was spinning out of control, but I was too far gone to do anything about it.

Aamir looked alarmed. But he knew better than to stop me now.

"What about me? What about what I went through? How come nobody is talking about that?" I stood and began to pace. There was too much anger coursing through me right now to sit still.

"Rukhsana, I'm sorry for what I said this morning," Aamir said. "That's what I came here to tell you. Maybe you shouldn't make it so easy for Mom and Dad. Maybe they do deserve to feel awful for a bit longer."

I stopped to look at him. What was he talking about?

"I don't really care about how Mom and Dad are feeling right now. At this point, I don't think Ariana will ever speak to me again. She told me she's moved on."

Just saying those words made the waterworks start again, and in anticipation Aamir quickly grabbed the entire box of tissues from my window ledge. He put his arm around me and pulled me close until my head rested on his shoulder.

"I don't know what to do, Aamir. What if she never forgives me? What if she really doesn't love me anymore?"

"C'mon, Rukhsana, you can't think like that. Once she knows what really happened and what you went through to get back to her, she'll forgive you."

My brother looked at me then, and there was an expression in his eyes that I had never seen before.

"And if she still doesn't understand, then she doesn't deserve you." He kissed my forehead and we sat like that for a while, just the two of us against the world.

chapter
thirty-eight

"Your parents have asked us here to talk to you, because it seems you are being quite unreasonable."

I was about to let loose on Aunty Meena, but her husband beat me to the punch.

"Meena, can you please just be quiet for once? You are only making things worse." I could have hugged Uncle Maruf, but I didn't because it was more fun to watch Aunty Meena sputter with indignation. "Rukhsana, ammu," Uncle Maruf said. "Come and sit down for a minute. Your parents have something to tell you, and they have asked us here because they want to say it in front of us."

So, it *was* an intervention. This would be fun.

"Rukhsana," Mom began. "I've made a very big mistake. I cannot undo what has happened, but I can promise you that things will be different from now on."

"Yes, and I also promise you the same thing," said Dad.

What did they expect me to say?

"So now I should forget everything you did and we'll all be one big, happy family?" I laughed bitterly. "You don't get it, do you?

You ruined my life. You took away a once-in-a-lifetime opportunity, and now I'm graduating from high school late like a loser."

I looked Mom straight in the eyes for the first time since she'd come back.

"Do you really think that I'll ever forgive you?" They had unleashed the monster and now they would all have to deal with it.

"Do you think that just because you've finally realized how narrow-minded you are, I should feel lucky that you're accepting me now? I'm sick, remember? And disgusting. Well, now *I* don't accept *you*."

I felt nothing as I looked at my parents, who were both crying.

"I'm putting my life back together, and I'll do it alone. I don't need you and I don't want you to be involved. So just leave me alone."

"Rukhsana, we're so sorry." Mom was sobbing, but it didn't move me one bit. I had shut off any feelings for her, just like she had done for me.

• • •

"Start from the beginning. What exactly happened yesterday?" Irfan asked after we sat down with our drinks.

"My parents thought it was a brilliant idea to hold an intervention for me. A freaking intervention. They even invited my aunt and uncle."

"What did they say?" Sara asked as she took a sip of her coffee.

"Just that they were sorry and that things would be different now."

"And you don't believe them?" Sara asked.

"No, not really. I mean, they lied about my grandmother being sick when they took me to Bangladesh, and we all know how that turned out. What if they're just doing this so they can convince me to forget all about being lesbian?" I would not go through that again.

"What if they're not though?" Sara said.

"What do you mean?" I couldn't imagine my parents not plotting to fix me.

"Well, you have to admit, it's a pretty radical change for them to admit that they were wrong, isn't it?" Irfan said.

"Maybe you should give them a chance," Sara said softly.

I wanted to get mad at her. But a part of me wondered if they were right. Could my parents be telling the truth?

"I don't know. I'm not sure if I can trust them again." I took a few sips of my coffee before setting my mug down.

"Why don't you talk to them? Give it a shot," Sara said. "If you feel like they're trying anything again, you don't have to keep going. You're graduating in a month anyway, and then you can leave if you want."

Irfan nodded slowly.

"I just think you might regret it if you don't even try."

• • •

Back at home that night, I was lying in bed, unable to stop thinking about my conversation with Sara and Irfan. What would it be like to not have my family in my life anymore? Would I regret it one day when I was older? I thought about Nani and never seeing her again. My heart ached, and my mind went to her diary. In the chaos of the last few days, I had completely forgotten about it. I pulled it out of my purse, sat on the edge of my bed, and began to read.

Today Arif went to Zubaida. I knew what he was going to do as soon as I saw him walk toward her room. I tried to stop him, but he pushed me away so hard that I hit my head

on the wall and fainted. When I was conscious
again, the door to her room was open and
Zubaida was on her bed crying. There was
blood on her sheets and her upper lip was split
open. I raged inside, but I didn't want him
to hear us. I took her to the bathroom and
showed her how to clean up. She would not look
at me. I have failed her as a mother. I didn't
protect her. But this will be the last time he
touches her.

I ran to the bathroom and threw up. I pressed a wet towel against my forehead and closed my eyes, but the image of my mother being violated by her own father was too much. I splashed cold water on my face and sat down on the covered toilet seat. How many more secrets were there in this family? It was horrible. I felt as if I'd been a stranger in my own life.

Never in my worst nightmares had I imagined anything like this. I would give anything to be with my mother right now and just hold her and try to take away the horror and pain the little girl in her had endured.

She had never spoken about any of this. At least not to me. Did Dad know? Was that the reason he always gave in to her? Because of what he knew she'd gone through? I knew he didn't agree with the way my mom had handled everything these past few months. If he'd really wanted to he could have stopped her. Now I wondered if he would do just about anything to make her happy. And I knew what I had to do.

I found my mom in the kitchen. She was cooking and didn't hear me come in.

"Mom," I said, "can we talk?"

She turned around and saw me standing there. Her face was tearstained; it was as if she hadn't stopped crying since she got back. Moving a large pot to the back burner, she turned off the stove before sitting down at the table. I pulled out a chair and sat across from her.

"Mom, I need to know the truth. Are you really being honest this time?"

She nodded slowly, as if she was afraid I'd change my mind and walk away if I didn't like her answer.

"Rukhsana, I know you don't believe me, but I made a mistake; I was wrong. I let other people's opinions influence me too much." She dabbed at her eyes with her orna.

"What changed your mind?" I had to know what it was, that defining moment when she realized she was wrong.

"It wasn't just one thing, ammu. When you didn't come to the hall that night, at first, I was so angry and ashamed of you. Then after all the people left, I started thinking. What if I never saw you again? What if you were gone from my life forever? But I was still angry."

"And what did you do?"

"We started calling, but you wouldn't answer. And then we heard the news about Sohail, and it was so terrible. His mother collapsed and his father, that poor man. No parent should ever lose their child in that way."

The tears were falling freely from her eyes, but she made no effort to wipe them away.

"You know, Rukhsana, I thought I was being a good Muslim, stopping you from committing a grave sin. But that night I realized I was the real sinner. In the eyes of Allah, I was doing wrong. To hate someone because of who they love, that is the worst thing I could do, as a Muslim, as a human being, but mostly as a mother.

When we found out that Sohail was killed because he was gay, I knew that Allah would never want that for anyone. And I knew that I still had the chance to make things right, but it breaks my heart every day to know that it took Sohail's death to open my eyes. For that I will never forgive myself."

At the mention of Sohail, my eyes filled with tears.

"Your father and I, we couldn't bear the look in his parents' eyes. They were broken, losing a son like that. That's when we realized what we had done. To lose your child is a horrible thing. But to push your child away the way we did with you? That is even worse. We didn't know where you were. But then Shaila told us about your whole plan. And we realized how close we had come to losing you forever. If you had been with Sohail, who knows what could have happened."

I swallowed the lump in my throat and reached out to hold her hand. That was all it took. She stood up and pulled me into her arms and sobbed like a child.

"I am so sorry, ammu," she said repeatedly, and then I was sobbing too.

I drew in a shaky breath. There was one more thing I wanted to ask her, but I decided that it could wait.

"Mom, I've cried enough for the last few months, and I don't want to cry anymore."

She nodded, wiping her tears. "I don't want you to cry anymore either. From now on I just want to see you happy and smiling. No more tears, okay?"

Just then Dad and Aamir walked back into the house bearing groceries. They both looked surprised to see Mom and me hugging.

"So? Is everything alright?" Dad asked hesitantly.

I smiled and went over to give him a hug. He buried his head in my hair and cried.

chapter
thirty-nine

Mom jumped into action and began to transfer the food into serving dishes while Dad and I set the table. Even Aamir helped by putting away the groceries. There was mutton curry, basmati rice with peas and carrots, and spicy eggplant. It was delicious, and I realized how much I'd missed my mom's cooking.

We talked about my plans for the future.

"Mr. Jacobs said I only need to finish math and chemistry to graduate. Then I can still go to Caltech in the fall. But I may have lost my scholarship."

"I can write a letter to Caltech and explain what happened," Dad said. "I will tell them it was our fault, that you didn't have a choice. They will understand."

If only it were that simple.

"Mr. Jacobs said he would explain the situation. And I'll explain it to them myself. As long as I get good grades in these two courses, they should consider me in the same way as last time."

"Then we will do everything to make sure that you have plenty of time to study," said Mom.

"Maybe Aamir can help out more?" I suggested with a grin in his direction.

"Yes, Aamir. From now on you are going to help with the dishes, okay?" Mom said as she stood up and began to clear the table.

Aamir nodded while simultaneously glaring at me behind her back.

"I think I'll go up and study now," I said innocently, sticking my tongue out at my brother. Things were already getting better.

I went up to my room and called Irfan.

"Hey, are you free to talk?" I said when he answered.

"Yeah, sure. Sara's here too. I'll put you on speaker. What's up?"

"I took your advice and talked to my parents."

"And what happened?" Sara said.

"I'm actually really glad I did. I mean, there's still a lot to process, but it's a start."

"I'm so happy for you," they both said simultaneously.

I smiled. "I just wanted to say thank you both. For being there and, you know, everything."

"Hey, we should be thanking you," Irfan said. "My parents are planning our wedding."

"I am so happy for you both," I said excitedly. "You guys, that's so great. Have you set a date yet?"

"Yes, it's in March," Sara said. "We didn't want to say anything because of everything else, but now I'm so excited I can tell you all about it."

● ● ●

My phone pinged the next morning while I was walking to school.

I'm ready to talk. I'll be at the recreation center after school.

303

It was Ariana.

I'll be there.

It was the longest day. When the bell finally rang, I sprinted the few blocks to the recreation center. Ariana was waiting outside the gym, the curls on her forehead slightly damp with sweat and her cheeks flushed.

I walked up to her and we sat at one of the tables in the lobby.

"Thanks for agreeing to see me," I said, wishing that my heart wouldn't beat so loudly. I didn't want her to know just how nervous I was.

"Well, Jen kept hounding me to talk to you so here I am." She wouldn't look me in the eyes, just like last time, and it scared me so much that the words just came tumbling out. I couldn't have stopped even if I wanted to.

I watched her eyes widen as I told her every sordid detail of what had transpired in the months I'd been away. It occurred to me that I should have done this a long time ago, like right after I got back. It wasn't really fair of me to expect Ariana to understand when she didn't have all the facts. But I couldn't then. Now, as I got to the part where Sohail was killed, the pain pierced me like a lance, going right through the scab that had formed over the wound in my heart. The tears fell and I didn't even care that people around us could see. All I knew was that Ariana was crying too.

We walked to the small park behind the rec center, stopping at the fountain and sitting on the grass.

Ariana took my hand and used her free one to wipe away my tears. Then she leaned over and kissed me.

It had been so long since I'd felt her soft lips on mine that my insides turned to mush. This was a kiss of forgiveness and acceptance, and by the time we came up for air, the weight of sadness I'd been carrying around for so long had dissipated.

We sat there holding each other, neither of us saying a word.

Eventually Ariana looked at me, her eyes bright with unshed tears.

"I can't believe I was so horrible to you. And you had to go through all that alone. I should have been there for you." She hung her head and a few fat tears trailed down her face.

"I wanted to tell you everything from the beginning. But I felt we were so far away from each other, and I don't mean just the physical distance. I didn't think you'd understand. Or maybe I didn't know how to explain it." I sighed, remembering all the nights I'd cried myself to sleep, wishing Ariana was with me.

"You know, Rukhsana, if I'm being really honest, I don't think I would have understood." Ariana wiped away her tears. "I was so angry, and I couldn't understand why you didn't just leave. And that's on me."

She took my hand and held it in her lap.

"I was thinking about your life, your family, and your culture and everything. And I realized that I was judging you for not being able to just walk away."

"You were? But you knew—"

"I did. But I didn't really appreciate what your family means to you and that there is a huge difference in the way you and I were raised. And if I truly love you, then I need to embrace that part of you. Not just the part that's like me."

I let her words sink in and thought about all the times I'd resented her for not getting it. And now, as I looked at her, I felt deliriously happy that I didn't have to be the one to point out that I wasn't only the person everyone saw me as in my regular life in Seattle. I had a whole other life, one that I loved, one that made me who I was. And that included my overprotective, often narrow-minded parents, who had sacrificed a lot to give me and my brother the lives we had. And while Ariana, Jen, and Rachel might think that it should be easy for me to just walk away from it all, that was not who I was. There were so many things I loved about my Bangladeshi side. I loved the clothes, the food, and the Bengali songs my mom listened to. I loved the old movies, the family friends dropping in unannounced and staying for dinner, and the sound of them speaking the language I loved but spoke with a ridiculous American accent.

But I also loved the part of me that wanted to kiss Ariana and hang out with my friends watching cheesy horror movies all night. It was not easy finding a way to reconcile these two equally vital parts of my identity, my life. But it was definitely worth fighting for.

● ● ●

"Rukhsana, your aunty and I wanted to talk to you about something. Can you please sit for a minute?"

Mom was waiting for me in the family room when I got back home. And Aunty Meena was with her. A feeling of dread came over me immediately. Not again. Nothing good ever came from Aunty Meena's visits, and it always took more than a minute. Much more.

"Yes, what is it?" I said nervously as I wiped my damp palms on my jeans.

"Well, we wanted to ask you something," Aunty Meena started. "We don't know anything about lesbians."

I stared at her, dumbfounded. What was she talking about?

"We were just wondering. And we had some questions," Mom said, looking mortified.

"Wait. I have written it down. All the questions," Aunty Meena said, pulling out a folded piece of paper from her bra. I did not want to know what else she kept in there. I picked my jaw up off the floor while Aunty Meena fished out her reading glasses from her purse.

"Okay, so number one: When did you first know that you were a lesbian?" She peered at me over the lenses.

I was trapped. They were both looking at me expectantly, waiting for me to answer.

"Well, I guess it was when my friends started going out with guys and I didn't have a boyfriend." I shrugged, having no intention of telling them that I'd known since my first crush in middle school. "I realized that none of the boys made me feel anything."

I didn't like where this was going, and I wasn't going to wait around for question number two. "Um . . . I've got a lot of homework to do actually," I said. "But we'll talk more later," I added, running out as fast as I could.

I was lying. I did not intend to take part in any more awkward conversations.

"Okay, but remember I have more questions," Aunty Meena called out as I disappeared up the stairs.

● ● ●

"Irfan, do you have any Bengali friends who are gay?" Mom asked casually.

Irfan choked on a piece of shrimp, but a few thwacks to his back took care of that.

I had invited Sara and Irfan over for dinner, but I didn't expect it to turn into yet another Bengali Inquisition.

"Yes, Aunty, a couple of my friends are gay," he said when he could speak again.

"How are their parents dealing with it? Are they understanding everything?"

"I'm not sure, but I can ask them."

I felt sorry for Irfan, but it was like watching a car crash. I couldn't look away.

"We were trying to read about it, but it is very confusing. All the different labels and orientations. I only knew about gays and lesbians. Now I find out that there are more. And all have their own letter. How am I supposed to remember them all?"

I was so thankful that there was no one around right now who would take offense. I knew she was trying, but clearly we couldn't take her out in public yet. And certainly not to Seattle Pride.

"Mom, I can explain everything later."

It was at times like these that I missed Ariana the most. And although I was deliriously happy that we were back together, I knew it would take time for her to feel comfortable around my parents again. Right now, I wanted nothing more than to laugh with her at the ridiculous situation I found myself in. She would have had so much fun with this.

After Irfan and Sara left, I sat down with Mom to answer more of her questions.

"So, Q is for queer or questioning?" she mused after I had explained what all the letters stood for. "Your cousin, Basheer, I think he is questioning. He's not getting married and he's not interested in anyone." She nodded, looking very satisfied with this analysis of her nephew.

"Rukhsana, if I knew about any other Bengali lesbians, then it would be easy to find a nice girl for you. But don't you worry, we will find someone." I wasn't worried, but she seemed happy so I kept quiet.

"I will ask Meena," she continued. "She always knows the latest gossip. If there are any lesbians to be found in our community, she will find them."

Not that I was looking, but sure, why not?

I didn't know whether to laugh or cry. Mom had gone from forcing me to marry a good Bengali boy to being my wing woman in search of the perfect Bengali lesbian. If she was going to embrace her daughter's lesbian side, then she would darn well make sure to find the best lesbian match Seattle's Bengali community had to offer.

"Mom, you don't have to find anyone for me. I'm quite happy right now. I have a lot to study, so I don't have time for a relationship now anyway." I wasn't ready to talk to her about Ariana yet. But I knew I would have to, sooner or later.

"That's true, you are very busy now, but don't worry. You don't have to do anything. Meena and I will take care of everything." Clearly, she was hearing what she wanted to.

I left her poring over statistics of LGBTQ South Asian teens. I had to admit, she had made quite an impressive turnaround.

I still wanted to ask her about Nani's diary, but there never seemed to be a good moment for it.

I found myself flipping to the page where I had stopped last time. I needed to know what happened as my mom got older.

Today Zubaida turned fifteen. When she looks at me I see nothing but hatred and shame in her eyes. I have failed to protect her from her father's evil. I have spoken to mother-in-law about it but of course she does not believe me. She thinks I am lying because Arif is threatening to take a younger girl as his wife. I told her I am praying to Allah that he will take another wife. Then he will not touch my Zuby. Every time I try to stop him he pushes me to the ground and kicks me until I am unconscious.

And then he goes into her room. When I am conscious again I hear her muffled screams. She is not fighting him any longer, but I know she is dying inside. I have tried to find Raju again. I have gone to the market several times looking for him, but he is not there.

I flipped through the pages to find more mentions of Raju and found one a few pages later.

Yesterday I went to the market to look for Raju and this time he was there. He caught me looking at him and when I went to check the spinach, he followed me and stood close enough that I could hear him. He told me to meet him by the paanwallah. I walked over there and told him about Arif and how he tortures us every day. Raju became very angry, saying he would kill Arif. I should have told him not to say such things about my husband. But I didn't say that. Instead I told him how Arif sometimes comes home very late at night from the city and the path he usually takes. Then I left quickly. If Arif finds out I was talking to another man, he will beat me to death.

The next entry was one brief paragraph.

It has been a month now since Arif died. The police said that some miscreants tried to rob him as he was coming home late from the city. When he didn't hand over the money they stabbed him to death. Mother-in-law has been in bed since the day the police came and asked us to identify the body. I was afraid that it wouldn't be him, but Allah heard my prayers and sent me Raju. I can never see Raju again. But he has saved me and he has saved my Zuby.

I flipped frantically through the rest of the pages only to find that they were blank. But I had so many questions. What happened to her mother-in-law? How did she end up in the city? How did she survive all alone with two young children? While I wanted to ask Nani, this wasn't exactly something I could talk about on the phone.

I snapped the diary shut and put it on my nightstand. I couldn't believe it. It was an act of a desperate woman, an act of survival for herself and her daughter.

I lay back against my pillow, picturing Nani. My sweet, gentle grandmother who sang to me and braided jasmine into my hair. That she could have such a dark past was not something I'd ever imagined. I wanted to talk to Mom about it, badly, but if she had buried the pain deep inside her, I couldn't open that wound. I couldn't do that to her.

chapter forty

"I have found a group, Ibrahim Bhai," Aunty Meena said excitedly as I walked into the foyer the following day. "It is here in Seattle."

She dug out a few brochures from her purse and handed one to each of us. It looked like a support group for South Asian parents and families of LGBTQ children, and the brochure promised to provide a safe and inclusive environment for everyone.

"Aunty Meena, where did you hear about this?"

She gave me a smug smile and waved dismissively in the air.

"Oh, I know many people in our community, Rukhsana. Do you remember that girl Seema? You met her at that birthday party last year?"

I didn't have a clue but it was easier to just go along, so I nodded.

"Well, I have found out that she is also a lesbian," she said triumphantly, as if she had just discovered the last two remaining in our endangered species.

"I told you, Rukhsana," said Mom excitedly. "I told you if there are any Bengali lesbians to be found, Aunty Meena will find them. Didn't I tell her that, Ibrahim?"

Dad just smiled, but Aunty Meena was practically purring with pleasure.

I had to admit this was a side to her I hadn't seen before. She was really looking out for me. It was a strange way of doing it, but her heart seemed to be in the right place. But she was about to be disappointed in a major way. I decided to wait until after Aunty Meena left to talk to Mom about Ariana.

"So, when shall we go to one of the meetings?" Mom was looking at the brochure again. "It says they have one this Friday evening."

"I'm pretty sure I'm busy that day," I mumbled, but no one was paying attention.

"Okay, then it's decided," said Aunty Meena. "Ibrahim Bhai, can you pick me up on the way?"

"Do I have a choice?" Dad smiled affectionately at her as she started to leave.

After dinner, I pulled Mom aside.

"Mom, we need to talk." Even to me, that sounded ominous.

Mom nodded, looking understandably nervous.

"Is anything wrong? I know your Aunty Meena gets a little bit too excited. If you don't want to go to the meeting, that is okay. I will talk to her."

I shook my head.

"It's not that, Mom. I wanted to talk to you about Ariana."

"Ariana," she said slowly. "I thought you two were not together anymore."

"She was very hurt and angry with me when I broke up with her. But we're working on it now." A smile spread slowly across my face.

"That's good, isn't it? So, you two are back together." I could tell that Mom was letting the information sink in.

"Aunty Meena will certainly be disappointed to hear that. She was very excited about finding someone for you. A nice Bengali lesbian girl."

"Mom, you really have to stop with this Bengali thing," I said, pretty annoyed now. "I love Ariana and she loves me. That's it. No more looking for anyone."

Mom nodded quickly.

"Okay, okay, I will tell her. But you should ask Ariana over for dinner."

Was she for real?

"Mom, do you remember what happened the last time Ariana was here? I doubt if she would even want to come over. And I can't say I blame her."

Mom looked at me in silence for a moment, and I wondered if she was going to try and deny that she had done anything wrong.

"Rukhsana, you are right. I treated Ariana very badly."

I could hardly believe what I was hearing.

"Please see if you can convince her to come over. I need to apologize to her. And I will make her favorite dish for dinner. Ask her what she likes."

This was almost funny. My mom really believed that cooking someone's favorite dish would be enough for them to forgive her. But I knew she was trying, and I also knew it wasn't easy for her to admit that she was wrong. So, I put my arms around her and promised I would try.

• • •

When I mentioned to Aamir that Aunty Meena was dragging us to the South Asian LGBTQ support group, he was ecstatic.

"I'm definitely not missing this," he said once he finished laughing. "I can't wait to go."

"I'm glad you find this funny," I said, pushing him off my bed. "You know they're trying to set me up again, right? If Aunty Meena says 'Bengali lesbian' one more time, I'm going to lose it."

"Your life is such a struggle," Aamir said as he got up to leave, closing the door quickly to avoid being hit by the pillow I threw at him.

• • •

An envelope was propped up against the napkin holder when Aamir and I got back from school the next day. It was from Caltech. My fingers shook as I ripped it open and scanned the letter.

"So?" Aamir said impatiently. "What does it say?"

"I'm still getting the scholarship." I beamed as I looked at my brother.

Aamir pulled me in for a hug.

"You think Dad had anything to do with it?" he said.

I shrugged. "I'm not sure. He did say that he would contact them to explain."

"I guess you can ask him tonight when we're all at that meeting," Aamir said with an impish grin.

• • •

"Hello, you must be Meena," a woman said to my aunt as we approached the community center where the LGBTQ support group was being held. She had an accent, but it wasn't Bengali. "I'm Jayanthi. I think I talked to you on the phone a few days ago?"

My whole family had decided to come to this first meeting with me, but Aunty Meena was the one who had set everything up.

As we entered the room, Jayanthi offered us some tea and pastries. There were several chairs set up in a large circle. Some were already occupied, but there were still people standing around getting tea.

When we were all seated, Jayanthi asked everyone to say a little something about themselves to the group. I looked around at everyone else. We were all South Asians in the room, from Bangladesh, Pakistan, Sri Lanka, and India. From the introductions, it was clear that we also represented the majority religions of the region. There were other Muslims, but also Hindus, Sikhs, and Buddhists. There was Jayanthi, who was from Sri Lanka. Her son was gay, and she was here with him. She was a group leader and had been with the group for six years. Then there was twenty-year-old Laila, a Muslim from Pakistan, who was there with her parents. After a while it became difficult to keep track of everyone's names, so I paid attention to their stories instead of trying to remember them all.

It was exhilarating to be surrounded by people who were in the same situation as I was. I didn't really know any other LGBTQ South Asians, not because they didn't exist but because we couldn't exactly advertise it. As a culture, we were a long way from being openly accepted, so this was as good as it would get.

When I thought about what happened to Sohail, I had to think that this was a big step in the right direction. And as much as I'd hated my parents for what they had done, I had to give them credit for turning things around and making an effort. Because looking at them now, I could see they deeply regretted how they had treated me.

After the meeting, Dad chatted up some of the other fathers in the group while Mom and Aunty Meena cornered some poor unsuspecting girl and her parents. Mom waved at me and I walked over to them.

"Rukhsana, come and meet Shilpi. She is also from Bangladesh. Her mother is just telling us how they found out that she's a lesbian."

I felt the blood rush to my face as I avoided eye contact with poor Shilpi. I couldn't believe my mom was being so embarrassing. Shilpi looked completely mortified, but I realized that was because of her own mother.

"One day, my son told me that he saw his sister kissing another girl at school," Shilpi's mother said.

"How did you manage after that?" Mom asked.

"At first, we were very upset," she said, patting Shilpi on the back. "We told her to get out of our house. But then she stopped eating and going to school. Then it hit us. We thought, why are we doing this? She is our child; we must love her no matter what. Then someone told us about this group, and so we started coming here. It's helped us understand a lot about our Shilpi."

She turned and kissed the top of her daughter's head.

Mom looked around the room pensively. Was she thinking about her own reaction? These days I tried not to dwell on that, but every now and then the memories came back unwittingly. No matter how good things were at home right now, I couldn't keep the bitterness from filling my heart. If my parents hadn't taken me to Bangladesh, maybe Ariana and I wouldn't have hurt each other so badly. And Sohail might have still been alive.

Dad came over and put an arm around my shoulders.

"Rukhsana, ammu, what do you think? Aunty Meena actually did something good this time." He smiled affectionately at me before turning to my mom.

"Zubaida, I was just talking to this nice family from Sri Lanka. They wanted to meet you too. Come, I'll take you to them."

They shuffled off to a group at the far end of the room, leaving me alone with Aunty Meena. I decided it was time to start being nicer to her. If she could do it, so could I.

"Aunty, it was really kind of you to bring us here. I'm glad we came."

She smiled, surveying the room for her next quarry.

"Irfan has been talking to me a lot these days. He was telling me that it's not right. How we treat people when they are different. He told me about that boy Sohail. Your mother said you two had become quite close. And then he was killed. Just like that?" She looked at me, and to my surprise, her eyes were misty. Could it be that underneath the caustic exterior she was human?

I couldn't bring myself to talk about Sohail with her. The wound was still too fresh. So, I just smiled and let her do the talking.

"You know, I have been talking to some of my friends back in Bangladesh. I have one friend who has been unhappily married to a gay man for thirty years. She could never tell anyone. Not even her closest friends." She shook her head slowly. "Not everybody is lucky like me or your mother."

I agreed with that much. As far as I knew, Mom and Dad had their share of fights, but it was usually about something trivial. And there was definitely no violence. Knowing what I did about my mother's childhood, I was sure she wouldn't have survived an unhappy marriage. And Uncle Maruf was a sweet man. In fact, in my eyes he was a saint since he had to put up with Aunty Meena.

• • •

"Rukhsana," Mom said a few evenings later as she began loading the dishwasher. "I was thinking . . . What about children?"

"What about them?"

"Well, how are you going to have any?"

She'd really been thinking about this.

"I'm not sure. There are a few ways, I think."

I hadn't really thought that much about it. I was going to turn eighteen in a week. Having children was not a priority at the moment.

"I asked Jayanthi. She said you could do virtuous fertilization."

Virtuous? Did she mean immaculate conception? It took me a minute to connect the dots.

"You mean in vitro, Mom. It's when they fertilize the egg in a petri dish and then put it into the mom's uterus."

This is why I'd taken biology. To explain the ins and outs of getting pregnant while lesbian.

"You're going to get pregnant in a dish?"

This was going to be a long conversation.

"No, Mom, no one is getting pregnant in a dish. They just take the eggs and the sperm and let them combine in a dish. Then they put the fertilized egg back into the womb."

She nodded thoughtfully, processing this information.

"Where is the sperm coming from? Do you have to have sex with a man? You can't have sex until you are married. That is against our religion."

There were so many things wrong with this talk, I didn't even know where to begin.

"No, Mom, I will not be having sex with a man, so don't worry." She relaxed visibly.

"Then where are they getting the sperm?"

"I don't know. From a sperm bank, I guess?"

"A sperm bank? Chhee. How will you know what you're getting?" She curled her lip in disgust.

"Mom, there are profiles of the donors. You can choose the characteristics you like and pick one. It's all anonymous."

She narrowed her eyes suspiciously. "How do you know so much about this?"

Because I don't live under a rock?

"I don't know . . . I watched a documentary on TV."

"How will you decide which one of you will get pregnant?"

Will the questions ever stop?

"Mom! Why are we even talking about this? No one is getting pregnant. Not for a long time."

I picked up a bulging garbage bag and walked out of the room.

"I just want to have my own grandchildren, that's all," she shouted after me.

chapter
forty-one

Mom paced back and forth between the dishwasher and the cabinet, carrying the same set of bowls but not putting them away. "That Suraiya thinks she knows everything about everything. If you hadn't stopped me I would have said something to her face."

She and Dad had just gotten home from the mosque, and they looked furious.

"Mom, what happened?" I said, gently taking the bowls from her and placing them on their shelf.

"You know Suraiya, that gossipy lady who knows about everyone else's business?"

I shook my head. I had stopped keeping track of them a long time ago.

"You know, the one who dyes her hair with mehndi. She walks around looking like a clown with her orange hair."

"Yes, yes. I think I know which one you mean."

I lied. I had no idea who she was talking about.

"She started saying nasty things about gays and lesbians very casually, as if I wouldn't know what she was up to. She thinks she's so clever."

"Was she saying stuff about me?"

"What? No, she'd never say anything to my face. No, no, she was just talking about it and looking at me. I understood very well what she was trying to do."

So, an orange-haired clown lady at the mosque was giving Mom some side-eye and she was all worked up about that? Or was it because she was talking about lesbians inside a mosque?

I was surprised it was still standing.

"Mom, it's okay. Who cares what she says? Let her talk. Sit down. I'll make you some chai."

"Thank you, Rukhsana," she said, pulling out a chair. "Next time she says something I'll tell her that everyone knows her daughter is running around with some white hooligan."

"Zubaida, I really don't think that we need to sink to that level," Dad said as he took a cup of chai from my hands. "People will say what they want."

"Yes, Ibrahim, I know we decided that from now on we will not care so much about other people's opinions, but that is only easy to say. Not so easy to do when they are talking about your own daughter."

"I know, Zuby. It makes me angry also. But I will not let them control how I live my life or how our daughter lives her life."

I hugged him from behind. There was no need for words.

chapter
forty-two

Movie night finally came, and I was ready to get out of my head and have a good old-fashioned girls' night. We parked ourselves in Jen's basement and argued over which movie to watch while we waited for Ariana to show up.

I'd been avoiding them since our sushi lunch, and I knew it was time to clear the air.

"I need to tell you guys something," I started, not really knowing how much I wanted to tell them. "I just wanted to explain why I've been so distant lately."

"You don't have to explain," Rachel said. "It's us, remember?"

"No. I think I do," I insisted. "The thing is, the last time we talked, it felt like you were taking Ariana's side. And I'd be lying if I said it didn't hurt."

The two of them exchanged a glance.

"We weren't taking sides," Jen said. "It's just that we were there when you broke up with Ariana and we saw what she went through."

Rachel nodded. "It was brutal. She missed a lot of school and her mom was really pissed at you."

I felt awful that I had caused her so much pain, and Ariana and I were moving past that. But there were still things that bothered me about my relationship with my friends.

"You know, things were pretty awful for me too." I knew I was being unfair because I had never told them the whole story. So, I did. And it wasn't easier just because I'd told it to Ariana and Sara and Irfan already. How could something like this ever be easy?

They both reacted as expected. With horror and disbelief.

"I can't believe you went through all that alone. How could your parents do those things to you?" Jen said, holding me in her arms.

"The same way people here throw their kids out of the house after they find out they're gay," I said. "It happens everywhere."

"No, I know, but I'm just saying . . . What your parents did was a little extreme, wasn't it?" Rachel said. "I mean, they wouldn't have done something like that here, right?"

I sighed. "Look, of course it's horrible, but I wish you guys wouldn't automatically judge my whole culture."

"We didn't mean to do that, Rukhsana," Jen said quickly. "We love you, you know that."

I nodded. "I know you do. But lately I've been feeling like I'm all alone in this. That's why I didn't tell you at first. I'm also really angry that you always made me feel like I was being dramatic about how my parents would react. I mean, you get it now because I told you everything, but why did it take all that for you to just believe me in the first place?"

They were both silent and I wondered if this whole movie night was still a good idea.

"I had no idea you felt this way," Jen finally said.

"Why didn't you say anything before?" Rachel asked.

"I don't know," I said. "I guess because every time I say something bad about my family, it becomes more about where I come from than just regular stuff that people go through with their parents."

"I'm really sorry we made you feel that way," Jen said.

"And you're right," Rachel added. "Maybe we do tend to jump to conclusions, and that's something we need to work on."

"Yes, you do," I said. "You have no idea how hard it is to constantly feel like you have to represent your entire culture. And to try and juggle all these expectations. I really don't want to feel like I need to be careful around you guys too. I mean, you're my best friends."

"I'm so sorry, Rukhsana," Rachel said.

We sat in awkward silence for a little bit and then Jen stood up suddenly.

"You know what we need right now? A group hug." She pulled us both up and we stood with our arms around each other. It reminded me of all the times we'd done this as kids after a silly fight and I knew then that we'd be all right. After a while, I extracted myself and went to grab a packet out of my bag. "I have something for you guys." I handed them each a box of the glass bangles I'd picked out at the Boishakhi Mela in Dhaka.

Ariana walked in just as Jen and Rachel were trying on their bangles.

"Aren't they so pretty?" Ariana twirled her wrist to show off her own.

"You're wearing them," I said, ridiculously happy that she liked them.

When we finished admiring them, Rachel took the remote from Jen and chose *Princess Diaries* again. I had to admit, it was a great movie. And I was just happy to be back home spending quality time with my best friends.

●●●

"Rukhsana, I was putting clean clothes on your bed and I saw Nani's diary on your desk." Mom sat down across from me at the kitchen table.

"She gave it to me before I left," I said, closing my notebook. "I'm sorry . . . I didn't know if I could talk to you about it."

"It's okay. If Amma gave it to you, she must have wanted you to have it."

"Have you ever read it?" She must have been curious as a child. Unless she didn't know it existed.

She shook her head. "I saw her write in it sometimes, but she always kept it hidden away. And after some time, I forgot about it."

"Do you want to read it now?"

She paused, thinking about it for a moment.

"I think I'd like to," she said softly.

"Mom . . . I read about what your father did to Nani and to you." Tears sprang to my eyes as I put my arms around my mother and held her close. "I'm so sorry you had to go through that."

"It was a long time ago. I buried it in my mind when I was young. I didn't want to think about it ever again."

"Maybe Nani would want you to read it now, to understand what happened." Did she know about Raju? Or how her father died?

"I will read it. Maybe it's time to put this to rest permanently."

I had one more question, but it took everything in me to ask it.

"Does Dad know?"

"No, ammu." She was quiet for a long time after that. "You know, your daddy has been very good to me. Knowing about this, it would break him."

"Then it will be our secret," I said, touching her face and kissing her cheek.

chapter
forty-three

"What's going on?" I said to Mom and Aunty Meena, watching them flit around the kitchen as if their rotis were on fire. Whatever was bubbling away on the stove smelled delicious. Mom had even taken out the nice dishes, and there was a huge bouquet of flowers on the dining table. "You think we'd forget your birthday?" Mom said with a huge smile on her face.

With everything that had been going on, my birthday had completely slipped my mind.

"Well, I promised you we would take care of everything. Ariana and her mother are coming for dinner tonight," Mom said triumphantly.

My mouth dropped. "Really? How did you convince her?"

"Rukhsana, that is a long story," Aunty Meena said. "Now don't stand around here getting in our way. We're preparing a feast for her."

"Yes, ammu, you go and get ready," Mom said. "I put out a nice outfit for you."

Some things would never change. But this time I wasn't complaining. I had no idea what the two of them had said or done, but my Ariana was coming over and that was all I cared about.

I went up to my room and had a long bath. I spent extra time on my hair, carefully styling it so a few curly strands framed my face. I looked at the outfit Mom had picked out and shook my head. The soft pink chiffon shalwar set with silver beading was exquisite, but a little bit much for tonight. I was not wearing that. I picked out a maroon blouse and paired it with some black jeans. I applied my makeup with more care than usual, lining my eyes with black liner and adding wings to the ends of my eyelids. I put on a soft pink lipstick and wore my favorite silver dangly earrings.

• • •

When I walked back into the kitchen, Mom was already waiting for me, a piece of paper in her hand.

"Rukhsana, can you please go with Aunty Meena to the store? I need a few more things for tonight and it will be faster if you go with her." She handed me a list as Aunty Meena ushered me out to her car.

"Rukhsana, I want to tell you something," Aunty Meena said as we pulled out of the driveway.

I waited silently for her to continue.

"As you know, I've been talking to Irfan a lot about you and everything that happened."

We approached a red light and Aunty Meena turned to me.

"I want to say that I'm sorry." She turned her attention back to the road as the light changed.

"For what?" I had a pretty good idea, but I wanted her to say it. Maybe it was petty of me, but after everything that I'd gone through, I deserved to be petty if I wanted.

"Well, your mother told me about you and Ariana. I'm glad that you worked things out. I'm sorry if I was being pushy about finding a Bengali girl for you."

Now I felt bad. She was trying to help in her own strange way, and I hadn't told her about what was going on with me and Ariana. Frankly, I was surprised that Mom had actually talked to her.

"It's okay, Aunty Meena."

"Good. I just wanted to make sure that you are not angry with me," she said, parking the car. When we got out of the car, I gave her a big hug.

It didn't take long to get the few things on Mom's list: cilantro, green chilies, curry leaves, plain yogurt, buttermilk, and papad.

When we got back home, I grabbed the grocery bags and walked to the front door, Aunty Meena right behind me.

Mom wasn't in the kitchen when I put the bags on the counter, so I assumed that she'd gone to shower and change for dinner. I went into the living room to wait for Ariana to arrive and nearly jumped out of my skin when a loud chorus of "SURPRISE" greeted me.

I reeled back in shock and by the time I recovered, I realized that our living room was full of people. Irfan and Sara, Jen and Rachel, Shilpi and the gang from the support group—they were all there. They all gathered around me, and there were hugs and kisses and introductions. Then I saw someone walk toward me from the far corner of the living room, and my eyes widened.

It was Shaila. I ran to her and threw my arms around her.

"I can't believe—"

I couldn't process everything that was happening. I was speechless. I couldn't understand how my mom had pulled this off or why she had even done this.

I turned and found her standing behind me with a big smile on her face. I wrapped her in a tight hug.

"Mom, wow. I don't know what to say. When did you—"

Just then the doorbell rang and I looked around. It had to be Ariana.

I ran to the door and opened it to find Ariana standing there with her mom. Ariana looked breathtaking in an off-white blouse and dark jeans. Her mom fidgeted nervously, and I quickly remembered my manners.

"Frances, I'm so happy you're both here. Please come in." I ushered them into the living room, and I could tell by Ariana's bewildered expression that she had no clue about what was going on.

Mom, Dad, and Aunty Meena all came to greet Frances and introduce themselves. Once everyone was seated on every possible surface, Mom stood and my stomach clenched.

What is she doing?

"There is something I must do and I would like to do it in front of everyone, because my Rukhsana is the most important person in my life and lately I seem to have forgotten that."

Oh no. I had never wished so desperately for a natural disaster of some sort. Anything to stop this from happening.

"Ariana, please come here," Mom said, and Ariana froze. Frances tensed up as well, and who could blame them?

But Ariana went to my mom nonetheless and stood in front of her. Mom took Ariana's face gently in her hands.

"Ariana, I want to apologize. From the bottom of my heart, I am sorry for what I did and that I hurt you. You make my Rukhsana happy and that's all that matters to me now. To us."

"We put other people's concerns over the happiness of our own daughter," Dad added. "And while we cannot take back what has happened, we can make a promise to both of you."

He turned to me. "Come here, ammu."

I walked over to them, the tears already rolling down my cheeks.

"We promise you that from now on we will support you both," Dad said. "And there will be those who will try to make you feel bad. But we will take care of all that."

"Yes, and if anyone tries to say anything to you, they will have to deal with me," Aunty Meena said emphatically.

I couldn't help but seek out Uncle Maruf in the crowd, and as I'd suspected, he had a huge smile on his face.

"We want to welcome you into our family, Ariana," Mom said. "From now on you will be like our own daughter. Please forgive us."

Ariana couldn't speak because she was sobbing, and my face was wet with tears. I knew Mom and Dad had been trying really hard lately and I appreciated it. But in my wildest dreams, I could not have anticipated this. And I could tell from the look on Ariana's face that she was stunned as well. We exchanged a smile and I knew we would have so much to talk about later. But now I just wanted to relish this moment.

"Now," Mom announced. "Who's hungry?"

Since there was so much food, the serving dishes had been laid out on the large kitchen island. Everyone helped themselves and then spread out in the kitchen, living room, and dining room.

I spotted Aunty Meena and Frances at one end of the kitchen, and it looked like Aunty Meena was pointing out the spice level of all the different dishes.

I grabbed Ariana and took her over to meet Shaila.

"Shaila," I squealed, and hugged her too tightly. "This is Ariana," I announced.

Shaila broke free from me and turned to put her arms around Ariana.

"I hope you know what you're getting into with this one," Shaila said teasingly, and Ariana grinned. "But, jokes aside, I am so happy for both of you." She kissed Ariana on the cheek and looked at her affectionately.

Irfan and Sara joined our group and we recounted the incident at the coffee shop. It was amazing that we could laugh about it now, when just a few months ago it had caused me so much panic and anxiety.

We took our plates and joined Jen, Rachel, Shilpi, and the other young people from the support group. I looked over to where the adults had all gathered and were having an apparently hilarious conversation. I caught Mom's eye and we shared a secret smile. She was having a great time, and I almost pinched myself to make sure this wasn't some dream. If it was I did not want to wake up.

I scanned the room and all around me were the faces of people I loved and wanted in my life. Watching them now, enjoying themselves here in my home, I felt a great weight lift off me and I could breathe again. Their presence tonight showed me their unconditional acceptance of who I was, and there could be no greater gift for me than this moment right here, right now. For the first time in a long while, I was truly happy.

acknowledgements

There are so many people who came into my life at just the right time and helped make this story what it is today. I am deeply grateful to each and every one of them.

First, my amazing Pitch Wars mentor, Natasha Neagle. Thank you for giving so generously of your time and talent to help shape this book. To Brenda Drake, who is a fairy godmother to so many writers, thank you for everything you do for the community. You have changed lives.

To my agent, Hillary Jacobson, for taking a chance on me. Thank you for your patience and your guidance and for believing so strongly that all our stories are important. I am so fortunate to have you in my corner. To my Hillary's Angelz: Adalyn, Ali, Astrid, Mel, and Tomi, I couldn't have asked for better agency siblings. Thank you for your wisdom and humor, your support and encouragement, and for making this a wonderful journey.

To my Scholastic family in the US and Canada: My brilliant editor, Jeffrey West, for loving Rukhsana's story as much as I do and for continually pushing me to make it better. Your connection with my characters transcends the barriers of culture, religion, and language and it has been truly amazing working with you; Crystal McCoy, Rachel Feld, Isa Caban, Vaishali Nayak, Lizette Serrano, Emily Heddleston, Melissa Schirmer, Josh Berlowitz, Preeti Chhibber, Alexis Lunsford, Erin Haggett, Nikole Kritikos, and so many others who have touched this book, my heartfelt thanks for all the hard work you put into bringing Rukhsana's story to the world; the designer, Maeve Norton, for creating such an amazing cover and perfectly capturing Rukhsana's essence; and a very special thank you to David Levithan for his support and encouragement.

To Nisha Sharma, Samira Ahmed, Tanuja Desai Hidier, and Sara Farizan for taking the time to read Rukhsana's story early and sharing your kind words. To Sandhya Menon, for patiently listening and being there for me throughout this amazing journey, and for answering my endless questions.

I would also like to thank Laura Silverman, Rachel Lynn Solomon, Sayantani DasGupta, Dahlia Adler, Julian Winters, Mason Deaver, Nafiza Azad, and London Shah; your friendship and support means the world. My heartfelt thanks to the many readers, bloggers, authors, librarians, teachers, and booksellers: Your enthusiasm for Rukhsana's story continues to fuel my passion for writing these important narratives that demand to be read.

To my mother, who sat with me for hours every day while I learned English as a little girl, instilling a love of reading in the process.

To my husband, who always puts my dreams before his own, thank you for providing me with the space and time to do what I love. To my two amazing daughters, who inspire me every day with their courage and conviction. I hope you are as proud of me as I am of you.

Finally, I would like to take this opportunity to honor all of the LGBTQ Muslims who have lost their lives far too soon, victims of senseless hate, prejudice, and violence. In particular, Xulhaz Mannan, cofounder of *Roopbaan*, Bangladesh's first and only LGBT magazine, and K. Mahabub Rabbi (Tonoy), both community leaders and LGBTQ activists, whose brutal murders in 2016 called attention to the very real dangers that the Muslim LGBTQ community face every day.

sabina khan writes about Muslim teens who straddle cultures. She was born in Germany, spent her teens in Bangladesh, and lived in Macao, Illinois, and Texas before settling down in beautiful British Columbia with her husband, two daughters, and the best dog in the world. She enjoys reading and spicy food and is obsessed with scented candles. She has a BA in political science and works as an educational consultant by day. By night she sings her heart out at karaoke and dances like no one's watching. You can find her on Twitter at @Sabina_Writer and online at sabina-khan.com.